*To Mum, thank you for starting my journey
with books, and in fond memory of my
very lovely Dad. You are much missed.*

Those known to be present at the Snakesmouth
Lighthouse on the night of the murder

SETH SEPPI — kitchen boy

NIGHTSHADE

INSPECTOR SAGACIOUS PEWTER (MagiCon)

MINA MINTENCRESS —

owner of the Snakesmouth Lighthouse

LARK SUNRISE — friend of Mina Mintencress

ALFIE MINTENCRESS —

brother to Mina Mintencress

HARI BROCKLER — lawyer for Mina Mintencress

ZACHARY RENDLETON — manager of the

Snakesmouth Lighthouse Hotel

CELESTE CRACKLING — maid to

Mina Mintencress

PART ONE

1. THE PROSPECT OF MAGIC

In the Last Chance Hotel, Seth Seppi was listening anxiously to the sounds of Mr and Mrs Bunn handing over ham and egg sandwiches to two hairy walkers who had been staying. They were offering cheery wishes for the next part of their journey.

Seth used to listen for the sounds of guests departing, just waiting for the chance to sneak into the quiet kitchen and secretly practise cooking. Cooking was his great love, learnt from his father, before his father had disappeared. But his recent discovery that he didn't work for Mr and Mrs Bunn at all, that they had been lying to him his whole life – and that the Last Chance Hotel belonged to him – had been astonishing. Seth could still hardly take in. It had changed everything.

But then he'd lately learnt so many astonishing truths that there was no part of Seth's life that he felt he truly understood any more.

The hairy and unexpected guests had stumbled gratefully upon the remote hotel, located in the sleepy depths of the Last Hope Forest. They had joyfully rested their blistered feet on the furniture, cheerfully left a skim of beard trimmings in the sink (accompanied by much singing), snored loudly and hadn't stopped eating everything put in front of them, including a very smelly goat's cheese everyone else had rejected and a Christmas pudding Seth had been trying to get rid of since last December.

And now they were gone. As he finally heard Horatio and Norrie Bunn slam the front door, Seth reached to the highest shelf to do what he *now* did in secret. Among the sacks of flour he had tucked a book, one with a bright pink jacket, covered in silly doodles and decorated with fluorescent lettering.

A Beginner's Guide to Really Easy-Peasy Magic.

It was only a few weeks ago that the arrival of a group of sorcerers had turned Seth's whole world upside down, not least because he'd narrowly avoided being arrested for murder.

Seth had discovered that magic was real, and the sorcerers had brought the tantalizing promise that he might actually be one of them – someone born with just a spark of magic. But just a spark was enough, Inspector Pewter of the magical police, MagiCon, had explained. Since then, Seth had been awaiting his promised visit, but so far the only contact he'd had from the inspector was the arrival of a small package. He'd unwrapped it eagerly to find it contained the *Easy-Peasy* book and a breezy note saying the inspector was unavoidably delayed and encouraging Seth to give the book a try.

Seth's shoulders slumped and his hands were shaking as he turned the pages.

Easy-peasy magic? Really?

The terrible smell of burnt, sour milk still hung about the kitchen as a constant reminder that his magic was an utter disaster.

Putting a very small wart on the end of a nose. After trying that one his nose had swelled to the size of an onion and had taken three days to return to normal, giving Horatio Bunn the best laugh of his life every single time he saw him.

He couldn't do this. He was never going to be able to do magic.

At least he now knew a little of his true history. The Last Chance Hotel had been passed down to him from his mother's family, and his mother had been a sorcerer.

Unfortunately, Seth had also had to stomach the seriously bad news that she had been a notoriously sinister sorcerer. And that she was wanted in connection with a grave event that had resulted in the deaths of countless magical people.

Now, as Seth stared at the book, he knew he was going to have to confront the most difficult truth of all. He was never going to be able to master a spell and be admitted into the magical world. He was never going to grow up to be a great and learned sorcerer.

And that meant he was never going to be able to discover if all they said about his mother was true, or look into a couple of other things that were troubling him.

To do all that he just needed to be able to perfect one spell. Just one. He pushed the book away. If there was easy magic, this was not it. He put his head in his hands and groaned.

Neither Inspector Pewter, nor his other new friend in the magical world, secret magical agent Angelique Squerr, had bothered to come and help. He felt all the powerlessness of being miles from anywhere, in the worst possible position of tantalizingly knowing about the magical world, but facing up to never being part of it.

He was growing desperate. Today, he had reached the last page. He was never going to get a spell right. Had he inherited any of his mother's magic at all?

And as he stood there alone, facing nothing but his failure, he found himself thinking something he'd promised himself he never would . . . was it possible that there might be magic he could do? Could it be that the only magic he would ever be able to master would be of the 'wrong' kind?

With a quick and guilty glance over his shoulder, Seth reached into a handy inside pocket of the bright-blue tunic he wore and took out a small black book. It was so old that the pages were held together with a scarlet thread. As he turned the cracked and stiff pages Seth felt, as he always did, that he was meant to use this book.

It was crammed with simple family recipes, mostly. There were weird instructions for creating perfectly innocent home-made boot polish and oven cleaner. OK, so it *was* sprinkled with the odd spell, and Pewter and Angelique had wanted to take this book away from him because *some* of it was 'disturbing' magic. Sure, there were banned spells in here and details of dark devices and sinister ideas. Yet it felt so right, so comfortable in his hand – reading it was like being close to a trusted friend.

Just looking at the book didn't make him some sort of sinister sorcerer, did it?

He turned to a well-worn page and found himself staring at the picture of the firefly cage, a dangerous and powerful device that terrified sorcerers.

Uncertainty and fear mixed together and crept into his stomach.

He knew he shouldn't even be looking at this book. But it had been his mother's notebook and the magic in it seemed to whisper to him in a reassuring voice, telling him he could rely on it. Here was a picture of someone stretching out their arms, as if beckoning something to them. *For capturing*, read the text alongside it. You said the words *Yma nam-well*. That one looked all right. That couldn't possibly harm anyone.

The magic seemed to whisper more insistently, it seemed to be saying that in a corner of the Last

Chance Hotel, in the middle of the Last Hope Forest, all alone, you may have no one to help, but there was also no one to see or care if you dabbled in just a little dark magic. Seth stretched out his fingers to give it a try.

There was a rush of cold air and a slinky black shape slunk in and wound herself around his legs, bringing in the dank and furtive smell of the forest.

Seth's black cat, Nightshade, was shimmying in from troubling the local wildlife. Seth hurriedly shoved the forbidden book back under his bright-blue tunic and tried to look at Nightshade with innocent eyes

'Can't leave you alone for a minute!' she cried, nudging at him with her pink nose. It was the only part of her that wasn't a glossy black. 'Let's see you do some tricks. Clean ones.' She leapt onto the worktop and clawed the bright cover of *Easy-Peasy Magic* closer.

Not for the first time, Seth wondered if it was really such a great thing that he had discovered his cat could talk. Most of the time she relayed stories of the bloodthirsty battles she had with her sworn enemies – the crows that circled endlessly above the hotel – but now and again she would break off from those to scold him. She fixed him challengingly with her big green eyes.

'I need a spell, Nightshade. Angelique explained it all to me. To join the magical world – the Elysee – you have to pass the Prospect. And to do that, you have to prove that you have the spark of magic inside you by demonstrating one spell done well. That's all I need. Then I've got a chance to find things out.'

Nightshade moved so close her green eyes bored straight into his. 'This isn't the way, Seth.'

'But—'

'What about spoons?' Nightshade clawed her way to the last page of the bright-pink volume. 'I mean, spoons – what can possibly go wrong?'

'You said that about boiling milk,' muttered Seth darkly.

'Well, show me something. Otherwise I've got a date with a particularly evil crow called Eric, who has a foul beak dirtier than a hare's behind. He needs teaching a lesson or two. Come on. You can do it.'

'It does look like a simple incantation,' muttered Seth.

They both took a shifty glance at the door to the hotel lobby, which was buckled and blistered and burnt around the edges, a relentless reminder of how every simple spell Seth tried not only failed, but led to disaster.

Nightshade took a step backwards, looking as if she wanted to put on safety goggles and a crash helmet. 'There won't be any blood this time, will there?'

2. Unfinished Business

Seth stood over a pan of still-hot potatoes he'd cooked earlier, now waiting to be mashed. A spoon stood amongst them. All he had to do was make that spoon move.

'Inspector Pewter told you it would be difficult,' said Nightshade, plonking her behind on the counter-top at a safe distance. 'It's not enough to want to do it, you have to believe you can do it.'

'Pewter's too busy hunting sinister sorcerers and murderers for MagiCon to help me. And Angelique is too busy being a glamorous top-secret magical agent, working undercover somewhere cool and dangerous,' Seth grouched. His hands hovered over the spoon as he readied himself.

His shoulders slumped.

'Perhaps,' he whispered, as he stared the spoon, 'I was better off before. I mean, it's worse knowing about magic, but not being able to do it. I might now be the boss of the hotel, but Mr and Mrs Bunn forget all the time and they still shout at me.'

'Come on. At least *she's* gone now – she was always the worst,' said Nightshade gently.

Seth tensed at even the thought of Tiffany Bunn – daughter of Mr and Mrs Bunn. For years he had put up with her schemes to humiliate and taunt him. He shuddered and tried to concentrate on the spell in front of him. But the words for that capturing spell from the black book were seared into his brain. *Yma nam-well.*

He read out the words on the page in front of him loudly and clearly, trying to sound more confident than he felt.

'*Effergy protogy noblio orgatory.*'

He swirled his hands around, trying his best to do it exactly as the picture showed. It felt good, actually. He got a waft of the soupy smell of the softening potatoes.

It felt somehow very magical. But the spoon didn't move.

He read out the words again, a bit louder this time.

And the spoon did a full slow circle of the pan. All by itself.

Nightshade moved a little closer to investigate, her whiskers almost touching the spoon. It twitched again. The tiniest slop of potato landed on her cheek. 'Seth! You've done it. You've got one you can show at the Prospect.' But the spoon wasn't stopping, it was gathering speed. 'Is it supposed to do that?' Nightshade got a splat of soft hot potato on her nose and miaowed in protest as she shook it off. 'I think you should make it stop now.'

A dollop of half-mashed potato flew out the pan and slapped Seth on the forehead. He felt it burn. Another sizzled past his left ear.

He grabbed the *Easy-Peasy* book for advice.

There was nothing between the spell and the back cover. *Unbelievable*. A swirl of the now well and truly mashed potato flew across the room in a graceful arc and dripped off the refrigerator like a dollop of snow.

'There's a page missing,' Seth said frantically.

'There's nothing here about how to make it stop.'

The mashed potato was bubbling up. Soon there were dollops on the ceiling and speckling the floor. Seth could only stare at it in futile panic – nothing was springing to mind except the certain knowledge that if all his previous disasters were anything to go by, there was about to be a terrible explosion.

'Do something!' cried Nightshade as she flew out of the door, narrowly dodging getting a large mash splatter on her rear end.

Seth did the only thing he could think of, which didn't involve any sort of magic.

He grabbed a towel to wrap around his head to protect himself from blistering airborne potato. Then he grabbed the saucepan and followed Night-shade out of the back door.

He ran with the pan to the edge of the forest and hurled the spoon, the saucepan and what was left of the mash under a tree. The whole lot exploded in a soft pluming firework and every leaf, every blade of grass, had a light white coating of potato, like frost on an winter morning.

'I can't do it!' Seth yelled at the top of his voice to no one in particular. Not Nightshade, as she had scarpered, nor the crows whose cries sounded exactly as if they were laughing at him.

He went back to the kitchen, mopped up everything, including himself, all the while muttering fiercely. Then he filled the sink with water, got a new pile of potatoes and started to peel again. Stick to what he was good at. Stick to what he knew. Put all those ridiculous dreams about magic behind him. He thumped potatoes on to the draining board.

A voice behind him made him leap about a foot in the air.

'What ho, young Seth.'

Seth swung around and was face to face with a tall, thin man in a shiny suit, with shoulder-length silvery hair, wearing glasses and a resolutely cheerful expression.

Inspector Pewter of MagiCon, the magical police, whom Seth had been convinced, not long ago, was going to arrest him for murder. The person who had led him to believe the impossible – that Seth himself might be magical. And had then left him to discover all alone what an utter failure he was.

At least Pewter hadn't been here a few moments earlier to witness his humiliating run into the forest, clutching a saucepan of mad potato with a towel wrapped around his head. At least it was his secret, as the last thing he wanted to do was to reveal to someone of immense and effortless magical talents like Pewter, how truly, utterly terrible he was at magic.

Seth plunged his hands back into the icy water to finish scrubbing the last potato. 'Hello, Inspector. What a surprise!' he said brightly, glancing around to see if any telltale splots of potato lurked anywhere. 'Are you on a case? Near here?'

'You'd be surprised where my work takes me. Just last week I was staking out an old isolated barn for days because some folk had reported seeing fairies.' Pewter shoved his hands deep in the pockets of his shimmering jacket. 'For a world that no longer believes in magic, it's incredible what people some-times believe they've seen. Now, you haven't got bad news for me, have you?'

Seth darted a suspicious glance at him.

'It's just that you haven't offered me tea,' said Pewter. 'You're not out of milk, are you? Or tea?'

Seth forced a smile and busied himself with the kettle.

'Take this case I'm heading off to,' continued Pewter. 'Right up your street. A lighthouse hotel. Sun, sea, sand and on-tap room service; food and drink brought to your room any time, day or night.'

'Sounds a small-fry sort of investigation for a MagiCon inspector,' said Seth glumly, handing

Pewter a mug before turning back to his potatoes. 'In fact, it sounds more like a holiday.'

'Ah, but no good for tennis.' Pewter loved the sport. 'What's a holiday without tennis? This place is on a bare rock in the middle of the sea. Doesn't even have a court. But at least there are some dangerous ghosts to liven things up.'

'But I thought you'd be . . . Aren't you on the trail of Red Valerian?'

Red Valerian was the code name of a sinister sorcerer who was causing plenty of trouble for Magi-Con, although he managed to stay hidden well behind the scenes, manipulating others to do his dirty work. His plot to acquire the firefly cage – by sending one of his followers to steal it – had led to the revelation that the dark device was hidden at the Last Chance Hotel. It had also led to the murder of the cage's inventor, and the truth about Seth's family history being uncovered.

Only Tiffany Bunn had outwitted everyone and had stolen the cage from under all of their noses before vanishing into thin air. To Seth, there was little more terrifying than thinking Tiffany was out there and might soon be able to wield the powerful magic of the firefly cage.

Pewter chuckled. 'Chasing down sinister dudes

like Red Valerian is way beyond my pay grade. Actually, I do have some news for you, though.'

Seth whirled around. 'Someone is on Tiffany's trail? You know where the firefly cage is? Red Valerian is unmasked?'

Pewter sipped his tea. 'You shouldn't worry, Seth. We have the very best people on all of that. I bring you news of your friend Angelique. Any chance of a biscuit?'

'Huh.' Angelique was another who had dangled the dream of magic, then hadn't bothered to even visit him.

'She teamed up with some young guy named Stormforce,' Pewter went on. 'You will be delighted to hear they have been receiving no end of praise and celebration. They solved a big case just yesterday. "The Case of the Walking Wardrobe" they're calling it. Lots of credit to them. Seems they make a good team. A perfect match.'

Seth scurried about, looking for any biscuits the hairy walkers hadn't munched their way through. He knew he should be pleased for Angelique, but all he felt was a deep dark stab of jealousy. She had a new friend and her career was flourishing. No wonder she hadn't bothered to visit him and his terrible magic.

He plonked some home-made shortbread down in front of Pewter.

'Ginger or chocolate-dipped?'

Pewter took two of each as his eyes flicked to the blackened frame and buckled door. They had been badly repaired with some planks. 'I am pleased to see you haven't been letting I dare not wait upon I would.'

'What does that even mean?' snapped Seth, without meeting Pewter's eye. He knew he would see a gleam there, glinting behind the inspector's glasses.

'It means I am delighted to see you have been practising your magic. Magic is a difficult thing to learn and most people don't have the patience for it.'

'It was a straightforward door-shutting spell,' Seth muttered, and added half-heartedly, 'I think I'm getting there.'

'Great to hear it.' Pewter rubbed his hands together. 'May I see?'

There. Pewter had asked the dreaded question.

Seth wiped down some more surfaces. The very last thing he wanted to do was to reveal his failure to Pewter, who'd had such high hopes of him.

He felt a warm hand on his shoulder.

'I feel I made a big mistake and I owe you an apology,' the inspector said. 'I told you that you might have been born with natural magic. That –' he shook his head and took a big bite of shortbread – 'was a big mistake. So easy to look longingly at others and only see brilliance. Not the hard work that went into getting there.'

Seth swallowed, hoping he hadn't heard right, trying and failing to hide how devastated he was. His heart was hammering.

That was why Pewter had left it so long before visiting – he already knew that Seth couldn't do magic. But for Seth, there was much more at stake than just being magical.

The black shape of Nightshade slipped back in. 'Whiskers and white mice! Inspector Pewter, thank goodness. Just in the nick of time.' She shook her whiskers. 'Hope you've got some ideas, because I'm surprised this hotel is still standing after Seth's attempts at magic. We are desperate.'

3. A BIG MISTAKE

S eth threw his cat a poisonous look.

'And,' went on Nightshade, 'you'll never guess
what I caught him with. That black book.'

Seth threw her an even worse look for betraying
this particular secret.

'You've not been using *that* book, have you?'
Pewter said in a low voice. 'I was hoping you'd buried
it in the darkest part of the forest.'

Seth's hand darted protectively towards his chest,
where he carried the book. 'I just like to look at the

recipes and stuff.' His words sounded unconvincing even to himself. He felt so utterly hopeless, stranded out here, feeling everything important was happening far away.

He discreetly wiped away a potato blob from the edge of the sink and then met Pewter's gaze as the inspector took him by the shoulders. Seth was really hoping that for once he'd get a straight answer and some proper advice. The inspector's glasses seemed to become clearer. Seth found himself staring into eyes as piercingly blue as the brightest sky. It was hard to look away.

'I think the reason people fail at magic, fail at anything,' said Pewter, 'is because they want it to be easy. The most important things in the world are reading and books. The right books. At my school we had to carry a book to read with us at all times – if we were found without one it was an automatic detention.'

'You studied magic at school?' Seth tried and failed to imagine Pewter in detention. Or a classroom.

A dollop of mash he'd missed on the ceiling flopped on to Inspector Pewter's head.

Pewter wiped it off without a word. 'Had to keep my magic a secret. I loved stories but there was one book that stayed in my school bag from my earliest days – a gift from my father. He'd learnt from it before passing it on to me. That book was like a secret best friend.'

The inspector checked a huge ornate watch on his wrist. 'Now, I'm afraid I've an appointment with a comfortable dinner and a sumptuous hostess,' he sighed. 'Maybe it's a sumptuous dinner, and a comfortable hostess.' He stroked his chin thoughtfully. 'See the sea from every window. I don't suppose you could spare more of that very fine shortbread?'

Pewter made his way outside, munching on shortbread as he strode into the trees that circled the hotel, towards a spot where the air was shimmering like a heat haze, as if part of what you were looking at wasn't real. Seth knew what it was – a teleport, the way magical people travelled about with great ease.

'By the way – the word to stop anything is *arosfa*!' he called. 'Worth practising that one – it's a goodie. If you shout it with enough authority it usually works, even if you aren't particularly a words person. And the other thing is belief. That's an important one; you have to believe you can do it.'

Seth blinked twice. *Not a words person? What did that mean?*

Pewter stopped and waved a hand in the air. 'But everyone should start with the basics.' And then he was gone, disappearing through the teleport before Seth could ask him anything more.

'Well, you handled that brilliantly,' said Nightshade as Seth headed back into the kitchen and the waiting potatoes. 'Why couldn't you have swallowed your pride, told him your magic is rubbish and asked for help?' She leapt onto the countertop and tucked her pink nose inside the easy-peasy book. 'You should follow his advice. Practise.'

'But Pewter said he made a mistake when he said he thought I had natural magic.'

'He was trying to tell you to stick with doing the difficult stuff and not to get lured into doing easy black magic, Seth.'

Was he? Instead of picking up the potatoes again, Seth opened the easy-peasy book right at the first page and he saw something he'd not noticed before. On the inside page, before the spells, someone had written an inscription. It was very faded, but he could make out the words: *Hope you have as much fun with this as I did, son.*

Seth stared at it. The writing was too faint for it to have been written recently. This must be the very book Pewter had talked about. The book Pewter's father had learnt from and had passed on to Pewter, who had carried it with him always. What had Pewter said? That when he had to keep his magic a secret and when no one else around him was learning magic, that the book was like having a best friend who truly understood him.

The book Pewter had given him to learn from was the inspector's own precious book.

Could that mean Pewter really did believe in him?

'You were too grumpy to listen,' went on Nightshade. 'Now he's off to some swanky hotel and you may not get the chance for months.'

Seth's mind was suddenly awhirl with an idea. One that involved plump pillows and someone bringing him cups of tea. And seeing the sea from every window. Seth had never seen the sea. He had never left the Last Chance Hotel.

For once, he could be a guest. And he could thank the inspector . . . and what better place to practise his magic undisturbed than as a guest in a remote lighthouse hotel? For the first time in his life he wouldn't be the one peeling the potatoes.

Seth tucked the book into his tunic, gathered Nightshade to him and began to run.

She gave an indignant miaow as he raced back

outside, hoping the teleport would still be open. He saw the haze still hovering. He ran as fast as he could, lifting his feet nimbly over tree roots, and flung himself after Inspector Pewter.

PART TWO

4. The New Kitchen Boy

It was like being in a whirlpool, not knowing which was way up, unable to breathe. The air was whistling past and there was nothing to see, not even blackness, just a blinding white. He could be hurtling, uncontrolled, through some distant corner of the universe; it had just been a few seconds, but they seemed to go on and on.

And then he was sprawled on the ground.

Seth had crash-landed awkwardly, his left leg twisting underneath him. As he tried to stand he knew that if he hadn't landed in something squishy, soft and very smelly, the leg would have been even more painful to walk on. He limped away from what he was sitting in, removing a long brown strand of it from his sleeve. Seaweed, he hoped.

He wriggled his toes and felt his nose, to make sure no part of him was left behind at the Last Chance Hotel, and looked about for Nightshade, aware of high, steep cliffs and a constantly moving foreground. Water, churning and boiling and racing towards him, then changing its mind and playfully racing back again, leaving a line of foam and a hushed whisper.

The tang of salt and a windy freshness snatched at him, bringing the taste of unknown open spaces. The air was raucous with the cries of seabirds and the constant roll and crash of the waves. It was so noisy. It was amazing to be somewhere so open to the sky, a never-ending blue reflected in the sparkling sea below.

'How come Pewter always looks as unruffled as if he's done nothing more difficult than step into a room when he comes out of one of those things?' snapped a voice behind him. Nightshade was checking her fur and whiskers.

Seth stared at the rushing waves, breathing deeply,

his senses aquiver at the avalanche of unusual smells. One particular smell . . .

'What's that terrible stench? Seaweed drying on the rocks? Or rotting fish . . .'

'Let's find a way off this beach,' said Nightshade, lifting her paws from damp stones with a little shake. 'Where's this bloomin' hotel?'

Seth had to shield his eyes against the glare of the sun as he looked upwards, searching the skyline and the towering cliff for some sort of path. As they climbed with difficulty up the steep shingle beach, the smell was getting worse. Ahead they could see that the high cliff was studded with brave and tough flowers, and a little way down the beach from the foot of the cliff was a huge wooden signpost that read 'PRIVATE. KEEP OUT.'

'How nice. Oh, very friendly,' huffed Nightshade. 'Pewter had better not have got this wrong.'

Seth suspected what she was really trying to say was that *he* had better not have got this wrong. He strode past the sign, slipping on the shingle, trying to appear confident, Nightshade close alongside grumbling on about sand in her paws.

Pewter must have stepped through only moments before. Where was he? Typical Pewter, landing a teleport on a beach with no way off . . . unless the inspector could fly. Could Inspector Pewter fly? As far as Seth was concerned, he could do anything.

'A load of dead birds.' Nightshade pushed delicately at the corpse of a gull with a paw. 'That's where that terrible stench is coming from.'

A live seagull pecked at something on the beach ahead of them and Nightshade tried to leap on it, but the loose shingle completely messed with her usual agility.

'Nightshade, you've plenty of birds at home to chase, please leave these ones alone.'

'Big birds are always trouble unless you show them who's boss from the start. And I promise to leave the birds alone if you leave the plant life alone.'

Seth was bending to pick some unusual plants growing at the foot of the cliff. 'But this is buck's-horn plantain. I've only seen it in books before,' he said, stuffing it in one of his many pockets. The tunic had always been perfect for foraging around the Last Chance Hotel. 'And I think this is wild carrot. Such great names, don't you think?'

Nightshade fixed him with her big green eyes. 'That carrot is not the only thing that will be wild in a minute. Just focus on finding this luxury hotel.'

They passed another five or six gull corpses, and when Seth looked back, he realized the air was no longer shimmering. The teleport had closed. There was no way back.

Things went wrong every time he did anything involving magic. They'd stepped into that teleport and now they seemed to have arrived in the wrong place. What on earth were they going to do?

A wet slimy lump hit the back of Seth's head. He investigated with his fingers and discovered a ball of seaweed. He then tried to scrape it off before any more slithered wetly down his neck. A pebble fell in front of him as if dislodged by someone scrambling away at the top of the cliff. He thought he heard an evil cackle and looked up.

Mistake. Another ball of wet seaweed slimed him, this time getting him in the side of the head and trickling into his ear. He felt sure the laugh that followed came from a small boy.

He squinted into the sunlight and could see the silhouette of a figure outlined against the blue sky.

He was about to yell something rude to the seaweed shooter when a young man's voice called: 'Guess you are here for the hotel?'

'Yes,' Seth cried, wiggling a finger in his ear to remove traces of seawater and a thin line of green weed.

He strode on more purposefully, and could just make out that the tall figure was extending a long arm and gesturing to a corner of the beach. Seth headed that way, struggling and slipping on the loose shingle. Nightshade followed him, still irritable, and finally they could see what the young man had been pointing towards. Steps, steep with no handrail, almost invisibly hewn into the rock. He started to climb.

Visions of those comfy beds and plump pillows returned. A few days with no kitchen duties, no vegetables to prepare and no washing-up. Visiting another hotel made him think he should start making changes at home. He could even employ a new kitchen boy to help him. That was an idea. It was going to take a while before he grew into his new role as the owner of the hotel.

At the top of the steps he was met by a young blond man over six feet tall, with a big white-toothed smile in a suntanned face. He looked about eighteen, and as if he'd be happiest chasing a ball on a sports field.

'I'm Zachary Rendleton, manager of the Snakesmouth Lighthouse soon-to-be Hotel,' he said with a big grin. 'Who the heck are you?'

'Soon-to-be hotel?' echoed Seth, not liking the

sound of this. 'I'm Seth Seppi,' he said nervously. 'You don't have guests?'

Thoughts of his luxury holiday were being shoved aside by a worry that if the hotel wasn't open, what possible excuse could he have for being here? He remembered that 'KEEP OUT' sign.

'Renovations are underway, but we've hit one or two snags.'

Seth was trying to place the young man's accent, as well as think of a reason to explain his presence, as he followed Rendleton's agile strides along a narrow path. He had difficulty keeping up. Australian, he thought. It was one of the things he liked about living in a hotel – you got to meet people from all over the world.

'You've worked in a hotel before?'

'Er – yes, I have.'

'Very glad you're here then, Seth Seppi,' continued Rendleton. 'There's a ton of work to do.'

A ton of work?

'You *are* the new kitchen boy?'

This was not what I had in mind, Seth thought, before realizing he should seize gratefully on this excuse for being here and answered with an eager, 'Yes, I am!'

But Rendleton wasn't waiting for an answer, as he

continued to lead the way.

'I think there was a small boy firing things? Isn't he a guest?'

'Ah, so you already got a taste of young Alfie's catapult? Bad luck.'

Seth rubbed the back of his neck. 'He's pretty accurate.'

'Plenty of time to practise. Young Alfie is brother of Mina Mintencress, who bought this old lighthouse. They sadly lost their parents in a car wreck, and moved here to be together while following grand plans to open the place as a hotel. Guess Jo just dropped you off at Gull Cove? I didn't think she'd find a replacement so quickly. Wasn't sure she'd even risk coming out with this storm brewing.'

Seth had no idea who Jo might be, but at least he might have chance to find Inspector Pewter and a way out of here. He was glad Nightshade had slipped unnoticed past them. Most people arriving at a hotel, for whatever reason, wouldn't bring a grumpy cat with them.

On the other side of the water Seth could now see a short, very narrow peninsula reaching towards them, with cliffs towering either side of what looked like a small harbour studded with low buildings.

'So has Alfie been killing seabirds and leaving

them on the beach?' asked Seth, thinking of the catapult and the evil cackle.

'Alfie and dead birds are the least of our worries, mate.' Rendleton paused to turn, raising a hand to point to where dozens of seabirds screeched anxiously overhead in a vast sky. 'I'm not an expert on the local wildlife, but I guess dead birds might have something to do with the biggest storm in years being on its way.'

Seth could see now that Rendleton wasn't really pointing at the birds, but at where the far-off sky was split dangerously in two. Directly above was cloudless blue, but leering towards them from the distance was a menacing black.

Seth gulped. He turned to see that Rendleton was already making his way further along the path at his rapid pace, and scampered after him.

He wasn't supposed to be travelling through teleports and getting himself a new job. The very last thing he needed was to be trapped, working in a totally unknown hotel, and with the most colossal of all storms on its way. However bad things had been at the Last Chance Hotel, this was a disaster. He was supposed to be practising magic. He had to get away, and fast.

Right now, though, Seth had little choice but to

follow, and tried not to dwell on his dark thoughts when he heard Rendleton ahead saying:

'My worries are more that we're all still here by morning.'

5. LUCKY IF WE ARE STILL STANDING

As they moved out the shelter of the clifftop rocks, Seth had his first sight of a cluster of white-painted buildings and the tall tower of Snakesmouth Lighthouse. It was almost cylindrical and painted in zingy orange stripes, the structure tapering upwards to huge windows from where a light would once have sent a piercing beam to warn ships of the rocks.

'Makes an impression, doesn't it?' said Rendleton. 'Though it'll be lucky if we are still standing by the time that storm's through with us.' The manager rushed on past a two-storey building made of white stone about as old and weathered as the rocks it was nestled into. 'That's our Sunrise Wing. Originally it was home to two families. Had to be here all year round to keep the light going. Course it stopped being a working lighthouse years ago. Plenty of room for guests when it's all converted.'

Seth could see now that they truly were on an island, a small, pretty one with seabirds whirling and calling above banks of tough plants. Beautiful views surrounded them, the air fresh and exhilarating. He was torn between admiring his surroundings and not being able to take his eyes off the darkening sky. Only minutes ago it had been like a roof of blue, with only that telltale black line of a storm brewing in the distance. Already both the sea and sky were a dark grey that warned of an approaching battle. The sky, massed with clouds, didn't just look darker – it looked closer.

'It's been deserted around eight years, after the last owner disappeared,' said Rendleton, keeping up a sharp pace.

'The people turning this into a hotel? Are they...' there was no easy way to say, but Seth didn't have a clue where that teleport had brought him. Did

Pewter only investigate crime in the magical world? 'This girl and her brother, are they a magical family?'

'You don't want to be worrying about dead sea-birds and magic,' muttered Rendleton, weaving his way along a path by the Sunrise Wing and reaching a sheltered blue door at the rear. 'But this is an unusual set-up, so you might fit right in with your strange questions. A pretty unlucky family, that's about all I know. Here is your new home.'

He led Seth straight down into a basement, bringing the smell of the outdoors, the sea and bracing air into a deserted kitchen. It wasn't vast, but it was well-equipped, with a long stainless-steel table and an oven so huge it made Seth wonder just how many guests they were expecting. There was no smell of baking or signs of any food being prepared.

'I – er, so tell me more about the job, the family I'm working for . . .'

Rendleton carried on through the kitchen on his long legs, pausing only to point to an open door and inform Seth it led to the staff accommodation. Seth caught a glimpse of a vibrantly purple corridor before he followed Rendleton up three steps opposite. Seth stopped in his tracks.

He'd emerged into an entrance hall papered in a soft lilac that looked shimmeringly beautiful, threaded with the faintest gold, picked out by sunlight streaming from a high window.

There were further doors, one leading to a lounge of brightly coloured chairs. Seth could see a dining room and a closed door to what he guessed might be a bedroom. But what really drew his attention was a narrow staircase twisting steeply from the centre of the entrance lobby into the tower above. It was covered in the sort of carpet that made you just long to take off your shoes and wiggle your toes in. The whole place had the aroma of fresh paint and a new-carpet smell of rubber and wool. As Seth craned his neck upwards to the topmost windows, he saw the wallpaper was decorated with a flock of birds that looked as if they were soaring right out to the sky.

'Wow!'

'That is the first reaction of most people.'

'This Mina Mintencress must really have a lot of money.'

'Yep – seriously minted. The second reaction is saying she clearly has plenty to throw around. The third is usually a comment that this is a lot of money to inherit at sixteen, closely followed by a judgement that this is a mad project to take on and they are bound to fail. But they were making a grand job of it . . . until lately. And Mina's got enough determination for a whole squad.'

The sound of a door being thumped or kicked made both Seth and Rendleton look upwards, from where an angry voice yelled: 'Open this door, Mina. You can't keep me locked out for ever.' There were two more thuds.

'Just a shame she doesn't always carry Lark along with some of her wilder decisions. A little trouble in paradise. I believe Lark and Mina may not yet have made up their differences, and the arrival of the blood-sucking lawyer doesn't help.'

'Differences?' said Seth over another thud. It sounded as if a solid door had received a heavy kick.

'Work lately hasn't been going altogether well. Just so you know. The builders have walked out. This lawyer, Hari Brockler, arrived, and unfortunately decided to hang around and stick his nose in. Now he and Lark are trying to talk Mina into just ditching the whole project. Perhaps not a bad idea, before anyone dies. Be warned – this new job of yours might not last for long.'

Seth barely had time to wonder why anyone might be in danger of dying before the door upstairs received another blow, but with less conviction than before. Seth winced nonetheless.

What must be Lark's voice cried shrilly: 'Stop

being so stubborn, Mina. You can't lock yourself in your room for ever. We need to talk.'

'I guess getting people to work on an island can be tricky. And getting guests,' Seth muttered, thinking of the difficulties faced by his own hotel, buried in the middle of the endless Last Hope Forest. 'Must be a difficult place to work if there are arguments like that. Is that why the builders left?'

Rendleton was speeding on up the stairs, and seemed not to hear Seth's question. 'It would be great if there was some sort of lunch in the dining room at one. Or soon after? Dining room's just next to the lounge, with a grand view of the sea. But then a grand view of the sea isn't exactly in short supply hereabouts.'

'Lunch? Isn't there a chef to do that?'

'Yeah, well, truth is, the cook left,' called Rendleton, taking the stairs two at a time.

'The builders, the cook and the kitchen boy all left? Because of the arguments?'

Rendleton paused to look at Seth over the polished banister of the spiral staircase, his floppy blond hair falling over his face as his voice trailed down from above.

'Well, yes, mate. They all left. But not because of the arguments. They all left because of the ghosts.'

6. The Village That Died

Now Seth remembered. Pewter was investigating some sort of mean ghosts.

He recalled the little the inspector had told him about the case: '*This place is on a bare rock in the middle of the sea. Doesn't even have a tennis court. But at least there are some dangerous ghosts to liven things up.*'

And all the staff and builders were scrambling to leave. Seth returned to the empty kitchen and looked around anxiously, half expecting something nasty to leap out at him.

Where was Pewter? However angry the inspector might be for Seth sneaking after him and getting mixed up in his case, Seth needed to find him. He needed to get back to the Last Chance Hotel. Why had he been so rash as to follow Pewter?

Seth ducked his head out of the back door. He didn't at all like the look of that threatening sky. And what had happened to Nightshade? She loved exploring and making a pest of herself to any local wildlife, but she loathed storms. He could only hope she had slipped in, found the warmest place in the lighthouse and settled there for a snooze – she was pretty good at that – because right then there came an almighty crack of thunder, and Seth felt the first huge splash of rain fall on his face. The storm had arrived.

Seth took stock. He'd lost his cat and Pewter was nowhere to be found. The biggest storm he'd ever seen was right on top of the ghost-infected lighthouse he was trapped in. He had a new job he didn't even want and he was expected to produce lunch for an unspecified number of people. The basement kitchen was already dark enough to need the lights on and a series of waiting candles told him losing the electrics might be a regular problem. And he was pretty sure he had both mashed potato and seaweed in his hair. What was he going to do?

He had no time to formulate anything that even looked like a plan before an untidy young woman practically tumbled into the room. She was trying to tuck her long brown hair under a ridiculous-looking white cap that was a little too small for the job. When her worried brown eyes focused on Seth, she nearly fell down the three steps into the kitchen.

Seth moved forward quickly to catch her before she went sprawling. 'I'm Seth – the new kitchen boy. Hope I didn't startle you. Are you all right?'

She was wearing a plain black dress with a small sprig of lavender pinned to the lapel. Her fingers twitched nervously as she still fiddled with her cap, pulling it down over her ears so it almost obscured her eyes. She smelled faintly of strawberries. 'I-I'm Celeste Crackling. I'm-I'm the maid.'

Seth breathed a sigh of relief. 'Well, I'm glad you're here! Rendleton said everyone would be wanting lunch. I guess it's down to us.'

He waited for her to tell him what he should be doing, but she didn't move.

'Is it OK if I explore the kitchen?' He opened and shut some cupboard doors. 'How many for lunch? Have we enough food to last the storm?'

'Storm?'

Celeste glanced nervously towards the back door and he decided not to add that Rendleton had said they'd be lucky if the lighthouse was still standing by morning.

Seth now saw there were four doors leading from the kitchen. He already knew one led back outside and one to the staff rooms. Then there was the door at the top of the short flight of steps that led to the entrance hall, but there was another door alongside that one. He approached it, hoping to find a larder.

Celeste practically screamed. 'No, not that one!' She recovered herself. 'Sorry, everyone gets a bit jumpy when that one's unlocked.'

Seth stood for a moment, staring at the innocent-looking white door, his mind already full of ghosts and hauntings.

'It leads to the Sunrise Wing,' said Celeste. Thunder rumbled.

'Rendleton pointed that out,' said Seth. 'Sunrise Wing is a nice name.'

Celeste snorted. 'Named after Lark Sunrise. She's been far too pushy in this project if you ask me. You'd think it was her money bought this place, but she's just a school friend of Mina's who didn't want to be left out. Lark said please could she take charge of the furnishings. Big mistake.'

'So is that the bit that's supposed to be haunted?' said Seth, nodding his head at the door as he began to forage in the kitchen cupboards.

Celeste tossed her head. 'Yes. *Oooh, the ghost of Soul Snakesmouth has returned to haunt us all.* Of course Rendleton wasted no time filling you in about that nonsense.'

'Soul Snakesmouth?'

'The guy who owned this place. He lived alone here for years and there was some mystery about his death, so it was left empty. There are lots of stories. Jo, that girl who drives the boat from the mainland, won't ever shut up about them. What are we having for lunch? I'm absolutely famished.'

Seth poked his head through the door to the staff rooms as he passed, guessing that with so few staff there would be space for him if he failed to leave tonight. The purple walls of the corridor had jagged metal artworks along the walls.

'Lark has a lively taste, doesn't she?'

'She just likes shopping, really.'

Seth was happy to find bread in a cupboard and discover a well-stocked, enormous fridge and freezer. He seized basics like butter and cheese gratefully and set about gathering something that might pass as lunch.

He hardly liked to take charge, but Celeste had slid out a chair at the long table, tucked in her feet – shod in a very delicate pair of pale-blue ballet pumps – laid her head on outstretched arms and closed her eyes. Within seconds she was breathing deeply, the thin skin on her eyelids fluttering. Was she going to sleep?

'Rendleton said the previous owner disappeared,' said Seth loudly, assembling more ingredients on the table.

Celeste sniffed loudly and sat up, blinking. 'Oh yes, well, Jo – the boat girl – always makes sure everyone knows that story. The village of Snakesmouth was a popular enough place – a pretty harbour nestled among the cliffs, that kind of thing. You'll have seen it from the boat.' She ducked as the thunder crashed again overhead.

Seth remembered the small huddle of buildings he'd seen across the water from the clifftop.

'But there was a terrible storm about eight years ago and a whole chunk of the coast fell away into the sea, leaving the village almost an island – you must have seen how narrow the peninsula is – supposedly shaped like a snake's mouth. The whole place is unstable and practically cut off. Cursed, some said. Everyone had to move out. And that same night,

Soul Snakesmouth disappeared and was never seen again. Well. That's one of the stories. Sure you'll have to listen to them all.'

Seth wondered how the stories might explain the ghosts. And Pewter being here. He slid a wrapped ham and carving knife in front of Celeste, who dutifully cut several thin slices, before devouring them all.

'Oh, I'm so hungry. Busy morning.'

'Glad to see someone's taking care of supplies.'

'I suppose Rendleton organizes things – Jo comes almost daily from Merricove on her boat. Mostly to eat as much of our food as she can. And pocket what she thinks we don't notice.'

'Maybe you wouldn't mind cutting some bread?' Seth suggested. Surely she couldn't be expecting him to do everything?

Celeste opened her eyes fully and scrambled to her feet. Slowly she drew a loaf of bread towards her.

'Erm – if you're going to help it's kind of usual to wash your hands first.' Seth wondered how her boss let her get away with being quite so lazy.

'Of course!' She headed for the sink.

'Tell me how you all ended up being here, turning this lighthouse into a hotel? Sounds a wild idea to me.'

He thought he saw movement in the corner of the room. But when he focused his eyes and looked properly, there was nothing there.

'Oh, now that *is* a great story. Mina's is the most tragic and romantic tale. She went to this horrific lonely boarding school, just along the coast from here. Her parents were always busy travelling abroad. If she couldn't sleep, she'd watch the lighthouse shining across the water. Almost a sign that her parents were thinking of her from far away.' Celeste sighed.

Lightning illuminated the basement kitchen through the high-up windows and her face looked suddenly frozen in terror. The storm was almost right above them now.

'We are in the highest building for miles around,' she whispered, and she gripped Seth's arm so tight it felt like she was cutting off the circulation. 'If lightning strikes it's going to hit us, isn't it? That storm looks evil.'

'This lighthouse has been here for years – this won't be the first storm it's been through,' said Seth, disentangling her fingers. 'Tell me more.'

Celeste still looked fearful, but she went back to slicing bread and telling her story.

'Her parents died in a car crash and she was

desperate for something to take her mind off the awfulness. She'd inherited buckets of money. Lark said to travel the world and go to parties. But that would mean abandoning Alfie at school. Then she found this place was up for sale. The place that had been a comfort for all those years. It seemed like it was meant to be. So Mina decided to save it.'

'And it was going well?'

'Of course. I mean, turning this place into a hotel is a great idea, surely? Why can't everybody see that? It's a real fairy tale. Just a shame that as well as being responsible for some terrible furnishings, Lark is now sneaking around behind Mina's back and plotting with that dreary lawyer, Brockler, who arrived and insisted on staying. His only purpose is to put a stop to all Mina's brilliant fun. Sneaky double-crossers, the pair of them.' Celeste waved the long bread knife dangerously.

Lightning flashed again, this time accompanied by a fizzing sound, and the kitchen was plunged into a very sudden and very deep blackness.

7. The Storm

Seth quickly lit the candles dotted around the room, which sent shadows dancing across the walls, transforming the kitchen with flickering light. Just for a moment, shapes seemed to loom out at them as if something was moving in the darkness. From the corner of his eye, Seth thought he saw a flitting dark shape. It was gone in an instant, and he wasn't at all sure he had seen anything. Maybe just a spider.

Partly to cover his own fears, Seth said loudly: 'So,

six people live here, including a small boy with a catapult. Alfie is Mina Mintencress's younger brother, right?' He was convinced there might still be traces of seaweed lodged in his ear.

Celeste's sigh of relief was immense when the electric lights blinked and decided to come back on.

'He is just adorable. A bit too into his rocks, maybe. And his catapult. Living on an island is perfect for him. So free. He found a fossil yesterday. And Rendleton's turning him into a really strong swimmer. This place has just been brilliant for him.'

'Is he bothered by the stories of ghosts?' asked Seth brightly, deciding he was keen to hear more about the ghost stories. He wasn't sure he believed in ghosts, but not long ago he didn't believe in magic either.

'Ghosts! You get one broken ankle . . . one hand sprain . . . I mean, doors slam in the wind. Electrics are bound to be dodgy on an island. And all that food going missing? Lark eats like a horse, and like I said, I reckon that boat girl, Jo, stuffs her pockets when she thinks I'm not looking. They all need watching, the lot of them. Things were going fine. But when builders moved into the Sunrise Wing . . . well, we hit a snag or two. I reckon all it needs is someone to watch Rendleton, Lark and now

Brockler for a bit, in secret, and find out who's up to what and who's lying.'

Seth nodded and watched her flinch as the lightning and thunder struck again, barely a second apart.

Celeste stuck out her tongue and very slowly finished cutting a single, wonky slice of bread with her soft hands and very long nails. Lunch might take a long time.

'I guess working for Miss Mintencress is a nice job.'

'Well, yes, but why do you say that? Most people just think she's mad, buying this place.'

To Seth, who had toiled all his life, it was obvious that Celeste's job involved doing little hard work, however crazy her boss was. 'Well, I guess you've never actually sliced bread before?' he said.

Celeste ducked at another flash of lightning, as a rumble of thunder rolled across the sky. She glanced up fearfully at the light in the centre of the kitchen as it fizzed again and they were suspended in near-darkness for a moment.

'I've been with her for years. But it's true, I'm more like her best friend than her maid.'

Seth thought this explained a lot.

'And who is Rendleton exactly? Not one of the family? He said he's the manager.'

'In charge of bookings, tours and marketing. Or so he says. I guess he's pretty useful.'

'Tours? For a hotel without guests?'

She snorted. 'Exactly. He's mostly one of Lark's ideas, which probably means she fancies him as a boyfriend.'

'Well, I'm sorry to hear about all of it.'

'Oh, we'll get new builders. Ones that aren't so stupid about ghosts.'

'I meant sorry about Mina's parents dying and the being lonely,' said Seth. 'And the arguing and staff leaving. But I see why she bought this place. I think it's brilliant.'

'You do?'

Seth would have liked to say how strange but also nice it was to hear that someone who had plenty of money had chosen to buy and live in a hotel. He had spent ages working out how he could get away from the Last Chance Hotel, but now he wasn't sure how he felt. Everything had become so tangled up with wanting to explore more of the magical world and all his unfinished business with Tiffany and the firefly cage. He wasn't going to go into any of that with Celeste, though, so he just nodded.

There was another terrific crash of thunder and lightning filled the room with a white glare. Celeste looked up, her dark eyes wide and fearful.

'Now this Mr Pewter has just arrived,' Celeste went on loudly, as if talking over the storm would stop her being afraid of it. 'Everyone's pretending he's here because the wiring is dodgy, but I'm pretty sure he's really here because of the supposed *haunting*. Hopefully he will tell everyone to stop being so stupid.'

It was a relief to hear that Pewter was definitely here, but Seth's mind was leaping along furiously– the inspector wasn't a ghost-hunter; he investigated magical crime. Apart from the ghosts, the only other puzzle seemed to be a missing person who disappeared in mysterious circumstances years ago. How did that relate to strange happenings once a new owner took over? Where *was* the inspector?

'Want to lay the table?' he said, thinking he really should focus on his work for now. As Rendleton had said, there was a ton of work to do and no one seemed to be doing very much.

'In the dining room?' asked Celeste uncertainly. She headed over to the sink where plates and cups were stacked and moved them around busily. 'Isn't it safer down here in the basement?'

There was another resounding crash of thunder accompanied by a splatter of rain against the back door that sounded like someone was throwing stones. A cup slipped out of Celeste's grasp, splashing her delicate blue ballet shoes. Seth caught it before it shattered on the stone floor.

'Have you got some better shoes for the kitchen?' he suggested. 'Don't want these to get ruined.'

'Do you know, I probably have.'

She sloped off through a door that led to the purple corridor and the staff rooms and returned wearing a pair of clumpy shoes.

'Look!' she said, kicking her feet giddily. 'Are these the sort of things you meant?'

'You really are the strangest maid I have ever come across,' Seth joked. Another crash sounded from on high – but Seth wasn't convinced this one was thunder. 'I think that crash came from inside.'

Even as he said the words, they lost the lights for a third time and for a few seconds were left with just the eerily playing light of the candles and the dancing shadows flickering in the corners.

When the lights came back on, they were accompanied by an ear-splitting scream.

8. Something Nasty in the Bath Tub

'Someone doesn't like storms,' commented Seth as the lights flickered madly.

But Celeste rushed towards the stairs, her eyes panicked. 'Was that Alfie?'

Seth followed her into the extravagant entrance hall. 'Perhaps you should wait here,' he said, trying to sound much braver than he felt. His mind was galloping with the talk of ghosts, cursed villages and mysterious deaths, not to mention his magic troubles back at his own hotel. And now a scream.

'Why? What do you think has happened?'

'Let me go and check.' Seth swallowed his fear and ran up the spiral stairs, looking around for the source of the scream.

He passed two closed doors on the first floor, reached the top floor and peeked through an open door, not liking to intrude.

The bedroom wasn't large, but had been decorated in the same lavish style as the entrance hall. There was a four-poster bed made of a reflective metal, festooned with frilly lilac pillows and drapes tied back with huge glossy bows. The same wallpaper of soaring seagulls complemented the huge windows surrounding them. This must be the room that had once housed the light.

The view of the storm was bewitching. He could instantly see that it would be stunningly beautiful here in the summer, but now it would appeal to anyone who loved to watch the savagery of wild weather. The sky was hard to take your eyes from. A mass of flashing light and rolling clouds over a grey and angry boiling sea.

'Who are you?' Standing by an inner door with her fists clenched stood a teenage girl, dressed in a purple-striped shirt tucked into tight black trousers. She looked at Seth suspiciously through eyes heavy with black make-up. She had a luxurious mane of long, brown curly hair and a cross expression.

'Er, is everyone all right? I'm the new kitchen boy. Just arrived. Someone screamed.'

'That was me,' said the man standing alongside her. He was in his thirties, well-groomed with oiled-back dark hair. He was wearing a stiff white shirt and well-tailored trousers. Brockler, the blood-sucking lawyer, Seth guessed.

He was fiddling with a sleek, expensive-looking watch on his wrist. 'The lights going out. All that lightning.' He shuddered. 'And Miss Sunrise and I have been trying to reach Mina.' His soulful eyes stood out, worried and watchful in his delicate face. 'She's locked in the bathroom.'

'She hates storms,' said Lark.

Brockler stared at the sturdy door as if just being angry with it would make it open.

Seth crossed the room and asked if was all right to look though the keyhole. 'Key's in the lock, sir.' He gave a sharp rap. 'Miss Mintencress, it's Seth, the new kitchen boy. We're worried about you. Can you let us know you're all right?'

There was silence.

'We have tried that,' snapped Lark.

Behind them, two others raced into the room.

First, a small boy with dark hair and a telltale catapult in his back pocket. Seth unconsciously
narrowed his eyes at Alfie and checked his ear for
more seaweed. Rendleton had arrived too. The one
person Seth really hoped would appear was Inspector Pewter. Why had he not come running at the
scream?

'What's going on?' Rendleton demanded.

'We're worried about Mina,' snapped Brockler.
'Something must have happened. I tried to bust in
there,' he wiped his long and delicate hands grace-
fully across his brow, 'but I couldn't shift that door
an inch.'

Another brilliant fork tore the dark sky outside.

'Could she have been,' began Lark nervously,
'struck by lightning?'

'Perhaps, Lark, you might want to take Alf downstairs,' suggested Rendleton. He rapped his knuckles
boldly on the door and called loudly, 'Mina? Miss
Mintencress?'

Even his voice could hardly be heard above the
howl of the wind. Rain hurtled at the windows as if
trying to break through.

'Lark, what's happened to Mina?' asked Alfie.

Lark seized his hand and spoke in a comforting
tone, too low for Seth to make out. He couldn't help

but fear Brockler was right. Why wasn't Mina answering? Something must have happened to her.

'She wouldn't want to be alone in a storm,' Brockler said, his big dark eyes standing out as he fixed them all with a worried glance, as if challenging them to contradict him.

'I could have a shot at it,' said Rendleton, sizing up the door. 'First, mate, it's not like we didn't all hear you arguing earlier. I'd look a right idiot busting into her bathroom if she's just trying to wind you up.'

Brockler looked annoyed and drew himself up, although he was almost a head shorter than Rendleton. 'She can't really be taking yet another bath. I instruct you to break the door down.'

Rendleton put his shoulder to it, and Seth did his best to help. Eventually there was a loud crack, the splintering of wood, and the door fell inwards. Rendleton staggered into the bathroom, followed by Brockler. Seth slipped in behind as a flash of lightning lit up the big picture windows like floodlights, showing waves that looked as if they were clawing their way up the side of the building.

An enormous white bath with a curling top, elaborate taps and ornate gold clawed feet, was elevated in the centre of the room. From its raised position you could admire the magnificent sea view while bathing.

Another flash of lightning showed something else very clearly.

In the bath was a young woman. She was completely immersed under foamy, bubbly water. Pretty much all you could see was her dark hair billowing out around her like a mermaid's. Only she wasn't a mermaid. Her face was distorted and unnaturally bloated.

And there was no doubt at all that she was dead.

9. A DREADFUL ACCIDENT

Seth's thoughts flew to Celeste, then shrunk from the fact that someone was going to have to break the news . . . and it was probably going to be him. She'd told him how she and Mina were more like best friends.

Another flash of lightning exploded into the high room, along with another crash of thunder that sounded like a car wreck in the sky. All three of them flinched. Seth felt himself duck, the lightning spotlighting just how enormous the waves had grown.

Brockler had slumped in an uncomfortable-looking gold chair in the far corner of the bathroom and put his head in his hands. He looked shocked and broken.

'A terrible, terrible thing,' Rendleton muttered, looking out of the window rather than at the dead girl, a puzzled look on his face. 'How could it have happened? She fall asleep – or what? She stand up to get a look at the storm and slipped? Or . . . what are we looking at here?'

Brockler stood. 'What are you saying?' he sneered. 'That this was the work of the ghost?'

'Nope, I'm not saying it's the ruddy ghost. But how did it happen? It's not like we don't know how you lot have been at each other's throats . . .'

It was easy to see what the manager was implying. Seth already understood that the place was a cloud of disagreements and difficulties, and now Mina Mintencress was dead.

Seth felt even more anxious – where was Pewter? The lighthouse shook as another clap of thunder rocked it, and he listened to Brockler and Rendleton discussing what to do.

Rendleton was insisting that there was something deeply suspicious about the death coming after a spate of ill fortune, accidents and arguments, and

Seth couldn't help thinking he was right. He knew that MagiCon had already thought the place worth looking into. And now the millionairess Mina Mintencress had died alone in a locked room . . . Seth could not help but remember he had so recently been involved in something similar. Someone had died, and that locked-room mystery had come so close to ending with him being arrested for murder. Well, if there was anything at all suspicious about this death, Seth was determined that this time the blame would not fall on him. But what exactly had happened here?

He knew he shouldn't leave it any longer to break the news to Celeste, and someone would have to tell Lark and Alfie, but Seth wavered. He stood in the middle of the tragedy, taking in the smell – damp with a tang of sour grapefruit; a sharp, unpleasant aroma from the shroud of bubbles lingering in the bath – and listening to Brockler and Rendleton carry on their low-level argument.

'Even if you call the police, the waves are the size of houses. They'll not get through until morning,' pointed out Brockler in his posh voice. 'And what are you going to tell them – blame it on the ghosts? And we can't leave her here.'

'I'll move her to the cellar.' Rendleton bravely

plunged his hands into the water and pulled out the plug; the foamy water started to gurgle away, allowing him to cover the body with towels and finally shoulder the bundle.

Brockler stood shakily, saying something about talking to Lark. He stared wordlessly at the empty tub. Another flash of lightning filled the room and his eyes widened. With a cry, he lunged into the bathtub and scooped up something up from the bottom before it drained away. Brockler stared at what he held in his hand, shaking off the clinging bubbles. Some sort of pendant on a leather cord.

'She loved this!' he cried. Brockler held it in his hands for a moment then tucked it in his pocket.

It struck Seth as a strange sort of jewel for a rich person to wear. From the quick glance he'd managed, it seemed plain, made out of a material like stone or wood, and not even a gold chain. A carved figure, Seth thought, with two small red gems for eyes.

Before Rendleton started down the stairs, Seth raced past him, needing to make sure Celeste was out of the way before the unfortunate burden made its way to the cellar.

When he reached the kitchen, Celeste was busy humming a little song. 'Look, I've done sandwiches.'

She looked up proudly from a small pile of badly cut bread. Her smile faded the instant she saw Seth's face. 'What's up? That scream – is Alfie all right?'

'Alfie is fine; the scream wasn't him.' Seth paused. 'Celeste, there's been a terrible accident. It's Mina, she's—'

'Accident? I only just left her.'

'I'm so sorry. There's no easy way to tell you this. She drowned in her bath. She's – I'm afraid she's dead.'

Celeste's eyelids fluttered, then her body simply crumpled, and only Seth rushing forward to catch her stopped her falling to the floor.

He tried to steer her to her room. Luckily she was only out for seconds, but she still leaned heavily on Seth as he led her down the short purple corridor to the staff bedrooms.

She seemed bewildered, not even sure which was hers, but the second room along contained a narrow bed and white coverlet and a selection of cosmetic bottles and jars arranged on a practical and sturdy chest of drawers. A similar outfit to the one Celeste was wearing hung on the outside of the wardrobe door.

'We've had so many accidents,' whispered Celeste, her eyes big and full of panic. 'She knew . . . she thought . . .'

Seth eased her on to the bed, squeezed her hand and said he was off to make everyone tea. But he had only just put the tea on to brew when there came a hammering on the outside door.

How could anyone be outside? No one could have reached the island in this storm.

Seth flung open the door and the wind rushed in first, followed by a dishevelled figure who staggered inside, rain running off him in rivers, his silvery hair as wet as if he was a creature from the sea. In his arms a black shape wriggled.

'Inspector Pewter!' cried Seth.

He slammed the door and the black shape the inspector was clasping squirmed again, revealing bedraggled fur. Nightshade leapt out of Inspector Pewter's grasp and landed on the floor with a damp plop and a hiss.

'Wretched cat,' growled Pewter, taking off his round glasses and giving them a wipe before squeezing water out of his hair. 'And Seth – aren't you just full of surprises?'

Seth wondered just how much trouble he was in.

10. NOT THE BEST WEATHER FOR CATS

'I was hunting for dead birds before the storm hit. Happened to see some cat had got itself stuck halfway up a cliff. Not the best weather for cats,' Pewter said, rainwater dripping off his nose and clothes and gathering in a puddle around his very wet shoes.

'Then the stupid cat refused to move and fought me. So we've been sheltering under a not very large rock until she finally agreed we'd get less wet making a run for it. I could really do with a cup of tea.' His hand was badly scratched. 'And maybe a towel.'

There was a clap of thunder so fierce the whole lighthouse shook again. Even down in the basement where they were away from the worst of it, it felt as if the sky itself was breaking.

'Thanks for rescuing Nightshade, Inspector. Sorry she put you to so much trouble. She must have been terrified.' Seth handed a large mug of strong tea to Pewter along with all the towels he could find. 'Sorry she's always so ungrateful and grumpy but I had no idea she was still outside. I assumed she was tucked up somewhere.' And before the inspector could even begin grumbling about Seth being here and bringing Nightshade with him, Seth pressed on. 'Something happened while you were outside rescuing Nightshade. It's Miss Mintencress. She's dead, Inspector.'

Pewter took the news more calmly than Seth had expected and continued to wring out his hair and remove his sodden shoes. Seth began to fill him in on what he knew – and how now there had been a suspicious death.

The inspector gave the occasional nod, and twice asked Seth to clarify a detail, but Seth felt he had hardly got started, when Rendleton, his grim chore complete, arrived in search of tea. Pewter's head was encased in a white towel and he was rubbing vigorously at his hair. He freed a hand, rummaged in an inside pocket of his suit and passed a business card to Rendleton.

Seth had seen the small white card once before. Words were arranged in a circle in the middle, as if they'd been stamped on.

MagiCon – all your magical crimes SOLVED*
*usually.

'Inspector Pewter, MagiCon. You'll have heard of us of course. We used to have this slogan "we make crime disappear" – you've heard of that, I'm sure? It was quite famous at one time.' Pewter's head emerged from the white towel like a chick hatching from an egg. 'I have been told of your most unfortunate news and have consequently put myself in charge.'

Rendleton looked at Pewter through narrowed eyes. 'MagiCon? Sounds seriously dodgy – what are you? Not official police? I thought you were the guy we called in to fix the electrics – what were you doing here in the first place? Seems a bit suspicious, mate.'

Pewter snaked a hand out from under a fluffy tea towel to take the card back. 'Let's just say you are in the unfortunate situation of having a dead body on your hands and no regular police available,' he said smoothly. 'In the circumstances, I think you will find you are lucky to have me in charge. I suggest you inform Mr Brockler and Miss Sunrise.'

Rendleton scowled. 'What on earth is magical crime anyway? Someone's been listening to the builders' scare stories about ghosts. All right, guess you're all we've got. MagiCon!' he scoffed, swinging out of the room.

All Seth could think of was to keep busy; they may as well take lunch through to the dining room. He went through and began placing plates on the glossy table. The room was painted a dark blood-red. The curtains were a heavy crimson, filigreed with delicate gold trim, and framed the storm that was still raging outside. A fancy antique clock on a polished sideboard joyfully chimed the hour in defiance of the thunder crashing overhead, ringing three times in unison with flashes of brilliant white.

Seth drew the heavy curtains against the grand force of nature raging outside, glad they were heavy enough to slightly muffle the wild sound as the residents began to assemble. Seth brought cake and a glass of milk for Alfie, who was sitting motionless, white-faced and silent; a deeply different boy to the one with the catapult and the cackle that Seth had first encountered.

Brockler also stared at nothing, adding several sugars to his tea. Lark took a slice of fruit cake and crumbled it in her fingers. Rendleton hovered solicitously and Pewter took a seat at one of the dozen mahogany chairs around the table, but seemed totally absorbed by his own thoughts.

Lark was the first to speak. She left the food and went to the window, pulling back the curtain. 'We can't get out, can we? We're trapped here. The place just gives me the creeps.'

'A boat will get through tomorrow,' reassured Rendleton gently.

The shock seemed to have almost sent everyone into a coma. Seth had expected Pewter to rush about, to visit the scene of the crime. Was it a crime, or just a terrible accident? Either way, the inspector was the only one eating. He started offering sandwiches and fruit cake and more tea to everyone, and gradually most of them accepted.

Seth hovered. He really needed to talk to Pewter. Had someone cleverly engineered Mina Mintencress's death? Was it possible that her lawyer, her best friend, or even the hotel manager was somehow responsible? And had Pewter really been brought in to investigate the supposed ghosts?

Seth felt pretty sure no one outside the lighthouse could have got here during the storm. If someone was responsible, it had to be someone here – one of the people closest to Mina Mintencress, the ambitious heiress with the crazy plan that had brought this party to this unlucky lighthouse. But which of them?

He looked at Brockler, trying to read if there was anything deeper in his troubled face. And what about Lark? She just looked blank, her dark-rimmed eyes telling nothing. Celeste had said those two were plotting – plotting what exactly? And what about Rendleton? Why had he come on board to this mad project at all? Pewter sipped a cup of tea and Seth waited outside the door, wishing the inspector would come out of the dining room.

'They're not saying much.' Celeste's voice whispering at his elbow nearly made him leap out of his skin. 'What are they doing? She's dead and they're all having a tea party.'

'It's not quite like that, Celeste. They're all just shocked, I think.'

'How is Alfie?'

Alfie had drunk his milk and they watched Lark cut him another slice of cake and bend low to say something quietly to him, her arm comfortingly slipping around him as he wiped his eyes.

'Celeste, what did you mean when you said Brockler and Lark were plotting against Mina?'

'Mina didn't know exactly. But she guessed something was up.'

'She suspected someone was going to kill her?'

'No!' Celeste shook her head vehemently. 'It was the ghost. She was beginning to wonder that maybe there was something behind all the hauntings. Or someone.'

Had that bathroom door really been locked? Was there another way in? What might he have missed? Seth saw he had a chance to take another look.

'Would you mind going and making some more tea, Celeste? And, er, call up the stairs if someone leaves the dining room.' He already had his foot on the first stair.

'What are you going to do?' said Celeste, following him. 'You're up to something, aren't you? If you're going to poke around and investigate, then I'm coming too.'

But they didn't get very far. This time when the lightning flashed, the thunder sounded not just like a collision in the sky, but like an explosion, as if the storm had come right inside the lighthouse.

'We've been hit!' roared Rendleton as he dashed out of the dining room and raced past them up the stairs.

11. BLUNDERING ABOUT IN THE DARK

There were cries, a thud. Seth was aware of people blundering silently in the darkness. This time there was no welcome return of the lights.

Seth fumbled his way back to where he knew he'd left the candles in the kitchen.

He bumped into Inspector Pewter cradling a ball of magical light in his hand and heading for the cellar steps.

'Electrics,' he said as he passed Seth.

'Er – you do know there's a dead body down

there?' Seth said. 'It's where they put Miss Minten-cress.'

Pewter looked startled just for a moment, then nodded. 'Thanks for the warning, Seth.'

Once he had a handful of candles and some matches, Seth remembered the tiny torch he carried in his tunic. He dug it out and moved much more quickly with the aid of its little beam, following everyone to the room at the top of the lighthouse. A chunk of the wall up by the ceiling was completely missing, exposing a direct view of the broiling sky. Rain was pouring through, running down the beautiful wallpaper of seabirds and pooling on the polished floor.

Brockler, Lark and Alfie watched on helplessly.

No one seemed to be doing anything, so Seth sprang into action, urging the others to help move the heavy bed to one side and away from where the rainwater could reach.

'Well, at least the windows didn't shatter,' he said, trying his best to keep everyone's spirits up.

But Brockler just slumped on to the bed. Alfie started splashing in the rainwater, which at least was better than seeing him so silent and unmoving during lunch

'We need a mop and a bucket,' said Seth. Nobody

moved. 'Where's Rendleton?' he asked with a sigh, lighting candles.

'Gone to the Sunrise Wing to get building supplies,' said Lark, biting her nails.

Seth handed Alfie the torch. 'You take charge of this.'

'What are you going to do?' asked Alfie, looking up at him. 'Are you leaving?'

'No, I'm going to help Rendleton and seal up that hole. Lark, I think it might be a good idea to fetch more candles when you get a bucket and mop. Can you try to mop up the water before it does too much damage?'

'I'll help you, Lark,' said Alfie, his small voice sounding eager.

Brockler still didn't move.

'Great!' Lark said as cheerfully as she could. 'Took me three days to decide on that wallpaper and it's all ruined. And I argued with Mina for three weeks over that flooring; let's see if we can save it. Come on, Alfie.' She held out her hand. 'Let's you and me get to work and clear this up.'

Seth raced all the way back down the stairs, but when he reached the door that led to the Sunrise Wing, he paused. Until now the door had always been closed and locked. Now, with just the flickering from the candles in the kitchen, the open doorway looked as dark and about as uninviting as a cave where you knew a bear lived.

No matter how much he told himself he didn't believe in ghosts, he had to clench and unclench his fists, trying to find courage to step through into the darkness. He cupped his hand around the candle flame and went through into a long corridor, where he could make out little except shadows dancing. He felt his heart hammering.

Then a gigantic shape loomed out of one of the side rooms, shuffling slowly but relentlessly towards him and gave a long, low wail.

'W-w-what the—?! Seth! You terrified the life out of me.' It was Rendleton, clutching a vast piece of board. 'For a moment there I thought you were— Never mind, thanks for coming to help.'

He passed Seth a hammer and nails and they manoeuvred the board with great difficulty all the way up the spiral stairs, and then somehow managed to successfully nail it across the hole in the wall so the rain no longer flooded in.

The lights flickered back on and there was a small cheer from Brockler and Lark.

'Perhaps that Pewter isn't half bad at those electrics after all. Next, I guess we could all really use another cup of tea,' said Rendleton, heading for the door.

Seth wiped his brow. His clothes and shoes were wet. 'I'll do tea.'

'Aren't you going to help mop?' asked Lark.

'When you and Brockler are doing such a grand job there?' grinned Rendleton. 'I need to make an urgent check there's no rain coming in any of the other rooms. Alfie, come and help me please?'

'Good idea, Alfie. You're in charge of spotting any more damage,' nodded Lark. 'But first, you should go and change,' she added, prodding him with the handle of her broom. 'I think your clothes did a better job of soaking up the water than the mop.'

Back in the kitchen, Celeste's small voice crept up behind Seth as he put on the kettle.

'Is everything all right? Is every*one* all right?'

She had found herself a pair of dark glasses to disguise the fact she'd been crying, and her white cap was pulled right down.

Seth nodded. 'The top floor took a direct hit. Rendleton's boarded it up and he and Alfie are checking the rooms on the other floors. So it's not so bad. It might even have helped take Alfie's mind off other things for a bit.' The thunder still rumbled and once more the lighthouse shook. 'The worst of it was that some water came in, but Brockler and Lark are sorting that out.'

Celeste nodded, and then cried out: 'Hang on – you mean Lark and *Brockler* are actually working? Getting their hands dirty?'

'With a mop and bucket. Yes.'

She looked as if she might start to laugh, then she frowned. 'Leave the tea, Seth. Come on. This I have to see. Plus, you had the right idea before; Mina was suspicious they were plotting against her, so let's be sneaky and find out what they are saying.'

12. Give up This insane Plan

Seth allowed himself to be dragged on the long trek all the way back up the spiral stairs and hovered while Celeste put her eye to where the door was slightly open on the top floor so she could watch without them seeing her.

'I can hear them!' she said in an excited whisper. 'And they really are doing something.'

Seth could quite clearly hear Brockler and Lark talking as they sloshed water into a bucket. But it quickly rose to an argument.

'If there was any chance of getting off this rock tonight I'd be gone already,' sobbed Lark's voice.

Brockler replied to another roll of thunder, but one that had lost its savagery. 'We've been pretty lucky. The storm is passing. There was one so bad eight years ago a whole chunk of coast fell into the sea and cut off Snakesmouth. I'm sure whatever damage has been done can be fixed. You'll be able to leave in the morning.'

'You make it sound like you're staying! You hate this place and this whole idea as much as I do.'

Brockler didn't reply. Celeste had the best view of the room, but Seth could see enough. Lark had rested her mop and was closing in on the lawyer.

'What are you up to?' she demanded.

'I'm not up to anything. I only wanted her to be happy. Now, I have no choice but to take charge. You don't need to be involved any more.'

'Happy? Huh! The only thing you were ever worried about was her wasting her inheritance on this place. It's not your money. Why would you hang around? And why are you so keen to get rid of me?'

'And I suppose you've stayed here on this isolated rock out of the goodness of your caring heart.'

'I stood by her. She was convinced this whole project was going to work. I just wish we'd been brave enough to stand up to her sooner, persuade her to give it all up. Because this place killed her. And you – I wish you hadn't terrified the builders into leaving with your stories of ghosts. We could have made it work, but we can't do anything without Mina.'

'*My* stories?' Brockler sounded incredulous. 'I did not make up ghost stories. It was you who really hated this place. Mina always thought it was you who moved that ladder when that builder broke his ankle. You certainly tried your best to make sure she gave it all up.'

'I only ever helped her!' cried Lark.

Celeste muttered in Seth's ear, rubbing her chin. 'Mina thought Lark and Brockler had started plotting together. Or possibly Rendleton. It was the reason I . . .' She trailed off.

'Well,' whispered Seth back, 'it doesn't sound quite like Lark and Brockler were plotting together.' They peered through the gap as the argument continued.

'You've really managed to ruin everything! Pleased with yourself?' Lark said to Brockler challengingly.

'Traitors,' muttered Celeste. She was breathing deeply and Seth was sure she was fighting an urge to burst in there and give them a piece of her mind.

There was a silence for a short while, with just the sound of water being sloshed into a bucket.

'Ruin everything?' came Brockler's posh tones again. 'Hardly. It's only the Sunrise Wing left to finish. This was Mina's dream, Lark. I feel it would be wrong to abandon it now.'

Celeste turned to Seth and gave him the thumbs up. 'Well, good for Brockler,' she said grudgingly.

'Finish the Sunrise Wing?' screeched Lark. 'You seriously still want to carry on with this? You are now actually thinking of running a hotel? Getting guests out to the middle of nowhere? You?'

'Maybe we should give it a shot. Don't we owe it to her, Lark?'

'I don't believe what I'm hearing. Yesterday you hated this place. Now she's met with this tragic accident and you, like, suddenly want to stay? I'll ask you again – what are you up to, Brockler?' said Lark slowly.

'I'm just—'

'Do you know, I think I can guess. You think that if all her money now goes to Alfie, he's young enough that you'll get control of it. Well, I am not going to let that happen.'

'Don't think *I* can't see how you've started to look after that boy,' Brockler replied with a low chuckle.

'Easy to step in, as Mina was far more similar to her parents than she liked to admit – much more excited by chasing a business opportunity than looking after children. You've been clever.'

'Just be warned, Brockler – you might find some surprises in her will. Yes, she made a new one without involving you. She didn't trust you. And I know she's left me enough money so that if anything happened to her, I'd be able to make my own life. She told me. Alfie does not get everything.'

'Well, that is so very fascinating,' said Brockler, his voice laced with icy menace. 'Thank you so much for telling me you had such a very strong reason to want her dead. So much for always having her best interests at heart. I'll be sure to pass that very fascinating detail on to Inspector Pewter.'

'What a stinking rotten thing to say,' scowled Celeste. She was biting her lip so hard it must hurt. She turned to Seth, her face blanched except for two bright spots of colour high in her cheeks.

'Time we moved,' said Seth gently, starting to ease her away.

They padded swiftly down the stairs. Celeste's face looked grim and had a set look about it. 'I've decided I like your plan, Seth. Someone's been plotting. Let's find out which one of the rotters killed her.'

13. MEASLES ACROSS THE MAP

The last thing Seth was expecting to discover when he went to collect the remains of lunch from the dining room was Inspector Pewter, sitting alone at the big table among a litter of abandoned cups and plates, with a big mug of tea in front of him and a thick slice of fruit cake to munch on. And he was poring with great concentration over a vast map he'd spread across the polished table, pushing aside the remains of the wonky sandwiches.

He looked up guiltily when Seth burst in, nearly

slopping the mug of tea he was slurping.

Seth glimpsed the outline of a long, thin bit of coastline that you could almost imagine was in the shape of a snake's head with an open mouth, and an island. Just enough to guess it was a map of the local area. It was covered with crosses marked in pencil, like it had measles.

From the way Pewter so hurriedly folded away the map out of sight, Seth could have believed the inspector was secretly on the trail of a vast hoard of buried treasure he didn't plan on sharing. He really longed to know what the inspector was up to.

'What ho, young Seth. Nice of you to drop in. Aren't Mr and Mrs Bunn missing you? And – perhaps I got this wrong – weren't you promising me you'd spend all your free time practising your magic? I must have misunderstood.' He shook his head. 'Because here you are.'

Seth avoided looking directly into his blue eyes.

'Um. you made it sound inviting . . . and the teleport was just shimmering there. Thought I'd just take a peek and go home, but then they needed help in the kitchen and I got . . . caught up with everything. And I'm pretty certain, sir, that someone here has been up to no good. We should—'

'You are right to be concerned.'

This floored Seth completely. He'd got so used to getting things wrong. So his suspicions weren't totally fanciful?

'You are correct that they are indeed desperate for help in the kitchen. Before you know it, it will be dinner time and I don't want to be the one telling them there is nothing more than a lot of very fresh and salty air to eat. Don't mind me if you've work to do.'

'Surely no one is going to be thinking of food?'

'In my experience there is seldom a time when no one thinks about food. Which makes your skills, young Seth, one of the most valuable in the universe.'

Seth had been longing to talk to Pewter and share all his thoughts about the mystery of Mina Mintencress. If he couldn't impress Pewter with his magic, he might at least show he'd picked up a few detecting skills. But he sensed it wasn't the time for sharing. The inspector was probably mad at him – he had every right to be.

But he couldn't quite stop himself asking questions. 'Why were you called in, sir? It can't really be the ghost . . . unless . . .' His thoughts were racing and he wondered why he hadn't seen it straight away. There could only be one explanation why a magical detective was on this case. 'Someone is using the haunting story to cover up magic! Sinister magic!'

Pewter began to place cups and plates on a tray as the sound of thunder grew more distant.

'Ah yes, I can see you have been listening to all the stories. What great stories they are too. The electricity failures, the slamming doors. But it is a sad truth that accidents happen all the time. And you have to stop yourself leaping ahead and reaching all sorts of conclusions based on very iffy evidence.' Pewter chuckled. 'Magic!'

Seth felt his face flush. It was a brush-off. He'd hoped that with the death of Mina Mintencress, Pewter might put aside any anger he justly felt about Seth's unwelcome arrival. But quite clearly he was determined not to discuss the case with Seth.

He took the tray from Pewter and headed for the kitchen, almost colliding with Celeste, who gave a half-hearted apology and slumped off to collapse at the big kitchen table.

Seth, muttering crossly under his breath, did what he always did when he was troubled – got cooking. He decided to whizz up a quick apple cake. He found butter, sugar and eggs, folded in flour. He put half the mixture in a cake tin and then layered in thin slices of apple, sprinkled with brown sugar and cinnamon, and topped with the rest of the cake mixture. He slammed it into the oven, not even responding when he heard Pewter's footsteps leave the dining room and head up the stairs. He longed to go with him, but fought the urge to follow and hung around the kitchen door, hoping he might get a glimmer of an idea about what Pewter was up to. He didn't have the heart to go where he wasn't wanted.

Only then did a thought strike him – had Pewter deliberately steered Seth away from talking about magic because right outside the door had been Celeste Crackling, listening in?

Another flash of lightning made the lights flicker feebly. It was like a parting farewell from the retreating storm, and revealed Brockler creeping down the plush spiral stairs, his perfect hair dishevelled and his crisp white shirt untucked and crumpled.

Seth darted back into the safety of the kitchen and then slipped after him, curious to see what he might be up to. The dining room was empty. But when Seth slowly pushed the door to the lounge, he spotted Brockler crouched low, going through a shelf containing a few books and board games that would provide some entertainment for guests.

Brockler looked around and started in surprise when he saw Seth framed in the doorway.

'Couldn't eat a thing when you brought lunch,' he said mournfully in his posh voice. 'Now I'm totally famished. Could you bring me a sandwich?'

Seth simply nodded and returned quickly with a small selection of sandwiches left over from lunch, although he was pretty sure the last thing on Brockler's mind had been food. It looked as if he was searching for something.

'I'm so sorry about Miss Mintencress,' Seth said, placing the plate on a low table in front of an uncomfortable-looking chair with metal arms.

Brockler had a fine face, the sort of face you'd call beautiful rather than handsome, with high cheekbones, dark brows, big, dark eyes and thick, glossy hair, and finery from his clothes to his fingernails.

He looked at Seth as he helped himself to a ham and mustard sandwich.

'She was a force of nature stronger than even this storm. Completely determined and always convinced she was right.' He looked upwards as another peal of thunder was heard in the distance, but it was a grumble now, not even a roar.

'So what will happen now?' asked Seth. 'Will this hotel ever open or should I start to look for another job?'

Brockler narrowed his eyes. 'Guess I have to decide

whether she was really on to something with this ridiculous get-away-from-it-all lighthouse-hotel plan.'

He started to eat another sandwich – tiny bites with a delicate little mouth – as Seth bustled about, plumping cushions and tidying.

'Mina insisted get-away-from-it-all should mean no television, just a few tedious board games, and all that nature and endless staring at the sea.' He flapped at yet another window, another view of still-enormous waves. 'Now, I could use a really good film. People need car chases, exploding helicopters and a really evil bad guy on holiday, a story where it all ends happily.'

His eyes misted over and he reached for a slice of fruit cake. 'Lucky I managed to get here before it got completely out of control. She'd have got through her family fortune in no time. Putting Lark Sunrise in charge of decorating! But for all that, Mina was smart. And she was convinced this place would be a little goldmine.' He looked at Seth with a self-satisfied smile. 'I don't think we need to talk about new jobs just yet.'

It was clear Brockler was convinced he now had control over the Mintencress millions. Lark had accused him of being behind the stories of ghosts that had spooked the builders and sabotaged the project. The big question was – were the two connected? And that still didn't explain Pewter's involvement. And how did that square with Seth's growing suspicion that it wasn't a ghost that was causing all the accidents, but that someone had been using magic? Surely that was the only explanation for Pewter being here.

'Do you believe the place is haunted, sir?'

A devious look crossed Brockler's face and his eyes narrowed. 'I believe there is much that we simply can't explain,' he said cautiously. 'I've been going into the history of this place. A really fascinating man, Soul Snakesmouth, the previous owner. A man full of secrets.'

'Secrets? What sort of secrets?'

'If I told you, they wouldn't be secrets. Besides, we all have the odd secret or two.' Brockler gave a little chuckle that only made him look more furtive than ever.

He finished the fruit cake, delicately brushed away the crumbs and grabbed something that had rolled out of his pocket while he had been sitting in the chair. It was that strange carved object he had taken from the bottom of the bath after they'd removed Mina's body.

'That's really interesting,' Seth said, slipping in a

little closer. He was fascinated to see now that the pendant was a carved giant snake winding around a lighthouse. It had wide-open jaws, as if it was devouring the building. Where the light would be at the top, were two disturbing red stones for eyes.

'Got some bits and pieces from the old hotel in Snakesmouth and turned this into a pendant as Mina wanted to wear it, for good luck. Poor, poor Mina.' Brockler placed it around his own neck.

Before Seth could ask the lawyer anything more, Alfie hurled himself into the room and on to one of the wide armchairs, crossed his arms and started moaning stubbornly about not being allowed outside to look at the storm.

'The best bit has passed already and you made me miss it!'

He looked tearful and scowled at Lark, who followed him in, throwing an imploring glance at Brockler.

Brockler cleared his throat and Seth guessed he might be remembering how he'd insisted that he was in charge of Alfie now Mina was dead.

'Now let me see,' Brockler said, tucking in his shirt and smoothing his dark hair. 'I think I know what someone's favourite is. How about we all play Pirate Pete's Party?'

Alfie instantly brightened and bounced forward eagerly. 'Oh yes. You're really, really good. I want to beat you.'

Brockler smiled and reached across tentatively to ruffle the boy's hair. 'That's my favourite too!'

'Thanks, Hari,' said Lark. 'It's good and noisy. Help take all our minds off things.' She added in an even lower voice. 'Perhaps this once you could actually let him win?'

Brockler offered Alfie his hand. 'Lead on, pirate! And tonight we're going to check your bedroom before you go to sleep. We'll check the wardrobe for ghosts, under the bed for nasty monsters.'

'I keep telling you, it's an angel. It's not monsters or ghosts. Get it right!'

'Whatever you call it,' said Brockler. 'We'll make sure there are no ghosts in your room who are going to come and get you.'

It was only after Lark, Hari and Alfie had left that Seth realized what the little boy was saying. It sounded very much as if he might be the only person here who thought he'd actually seen the ghost.

14. Strange Happenings

'Whiskers and white mice! Now did that sound to you like someone upset that Mina just died?' purred a voice from under a low table across the lounge. 'There are mysteries to be solved here and I have a feeling you've got ideas.'

'Nightshade! You've dried off nicely,' said Seth, bending to stroke her soft fur. 'Hope you thanked Inspector Pewter for rescuing you. What did he say when he saw you?'

'You mean, how livid was he?'

'Exactly.'

Seth could sometimes imagine Nightshade was shrugging, although he wasn't completely sure cats actually could shrug.

'You know Pewter – I never have a clue what the heck he's thinking.'

'No, but do you know what I'm thinking, Nightshade? I'm convinced Mina's death is murder.' Seth's many thoughts tumbled over themselves as he tried to get them into some sort of order. Brockler was right about one thing. Everyone seemed to have a secret.

'Celeste was convinced Brockler and Lark were plotting against Mina. Lark will come into a chunk of money and can make a life for herself, rather than tagging along with Mina, and she definitely doesn't want to be here any more. They all seem to be upsetting each other. Alfie's troubled and thinks he's seen the ghost, an angel or something. He's the one who gets most of the Mintencress millions . . . so whoever takes care of Alfie gets control of the fortune.'

'Hmm, yes, but none of that matters if you can't work out *how* Mina Mintencress could have been killed. You were also thinking about Angelique, weren't you?' said Nightshade, cleaning herself with her rough pink tongue.

'I was not!' It felt like someone had knocked the wind out of Seth. 'She's not bothered about me, why would I waste my time thinking about her?'

'Maybe because she's the best thing that ever happened to you. And someone dying in a locked room – don't tell me it's not making you think back to the reason she first turned up at the Last Chance Hotel. You don't believe there are ghosts here. You think there's someone stirring up magic at the bottom of it all.'

'All right, I do.' Seth pulled out a chair and Nightshade snuggled onto his lap. 'Anyway, I am going to do magic perfectly well by myself, without asking Angelique for help. And I'm sure I can solve this case even if Pewter's not speaking to me.'

'Sure. Just don't call me next time you try to get a door or a spoon to move, or to boil milk. Right now, I think you fancy yourself as a bit of a detective. You're enjoying yourself. Come on then – which of them is it?' she asked, sticking his legs with claws as sharp as needles as she got herself more comfortable.

Seth often felt he was only floundering on the very edges of understanding the magical world, but his understanding was definitely growing, and he was trying to work out how magic might have been used here.

'Remember why Angelique Squerr was working undercover at the Last Chance Hotel? She was investigating my mother.'

'And you found out your mum was one of the dead sorcerers' club?'

'The what?'

'Missing Feared Exploded – that's what they call those forty-two sorcerers who died in that explosion or battle or whatever it was, the one they only ever refer to as the Unpleasant. Their status is Missing Feared Exploded because it's impossible to figure out exactly who died. I do pay attention, you know. Mostly because no one ever pays any attention to me. That's Angelique's job, right? To identify exactly which of those forty-two MFE sorcerers are definitely dead, and not just lurking about and planning more trouble.'

Seth was nodding. 'The Unpleasant was all because of a crisis in the magical world. Magical folk were once everywhere. They took on apprentices, training up anyone who showed they might have a spark of magic. But belief in magic started to dwindle, sorcerers became more secretive and seeking out those who might have a spark of magic – all that bringing fresh people in – stopped. And the real trouble is, there's no guarantee you pass magical ability on to your children.'

'Magic is starting to die out.'

'Exactly.' Seth tried to think everything through as he stroked Nightshade's glossy fur.

'Some of the magical families didn't at all like a move to bring back apprenticeships that are open to anyone,' finished Nightshade, at last in a comfortable position and beginning to purr like a kettle as Seth tickled her behind her ears. 'And it all led to one huge row, the Unpleasant, and all these sorcerers Missing Feared Exploded. And one big old mess that Angelique's department has the misfortune of trying to sort out.' She purred deeply. 'But, come on, that's all very well, but what has that to do with Mina Mintencress?'

Seth scratched his own ear. 'I was thinking how Angelique uncovered all sorts of magic at the Last Chance Hotel, didn't she? Leftover magic from when my mum was alive. Things we never realized were magical artefacts and didn't have a clue what they really did. What if exactly the same thing is happening here? Some sort of leftover magic causing electrics to fuse and accidents?'

'You think a sinister sorcerer used to live here, Seth?'

'I do. There are stories about Soul Snakesmouth. He disappeared one night about eight years ago and was presumed dead, and I think he could have been one of the forty-two – an MFE.'

Nightshade stopped purring. 'I can see how all of that makes perfect sense, except for one problem. Think about Angelique's lot, S3, the Sinister Speculation Services, and what they do. Their job is to swoop into a house with a magical history, right? They have a good old rummage about. And if they decide the sorcerer is definitely not coming back, they have a clear out of any magic lurking and make the building safe for other people to live in. They call it cleaning. Angelique calls herself a cleaner – right?'

'Yeeesss. Angelique is brilliant at finding out if there are signs of recent magic and spotting evidence that an MFE is likely still alive.'

'Well then, if this was once the home of a sinister sorcerer and an MFE, wouldn't S3 have been all over this place, cleaning?'

'You'd think so,' said Seth slowly.

'But Pewter's here,' Nightshade pointed out. 'Why Pewter? He investigates magical crime, doesn't he? He's MagiCon – not S3. He's not after the dead sorcerers' club.'

Seth considered this, forced to admit what Nightshade said made sense. But he was reluctant to abandon all his careful theories – he'd been so sure it made sense that Mina Mintencress's drowning might have been down to magic. The door had been locked and there was no way into that room at the top of the lighthouse.

'All right. Unless it's not Soul Snakesmouth's leftover magic causing all the problems,' he mused. 'Maybe someone here is a sorcerer? Maybe it's recent magic.'

'I leave the magic to you, Seth,' sighed Nightshade. 'I'm more bothered that there are a lot of unpleasantly cheeky seabirds on this island and if it weren't for that horrible storm I'd be outside, teaching them all a lesson or two. But I'm stuck in here, and I haven't had a single bite of supper.'

Seth took the hint. He got to his feet and they padded together to the kitchen to find a few scraps for Nightshade. 'Didn't Pewter say he was outside looking for dead birds? Why d'you think there were so many dead birds on the beach? Just another strange thing about this place.'

'You are starting to suspect too many secrets, Seth. MagiCon inspectors don't get called in for cleaning jobs and they don't look into the unexpected deaths of gulls.' She chewed on a leftover ham sandwich. 'I hear what you say, but it doesn't all quite add up, does it? I think you can safely leave the gulls out of it. You need to be concentrating on this – if you think the magic might be recent and someone here is a sorcerer and causing all this with magic – which one of them is it?'

15. SURPRISED I ONLY LOST MY WHISKERS ONCE

Seth felt a hand clap him on the shoulder.

'Now, my superior detecting skills are telling me something of great importance,' said Inspector Pewter, fixing Seth with one of his looks where it was impossible to tell what he was thinking. 'You haven't yet made a start on dinner. Anything I can do to help?'

'I'm sorry about crashing through that teleport and intruding on your case,' said Seth quickly. A late apology was better than none.

'No matter. I've been told more than once – or maybe it was just once – that I'm brilliant in the kitchen,' said Pewter. 'You just tell me what to do.'

Seth knew he had to swallow down all his questions for now. He'd upset Pewter enough already.

'I'm pretty good with dinner,' went on Pewter. 'As long as it's spaghetti Bolognese. Which is good news for you, Seth.'

'Why's that?'

'Because it doesn't involve peeling any potatoes. I know you better than you think, young man.'

'Spaghetti Bolognese it is,' muttered Seth. He watched as Pewter put on a pan of water to boil.

'Admiring my technique?'

'I thought perhaps . . . maybe it was a dish you could make with magic?'

Pewter gave a deep chuckle. 'Most humble sorcerer folk like me know magic is a privilege, Seth. It is never to be used lightly. It can go very badly wrong. Anyway, how would it look if I had friends over for dinner and then started chanting a spell so that the onions chopped themselves?'

Seth tried to picture Pewter sitting in a kitchen in a normal home with non-magical friends. He failed. 'Do you *have* regular friends? Do you cook them dinner?'

Pewter looked up from where he had started dicing carrots. 'Course I have regular friends. Of course I have people around for dinner. All the time. Well, some of the time. Well, perhaps not that many "regular" friends, as you put it. Now, I guess we need some type of pasta. That long stuff. And what's that handy, ready-chopped meat called? We could almost definitely do with some of that.'

'I think the pasta you are thinking of for spaghetti Bolognese is spaghetti,' said Seth patiently. 'And mince?' He placed portions of both on the table behind the inspector, who was already shovelling carrots into a frying pan with a flourish and a sizzle and giving them a vigorous stir that sent plenty of them tumbling to the floor.

Nightshade started batting around the bottom of Pewter's legs.

'What Seth really wants to say is that he's sorry he was so grumpy earlier,' she said. 'And I'm going to say this because he is too proud to tell you, but he would really appreciate some help with his magic. Frankly, I'm surprised I only lost my whiskers once. But he's worried, because if he fails to pass the Prospect and get into the Elysee he will never find out his mother's real story. He hasn't even had time to think if he should start looking for his dad. And, oh, he also thinks MagiCon isn't working hard enough to track down Tiffany and the firefly cage. Was there anything else, Seth, or does that just about cover it?'

'Erm...'

'And he's been having suspicions about all that golden light coming from the firefly cage when Tiffany escaped with it and what it all means.'

There was a pause where all Seth could do was watch Inspector Pewter chop more vegetables. Nightshade sniffed the air and unceremoniously fled the room.

'She always does that when I chop onions,' said Seth.

'What, asks a load of really tricky questions?'

'No – I mean— Never mind that.' He could bear it no longer. 'Tiffany's got to be found! She's got that firefly cage. You can't imagine the havoc she'll wreak if she finds out how to use that thing, but I can – there was magic coming from it already.'

'Seth, I understand you have questions.'

'But you never answer them.' Seth tried to breathe more calmly. 'Inspector Pewter, do you think there is any chance my mother is alive?'

'I told you if I had any information that you would be the first to know. I can give you answers – it's up to you whether you choose to believe me. Be assured, the very best people are after Tiffany and Red Valerian and the firefly cage. Seth, I understand you long for answers. But I am but a humble inspector. I don't have all the answers. Sometimes you can only work slowly towards the truth and it can reveal itself quite by chance.'

'Well how about you answer this then – do you think Mina Mintencress was murdered?'

'Honestly, Seth, I do not know.'

It wasn't quite what Seth might have hoped for, but it gave him the courage to continue.

'I think there is a really good chance that Soul Snakesmouth, who used to own this lighthouse, was a sorcerer,' blurted Seth. 'I think he might be one of those who died in the Unpleasant. I think there might be magic he left here and that it might even be causing all the trouble and rumours of ghosts. Not a haunting, but leftover magic, just like there was at the Last Chance Hotel. It might explain how Miss Mintencress died alone in a locked room.'

He wasn't expecting Pewter to react with a chuckle, but that's exactly what he did. He turned to Seth, his eyes crinkling, although his expression was always difficult to read, particularly because of the way his round glasses reflected the light.

'Your instincts are extraordinarily good!'

'You mean there is leftover magic here? Are you going to call in S3 and get the lighthouse cleaned?'

'No, Seth,' said Pewter quietly.

'But can't you see what's going on?' cried Seth, a flash of annoyance with Pewter flaring. 'It's quite possible Soul Snakesmouth is an MFE. He might not even be dead. You can't just not investigate.'

'Investigate what, exactly? That his ghost has come back to stop anyone else moving into his lighthouse?'

Seth wasn't sure how to answer as he wasn't sure how serious Pewter was. Was that even possible?

Pewter turned from the stove and said gently, 'You know how it is. It's way above my pay grade to track down MFEs.'

Seth felt utterly confused. 'But then why are you here? Are you really investigating ghosts now?'

'I told you your instincts are good, Seth,' replied Pewter eventually, tasting a little of the sauce with a teaspoon. 'Your trust and faith, admittedly, are lousy, but you are partly right. Look at the evidence and see if your theories fit. Do it the other way around and you'll never make a good detective.'

Seth could only shake his head as Pewter went on.

'I can tell you this much. This place does indeed have a magical history. I don't think I am telling you anything top secret if I let you in on the fact that, yes, this was indeed the home of a very well-known sorcerer, one of those wanted MFEs, exactly as you say.'

Pewter didn't sound in the least bit excited, but Seth felt his heart start to beat faster. He'd guessed right! 'Soul Snakesmouth!'

'He practised a very shadowy brand of sinister magic. There was a lot of experimenting with dark-witching. Which, to be clear, is definitely banned magic.'

'Darkwitching? What's that exactly?' It sounded dangerous.

'The sort of thing likely to get you killed if you don't know what you are doing.'

Seth's thoughts went back to the explosions he'd suffered just trying to do a simple door-shutting spell and thought uneasily of how Pewter and Nightshade kept trying to steer him away from experimenting with his mother's tempting spells.

'This place was put up for sale. Now, if you think about it, you should be able to work out what that means,' went on Pewter, his blue eyes glittering. 'Surely, first, S3 should be called, it should be cleaned; declared safe and magic free? Wouldn't that be the responsible decision for the Elysee for an empty former home of a sinister sorcerer?'

Seth could only nod.

'Then understand this. I don't need to call S3 because S3 have already been. Before it was sold, rest assured that the Snakesmouth Lighthouse was completely and thoroughly cleaned.'

PART THREE

16. DREAMING OF TIFFANY BUNN

Seth woke with a start, sweating. His heart racing, fearing that there was someone in the room. He looked about and it took him a few moments before he realized he was no longer at the Last Chance Hotel, the place he had lived his whole life.

It was weird to wake in a strange room, but his fears had all been in his dreams. He'd been dreaming of Tiffany Bunn. Tiffany, whose greatest joy in life had been to find ways to torment Seth. Seth may have learnt about the existence of magic, but it was one of the most devastating things ever that Tiffany had too. And she had been determined to get some for herself. And Seth had not been able to stop her stealing the firefly cage, one of the scariest and most powerful devices of sinister magic ever invented.

Seth moved his legs carefully so as not to disturb the sleeping form of Nightshade, curled on the end of the bed giving little snickering snores.

He was thinking about the firefly cage. It was a terrifying prison that trapped a sorcerer and gained access to their magic. It was one of the most feared of all sinister magical devices and one had been kept in secret at the Last Chance Hotel. Now it was in the mean hands of the wicked Tiffany Bunn. Seth remembered his horror as he'd watched her using it, how a mesmerizing golden light had seemed to spill from between its intricate bars as she'd commanded dark magic to her will.

It was difficult to shake off that dream of bright-haired Tiffany. He'd dreamt she had approached his bed, tiptoeing forward, leaning right over him with a gloriously triumphant smile; leaning so close that they breathed the same breath. She'd been muttering about how she was pleased to see him so her games could start again and she had been holding a thick slab of cake. She had been munching her way through it, watching him sleep, smiling her evil smile. Reminding Seth that he had failed and that Tiffany was still out there.

Seth suppressed a shudder and swung his feet on to the floor. He should ask Pewter for some sort of spell to stop nightmares.

Surprisingly, having had such a terrible dream, he'd awoken with renewed vigour, and was determined to get back to his plan of finding one spell he could demonstrate to the Elysee. He needed to practise his magic. It was the only way to stop Tiffany. He couldn't just let her get away with it.

Years of working in a hotel meant Seth was an early riser and he guessed he'd have a little time to practise some magic before anyone else surfaced wanting breakfast.

After dressing in his bright-blue tunic, he took out his copy of *A Beginner's Guide to Really Easy-Peasy Magic*, took a deep breath, flexed his fingers and promised himself that this was the day he would get something right.

In the silence of the kitchen, he pored over the book. He could try that door-shutting spell again. This time he would really believe he could do it. He had to concentrate, because he could not afford to cause an explosion and blow the door off its hinges here.

Nightshade padded in. 'Ready when you are.'

Seth grimaced at her. Deep down he felt this was going to be as big a disaster as ever. He was supposed to create a rush of air just by moving his hands. There weren't even any magic words to utter.

He tried several times, feeling Nightshade's unwavering stare from her bright green eyes. He muttered something about the door being simply too big. He experimented with one of the smaller cupboard doors, but after ten minutes the strongest breeze was from Nightshade's weary sigh. He then tried rolling some spherical fruit across the table, thinking surely that would be easy, but then downsized to a pea, and couldn't so much as get that to the edge with the amount of air he could get to *rush* from his fingers.

He closed his eyes and concentrated furiously, moving his hands, not too much, remembering the flames when he'd done this before. He thought he felt a rush of air and lifted his hands towards the door. The door moved!

'What ho, young Seth.'

The door closed with a slam and Pewter had to open it again to step through, looking momentarily confused. He could only have narrowly avoided squashing his nose. Had Seth done that? Or was it Pewter?

'Good to see you practising. Was that your door-shutting spell?' Pewter was dressed in his smart grey suit as usual and managed to look fresh – as if he'd got a several hours' head start on the day.

Seth hurriedly tidied away the apples and oranges he'd failed to move across the kitchen table and busied himself with making Pewter a cup of tea.

When he got milk from the fridge, he noticed the remains of the fruit cake had gone. And most of the rest of the apple cake he'd made the day before. Someone must have been hungry and sneaked down in the night. He wasn't surprised people had trouble sleeping after the storm and Mina's death.

Seth poured himself a tea too and sat alongside the inspector, who was turning the pages of the easy-peasy book, a small smile on his face.

'This is the one you talked about, isn't it?' Seth asked. 'This book was a present from your father. You learnt all your own early magic from it?'

Pewter smiled. 'Hope you get as much fun from it as I did.'

Fun? Seth smiled weakly and began to make toast, wondering if this was the moment he should simply confess that he was an utter failure at magic. Confirm everything Nightshade had said, and ask for help. Deep down, he feared Pewter might abandon him if he knew just how bad he was.

Instead, he muttered, 'I can't quite work out why anyone would need a door-shutting spell anyway.'

Pewter added more milk to his tea and slathered his toast with butter and marmalade. 'Ah yes, but that is the beauty of beginners' magic. Think about it. What is it really? When you have mastered it, you will discover it's a spell that gets things moving without you having to touch them. Useful! Doors are just perfect for practising. If novices started with something that wasn't securely attached to a building it might lead to all kinds of difficulties.'

Pewter poured more strong tea into Seth's mug. 'Ready for the day, Seth?' he said. 'A doctor is on the way from the mainland. Let's go meet her. Rather her than me – the sea's still pretty rough out there. Hope she hasn't swallowed down her breakfast just before leaving or she might be seeing it all over again.'

17. The Raw Salt of the Sea

The sky was clear and innocent today. Seth waited on the beach at Gull Cove and the sea here looked pretty playful, making him think of a naughty child determined to show everyone how well behaved it could be.

He put up his hand against the glare of the sun and saw Rendleton approach, his hair wet and tousled; he was drying it with a towel.

'Fierce morning for a swim!' he yelled over the wind. 'Can recommend it! Those waves are amazing. Nothing like it for getting the day off to a bracing start.'

'Think I'll leave you to it,' said Pewter, hands deep in his pockets.

Seth could only wonder at and admire anyone who would see it as an enjoyable challenge to swim in those waves, and was even more astonished to see Alfie bob into view behind Rendleton, scrambling over rocks, also in wet trunks. He must have been swimming too. Alfie was clutching a large pair of binoculars along with his beach towel. He had a huge smile on his face and looked much more like the confident boy who'd been so accurate with his catapult only yesterday.

'Been getting him to come out with me most mornings,' said Rendleton, as he drew level with Seth, his words no longer whipped away by the wind. 'He's turning into a pretty strong swimmer. We'll have him racing me yet.' He turned to grin at Alfie, his teeth standing out white in his bronzed face.

Alfie looked up at Rendleton and give a shy smile. Seth hoped he'd had a peaceful night's sleep, but also wondered if he might be the night-time cake thief.

'Going to check out the seabirds?' said Seth, nodding at the boy's binoculars. 'Good day for it.

Guess quite a few might have been blown here by the storm.'

'I'm getting good at telling them apart,' responded Alfie proudly. 'Most people can't tell a cormorant from a shag, but I can now.'

'That's brilliant,' said Seth. 'Must be a big adventure, living on an island.'

The cliffs and the air above them were constantly moving with twirling and calling seabirds. Seth watched one swoop down towards the beach then peel away to land on a ramshackle wooden building on the edge of the cove. 'What's that little house there?'

'The boathouse,' replied Rendleton. 'Like most things here before Mina took charge, a bit of a wreck. Only an old rowing boat there now. Not one anyone would use in anything except a dire emergency.'

Over the sound of the sea, the waves and the birds, they could begin to hear the hum of a motor and could just make out an old wooden boat approaching, large enough to be carrying four buffeted figures, but looking like it was probably more often used for fishing. The waves looked pleased to have something to play with.

Four figures?

Seth felt his insides shiver as he remembered he

was here entirely uninvited and only pretending to be the replacement kitchen boy. What if the real boy was arriving on that boat and he would be revealed as an imposter?

He shielded his eyes against the sunlight again, watching the rolling waves reach the shore, where they crashed on to the shingle before retreating with a sizzle. He could taste the raw salt of the sea on his lips as he shifted his gaze to the boat, now rounding the rocky point and into the cove. Its prow was lifting clear of the water, then thumping down into the foam.

At the wheel of the boat was a girl enveloped in a vast orange waterproof jacket, her short blonde hair tormented by the wind as she steered towards them.

Of the figure huddled at the back of the boat, Seth could make out little, as she had an oilskin hat pulled well down over her ears and her jacket collar was turned up. The heaviness in the way she sat told Seth she was not enjoying the journey one bit.

One figure wasn't huddled down – a boy who looked like he was enjoying every moment of the gusty, stomach-flipping journey, his long brown hair tossed about by the wind. He had such a wide and confident smile that Seth could practically see his perfect teeth flashing from the beach.

Of the fourth figure he could see nothing but a dark coat and a face concealed by a hood.

It was only as the boat swerved suddenly and expertly to finally swoop past some rocks that Seth could see the hood was lined in a bright crimson, like something out of a fairy tale. Seth caught only a brief glimpse of her profile, but he would know that long imperious nose anywhere. The very last person he'd been expecting to see here: Angelique Squerr.

His heart rose. They'd shared such an adventure.

Then he felt a knot growing in his stomach. Pewter had said she'd teamed up with some other young S3 agent making a name for himself, someone called Stormforce. So what was she doing here? Another cleaning job? Did that mean there was left-over magic at Snakesmouth Lighthouse after all? Seth felt his suspicions that Pewter was concealing much from him rise again.

And what would Angelique say when she found Seth here?

The boat slowed and carefully edged towards a short wooden jetty on the opposite side of the cove to the boathouse, making several futile attempts to approach the jetty, which didn't reach out very far. Each time the waves played with the boat, tossing it back again like it was a stick, rather than full of people.

Seth could only watch helplessly.

Rendleton quickly sized up that the boat was in trouble and without hesitating, he sprinted to the water's edge. The boy in the boat – who Seth could now see was wearing a dark-brown leather jacket – grabbed the rope from the pilot and started to twirl it above his head like a lasso. Pewter watched, his hands shoved even deeper in his pockets. Surely there was no way to get the rope to travel far enough so they could catch it.

Rendleton was up to his waist in water, swimming towards the erratically bobbing boat and Alfie plunged in right behind him. But the boat was still a way off. It all depended on Rendleton. Could he reach the end of that rope?

Then the young man with the confident smile released the rope and it shot out in a straight line and just kept on going, like it had been fired from a bow. Seth watched, expecting it to ditch into the sea at any moment, but it carried on, straight into the strong waiting hands of Rendleton, who caught it deftly and swam to the jetty. Seth finally snapped into action and soon Pewter was there with Alfie too. Between them they began a tug of war with the sea, bringing the little boat closer and closer until Rendleton was able to secure it tightly.

The girl in the orange oilskin leapt out first, checking Rendleton's knot and finding it to her satisfaction. She beamed at Seth from beneath a thatch of blonde hair, as if she'd relished the challenge of bringing her passengers in safely.

'Hi, I'm Jo Crow.'

Seth mumbled his own name, keeping his head down, aware that Angelique was now stepping off the boat, leaning on the red cane she was never without as the boat rocked dangerously.

He chanced a glance up and saw that Angelique was looking straight at him. Was she amazed to find him here? Annoyed? Would she give him away?

He gave a nervous nod, hoping he might at least see recognition and pleasure appear in her eyes. But she turned to Rendleton, held out her hand and said: 'Very pleased to be here, I'm your new cook.'

18. BRINGING UP MY BREAKFAST

Seth was confused for a moment, but then he remembered that Angelique was a secret agent – she always worked undercover. And if she was working, that could only mean one thing: S3 must be investigating if there was still leftover magic here. The boy in the brown leather jacket stepped off confidently on long, agile limbs. He reached for Rendleton's hand and shook it.

'Great to be here! Dexter Stormforce. Call me Dex.' The boy shook Alfie's hand next and flashed his perfect teeth at Seth and Pewter. 'Can't get enough of this fresh weather after that storm I heard you had here last night. Incredible. Mind you, thought I'd be bringing up my breakfast in that boat for a minute.'

Stormforce? So this was the agent Angelique had been working with on her big cases.

Stormforce was wearing skinny black jeans. He had annoyingly high cheekbones, and wavy brown hair just long enough to tumble roguishly in the wind. His intelligent, green-flecked eyes were taking everything in with cheerful curiosity.

'Hope I'll be the answer to all your troubles. Well, some of them.' This was met with silence, except for the howling of the wind. 'I'm the new builder!' added Dex unconvincingly, brushing a little stray seaweed from the arm of his expensive jacket.

'When the builders are even younger than me I start to worry,' said Rendleton, his eyes widening in surprise. 'Shame you didn't think to bring a friend to lend a hand, son.'

Stormforce flinched a little at the 'son'. 'Well, I'm here more by way of an assessment of what needs to be done –' he waved generally at the island, taking in everything from the boat to the cliffs – 'unless you feel you don't need me . . .'

'Didn't say that, mate. I'll give anyone a chance. And I won't say there isn't a bit to do. A few days ago we were on schedule to open in two weeks, but then work stopped and we suffered a direct lightning hit last night as well as a tragedy. Now you're here, I guess everything will be back on track in no time.'

'When's breakfast?' asked Jo, trying to lift spirits as she helped the final shape huddled right at the back of the boat to disembark. A dark woman with neatly tied grey hair started to unfurl herself.

'Welcome, Dr Malinger,' said Pewter, as the woman waddled unsteadily down the jetty.

'If I'm lucky, I can be away from this place before breakfast,' she announced clearly over her shoulder.

Everyone fell in behind her and set off towards the lighthouse, Pewter and Seth bringing up the rear.

'I am slightly disappointed they sent us Storm-force,' muttered Pewter, as much to himself as to Seth.

'I can see what you mean,' Seth replied. 'Why didn't you warn me Angelique was coming?'

'That would be because I had no idea she *was* coming. Thought they would send Copious Bladderwrack.'

'Who?'

'The agent who cleaned this place.'

'But you said you weren't calling them in, that the job was already done.'

'Ah yes, but as you so rightly pointed out during our chat yesterday, with sinister magic, it always pays to be sure.'

When they got back to the lighthouse, Seth guessed that Brockler and Lark were still sleeping – and Celeste too – as it was all quiet when they walked into the entrance hall. He had listened at the maid's door first thing that morning, guessing that, like him, she would be an early riser out of habit, but all he'd heard was loud snoring.

Dr Malinger was clearly keen to get right on with what she had come here to do. She grabbed the heavy bag that Jo had carried for her from the beach and plunged straight down the cellar steps. Seth tried not to think of the grim remains of Mina Mintencress lying below, but felt himself shudder.

He made to follow the doctor but Pewter put out his hand to stop him. 'Don't think we need you for this, young Seth. Besides, the new cook will be wanting to inspect her kitchen, and I'm sure everyone will soon be ready for a cup of tea. And a biscuit, if you had such a thing.'

Seth didn't have the chance to show the new

'cook' around, or exchange more than a brief nod with her, as Pewter and Dr Malinger quickly reappeared.

A disgruntled frown had settled in the soft folds of the doctor's face. 'How am I supposed to conduct any sort of medical examination in these conditions?' she was saying to Pewter. 'There's hardly enough light to get down the steps without breaking my darned neck. If this is the best we can do I shall have to arrange for the body to be removed to a hospital and you won't get even a rudimentary analysis today.'

Everyone turned to Rendleton. If you wanted to get anything done around here, he was your man.

Rendleton rubbed his square chin thoughtfully. 'Builders had some monster lights, so they could carry on work into the evening. They left in such a tearing hurry, it's got to be worth a shot to see if they're still there. They're heavy brutes, so I'll need a hand. And they'll be over in the Sunrise Wing.'

Seth's gaze slid towards the door to that wing, as firmly closed as ever.

Jo looked up from where she was busy with a tin of biscuits. 'Sunrise Wing? That what you're now calling the derelict old hovel built into the rock? Yeah, yeah, count me in,' she said cheerfully, through a mouthful of crumbs, putting the lid back on the tin reluctantly. 'Builders didn't just leave in a hurry, they scarpered, cos the place terrified them. Who's up for seeing this ghost then? I'm up for it.'

Dex's confident grin grew even wider. 'We're ghost-hunting? Awesome,' he said excitedly, before moderating his tone to add, 'And, you know, I should see what supplies are available to me, should I take this project on.'

Seth immediately volunteered too, but Angelique didn't follow suit.

Since more or less the moment he'd arrived Seth had heard stories about the wing that everyone avoided. It had spooked a bunch of tough builders so much they had downed tools and fled in such a hurry they'd even left their equipment behind. Now he'd get his first chance to have a proper look at what was behind that closed door.

19. WHAT DID THE BUILDERS SEE?

Did Seth imagine it, or did even Rendleton, who seemed fearless enough to tackle anything, pause slightly before unlocking the door?

The four of them stepped through into a long corridor painted a stark white with terracotta tiles on the floor, although not much light filtered in and there was a general feeling of cool gloom and darkness.

Rendleton fumbled along the wall and flicked a light switch, but nothing happened. He clicked it a couple more times and swore lightly under his breath.

'We've come in here to fetch lights but we need more lights to get the lights,' said Dex with a wry chuckle. 'Let me try.'

Seth felt a rush of air as Dex moved, and saw a crackle of blue light. This time, when Dex flicked the switch, the lights came on.

Dex surely had just used magic to fix the lights. It had been effortless. Seth fought a stab of jealousy.

'Great, mate,' said Rendleton, stepping through into the corridor. 'Guess you're not as useless as you look,' he joked.

'Well, I hadn't got you figured as someone who'd go completely pale at the first mention of the word *ghost*,' responded Dex with a grin in his voice.

'This is a bit different to all that fancy stuff up in the lighthouse,' commented Jo through a mouthful of biscuit she'd managed to smuggle from the kitchen. 'Entrance lobby is full of all that gold shimmery stuff.'

Dex strode forward eagerly, rubbing one hand along the smoothness of plain walls. 'Someone have the jitters it was all costing a bit much?'

'Going for a more reflective look here, I think Lark said,' muttered Rendleton, throwing open the first door and hesitating a second before stepping through.

'I think I'd reflect that I could do with a nice log fire and a couple of cushions,' suggested Dex. 'This place in winter might be a bit stark.'

Seth had to agree. He could feel cold creeping in, as if someone was touching the back of his neck with ice-cold fingers. His ears pricked up as he heard the faintest of scratching, scuttling sounds, but no one else reacted. He was probably just imagining things.

The couple of rooms they looked into were bare brickwork with exposed pipes and rubble on the floor.

'Thought you were opening soon,' said Jo, pushing back her mop of blond hair and pausing to examine what looked like a brand-new drill abandoned on the floor.

What was it that the builders had seen that had made them leave in such a hurry?

'The top rooms are getting there,' said Rendleton. 'Just need to knock a wall down here and there, pipework, finish the plumbing for the bathrooms. Plastering. Then it's just a sweep through. Bit of paint, carpets and furniture, and we're in business.'

'Just a sweep through,' echoed Dex, poking a toe at a pile of cement still with a spade stuck in it that was blocking the entrance to one of the bedrooms. 'These builders sure did leave in a hurry. You seen anything of what exactly upset them?'

Rendleton shot him a quick look. 'You'll find it best to ignore stories. I've been down here loads of times and nothing's ever bothered me. Let's get on and find those lights.'

'Talking of stories,' began Jo, as they all crept along the corridor. 'I could tell you all sorts about this place. Did you hear there was a sign things were going to change, just about the time the Mintencresses moved in?'

'A sign?' repeated Seth, curiosity piqued. 'What sort of sign?'

'Aye. Right in the same place where the rift is. That's where we lost the coastal path. Did you hear about that? But anyways, one night not long ago there was this bright light. It was like one of them stars actually dropped out of the sky, right where we lost our bit of coast a few years back. Or thereabouts. A portent, some called it.'

They had all started to creep even more slowly as she'd begun her story. Now, once again, Seth thought he heard a soft, scuttling sound from above. This time, all their heads snapped upwards towards the ceiling.

'Course, others said as how that bright light was Soul Snakesmouth returning. Or his ghost, I mean.'

They all stopped, still looking upwards.

'Sounds more like mice than something that goes bump in the night,' said Rendleton cheerfully.

He thrust open the last-but-one door at the end of the corridor. They all stepped carefully, as there was not just dust, but mess everywhere. This room was in a much worse state than the rest, littered with abandoned builders' equipment, including trowels, a spirit level, a single glove and an open bag of cement that had started to spill on to the concrete floor.

'Reckon the lights must be in the next room,' said Rendleton. He headed in there and gave a cry of triumph.

Jo lingered, clutching a large abandoned spanner and the spirit level, shoving her finds in a deep pocket of her voluminous coat. Seth was pretty sure she'd swiped that drill too. She gave Seth a cheeky grin when she realized she'd been observed. 'Shame to waste them.'

'I think I should have a quick squint upstairs,' said Dex, his green eyes lighting up as he headed for the stairs.

'Not now you don't, son,' said Rendleton, grabbing him by the shoulder.

Seth could see Dex's jaw clench again at the word *son*.

'If mice have got into the upper floor already, then there'll be plenty to worry your head about. But for now, we don't want to keep the doctor hanging around. Here we go.' He handed the heaviest end of the first of two big lamps to Dex, who grunted as he shouldered the weight.

'If there's damage from the storm, something's bound to have got in. Maybe even birds,' said Jo, taking the lamp by the legs at the other end.

Rendleton groaned.

This time there was no mistaking the soft but insistent scratching noise from the floor above them. They all stood there, just for a moment, listening.

'OK, set?' said Rendleton loudly, and they made their way much more slowly back along the corridor, struggling with the heavy, awkward lights.

Seth couldn't help but take a few quick glances back over his shoulder, listening for the sounds

'How did you end up doing odd jobs in a remote lighthouse?' Dex asked Rendleton.

'"Odd jobs"? I'm the sort-of manager, mate.'

'Yes. It's the "sort-of" bit that's interesting. I bet there's a story behind it,' went on Dex.

Seth's arms were not just beginning to ache, but

felt like they were being stretched from their sockets. Even though he was concentrating on not dropping his end of the lamp, he kept his ears open. What was Rendleton's story?

'You're the only member of staff who hasn't run off terrified of the ghosts. That's interesting too,' Dex repeated.

'I was at a loose end. Met Lark at a party and she suggested I tag along,' he answered easily. 'Think she knew they could do with the help. I needed the work. If it's any of your business.'

'There I was imagining all sorts. I thought you were going to say something thrilling, like this is a great sort of a place to hide out,' said Dex jovially. 'I mean, it's exactly the sort of job I'd look for if I were on the run, say. You sound like you've come here from pretty far off. Australia, is it, from that accent? What better place to come if you didn't want to be found in a hurry? If I happened to be a wanted criminal, this would be the perfect spot to hide out – remote, anonymous . . .'

'Plenty of anonymous places that would be far less trouble than this,' said Rendleton easily.

'Just saying!' grinned Dex.

Seth was struggling with his share of the weight, which was heavy enough to stop them speaking easily.

But that wasn't the reason everyone was suddenly silent.

That noise had come again, that small, scratchy-scrapy noise from upstairs. But this time it was followed by a definite thump.

Was everyone thinking the same thing? That sound hadn't come from birds or mice.

20. NOT EXACTLY POPULAR

Angelique's head bobbed out of a kitchen cupboard. She was dressed in a neat dark suit with a red lining to the jacket and she was staring with curiosity at a jar of pickled onions.

'I have probably never seen anyone who looked less like a chef,' said Seth.

He was glad to have delivered the lights. Now Dr Malinger was busy examining the body in the cellar. But he felt incredibly shy of talking to Angelique. He couldn't help but wonder why she had not kept her promise of staying in touch. Why had he heard nothing from her for weeks?

He really longed to hear all about the cases she'd been working on. Her department was on a long-term quest to investigate all of the forty-two sorcerers Missing Feared Exploded in the Unpleasant. She did secretive and excitingly dangerous work and she possessed unbelievably strong magical ability, even though she was only a couple of years older than Seth.

'They needed a cook,' Angelique said simply. She was peering into another cupboard. 'You probably know where everything is by now. I guess we need eggs and things?' She wrinkled her nose. 'How are things? Much better at the Last Chance Hotel now you're in charge? And without Tiffany?'

Seth hated how even the mention of the name made his stomach clench in a cowardly knot. It also reminded him of the many reasons why he so desperately needed to be magic and how let down he felt by Angelique. He bit back replying that if she was really interested in how he was, why hadn't she visited?

'I suppose you're pretending to be a cook because you're here *cleaning*?' he said. 'I guess it freaks people out if they think you're in their home to investigate dangerous magic.'

'That's not why I'm here. I came to see you, Seth.'

Why couldn't she be straight with him and admit what she was really doing here? He understood that magical people felt the need to be secretive. But did he always have to be shut out?

'Things are pretty much the same with me,' he said noncommittally. 'Pewter mentioned you'd hooked up with Stormface. Glad to hear you've been making a name for yourself.'

'Storm*force*.' Angelique gave a small smile. 'Pewter suggested I make a start on breakfast. Would you help me?'

She stared at the bread he put in front of her in a way that informed Seth that breakfast was going to be down to him.

'Toast,' he explained. 'What is it with people? Am I the only person left alive who cooks anything any more?' He emptied the fridge of bacon, eggs and sausages and slammed a pan on the stove.

'Tell me all about what's happening here,' began Angelique, frowning as she fiddled with switching on the stove. 'I've heard Mina Mintencress was really young and incredibly wealthy and took on this lighthouse and things have gone badly.'

'Sounds like you know it all already,' snapped Seth, watching her load sausages into a fiercely sizzling pan. 'I guess we'll soon find out if there's something more behind her death, although I'd have thought Pewter would want to call in a magical doctor if he wants to see if Mina Mintencress was killed by magic . . . Are there magical doctors?'

'Pewter's cousin is one of the best magical doctors. But magical people pretty much die in the usual ways.'

'So what's with bringing Prince Charming?' Seth said as he rescued the sausages, which had started to blacken. 'Don't you go anywhere without your new friend?'

'Actually, it was totally the other way around. It's his case. I told you, it was just a chance—'

There was a loud yawn behind them and in drifted Celeste, her cap askew, dark glasses on and back in her delicate little pale-blue ballet pumps. 'Cream cheese and crackers! I could really do with some coffee.' She sank on to one of the kitchen chairs.

'I'm Angelique Squerr,' said Angelique.

Seth went about putting on coffee, while keeping an eye on the frying pan.

'Don't mind me,' said Celeste. 'Is there any coffee? Pretend I'm not even here. How do you two know each other? Because you sounded like you were having a teensy bit of an argument.'

'I'm the new cook. And you are?'

Celeste removed her dark glasses to look her up and down disbelievingly. Angelique appeared as immaculate as she always did – her long hair was glossily smooth with a long stripe of red down the right side that matched the lining of her jacket. Her suit was tight-fitting enough to show how lean and fit she was.

'Really? Good. That means I don't need to make breakfast.'

'And you are?' repeated Angelique, moving closer and looking down her long nose at Celeste, taking in the beautiful white hands and perfect nails spread along the table as she rested her head.

'Celeste, maid to Mina Mintencress.'

'Maid? Great, you can help then.'

Celeste lazily stretched out her arm so she could lay her head comfortably on it. 'Please don't expect me to be in any state to do breakfast. You have no idea the sort of day I had yesterday – and that bed! I hardly got a wink of sleep.'

'We all had a bad day with a lot of shocks yester-day,' said Seth. He *had* heard plenty of snoring coming from Celeste's room, which was next to his. 'But Celeste particularly,' he added kindly, giving her a smile. 'And I think you need to change your shoes again.'

He pushed both Celeste and Angelique a cup of coffee, with a jug of cream and a sugar bowl. Celeste poured in a generous glug of cream and four lumps of sugar without lifting her head, but looked down at her gorgeous little blue shoes and wiggled her toes. 'Oh, I've put the wrong shoes on again, haven't I? Believe me,' she said, stirring, 'it's not every day your boss gets murdered. It gets you all muddled up.'

'I know she wasn't exactly popular. But murdered?' said Angelique, wrinkling her nose.

'We don't know yet,' said Seth, beginning to cook eggs and brown toast.

'Not popular?' declared Celeste stoutly. 'She was incredibly brave to take on an ambitious project and restore this lighthouse to something spectacular. She had to constantly stand up to Lark, and then her lawyer tried to stick his nose in. If Lark thought the lighthouse was so awful, she could have taken off, couldn't she? Is that bacon ready yet? I'm starved.'

The trouble was the Mintencress millions, thought Seth. Lark couldn't really go off on her own, she had no money. At least . . . not until Mina had died.

'That irritating Brockler was always talking to Jo and getting all these terrible lurid stories about this place. Gave him ideas. Everyone became convinced there was something wrong here.' A big glassy tear appeared in the corner of Celeste's eye.

'You really should go back to bed,' insisted Seth. 'I'll bring you something on a tray. Leave the coffee. Why don't I make you some chamomile tea? It might help you rest.'

Celeste's eyes were dark and ringed with grey smudges. 'Don't you need me?'

Seth smiled kindly at her. 'Course I do, it's why you have to look after yourself. No one's expecting you to do anything today. We've got a cook!'

Seth felt Angelique nudge him and she slid a plate heaped with breakfast in front of Celeste. Seth hoped everyone liked their bacon really crispy. Then Angelique did the same for Seth, sliding him another loaded plate.

'Eat,' she instructed. 'Then I want to tell you about—'

There was a noise from the cellar, which extended below them, and Celeste leapt to her feet. 'What was that?' Her over-large dark eyes turned fearful.

It would be Dr Malinger, Dex, Pewter and Rendleton coming up the steps. Any minute now they'd be here and they'd probably deliver more upsetting news.

Perhaps Celeste had worked this out too, as she

practically threw down her cutlery and raced to her room. Seth shoved in another mouthful of his own eggs and bacon – he hadn't realized how hungry he was.

Dr Malinger came in first, wiping her hands and looking grim. She was followed by a serious-looking Pewter.

'Hope we did a good enough job with the lights?' said Rendleton. 'You were very quiet down there. Didn't know as how you could tell anything for sure.'

He sounded anxious. But then it was going to be a big deal if the doctor had found any evidence there had been foul play.

But Dr Malinger was nodding. 'Oh yes. I know exactly how she died.'

'I'd imagine it's difficult to work out with just a quick look,' went on Rendleton. 'I guess she drowned, but was it—'

Dr Malinger cut him off with a withering look.

'What we'd really like to know is if it is possible to even tell if there was anything suspicious about her death,' said Pewter.

'Oh yes. Miss Mintencress's death was most definitely murder. How can I be so sure with just a quick look? Because she didn't drown, Inspector – she was strangled.'

21. ALONE AT THE TOP OF A LIGHTHOUSE

Jo appeared, loaded up a plate and started to eat hungrily at the kitchen table. 'It's a proper mystery, innit?' she said with relish, slathering her plate with brown sauce. 'She was alone in the top of this lighthouse. And the door was locked. Spooky or what!'

That was it. Seth was now convinced magic had to be at the bottom of it. Strangled? Alone in a locked room at the top of a lighthouse? He looked at Jo and was keen to learn what stories she might have shared. Had the local people any suspicions that this lighthouse had once been home to a sorcerer?

'Is everyone thinking what I'm thinking – that this is the work of the ghost?' went on Jo. 'Be nice to have a tea to wash all this down. Any chance? I mean, I will have coffee if there isn't.'

Seth made tea. He thought of Celeste's determined face: *Let's find out which one of the rotters killed her.* Somehow they'd both known there was more to her death than it had appeared.

Dexter Stormforce's finely chiselled face had been the last to emerge from the cellar, looking less rugged and more a chalky white. Rendleton put his hand firmly on Dex's shoulder and began talking about the urgency of inspecting storm damage.

'Need to get a proper fix on that brickwork. We'll start outside. You look like you could do with a blast of fresh air, mate.'

Dex's eyes had the desperate look of someone looking for an escape. But Rendleton had him in a grip that wasn't going to be easy to wriggle out of and Dex was steered away in a drift of conversation about structural damage, loose pipes and rendering. He made a feeble request for breakfast.

'I have two suggestions,' said Pewter, hauling a huge platter of bacon from where it had been warming, and steering Dr Malinger towards the dining room. 'One, we leave breaking the news to everyone else until after breakfast. Two, maybe save a rasher or two for Stormforce. I think he might need it.'

Seth called Pewter back to hand him some coffee, and managed to say in his ear, 'But Inspector, no one could have strangled her. She was alone at the top of the lighthouse. We had to break down the door.'

'Fascinating, isn't it?'

When Brockler, Lark and Alfie all finally made their way to the dining room, it occurred to Seth that the upstairs rooms were clear.

Slipping past the dining room unseen, he sprinted for the room at the top of the lighthouse. He thought he'd been really stealthy, but when he turned he saw Angelique closing in about six steps behind him.

'What are you up to, Seth?' she demanded once she got to the top, setting her black jacket straight and tucking her silver-topped cane under her arm after her dash up the spiral stairs.

Seth cautiously pushed open the door of the top-floor bedroom. 'I knew there was something suspicious about her death,' he said. 'But I've no idea how it was done. What could we have missed?'

He turned and saw Angelique's eyes widen as she took in the floor-to-ceiling windows and the gaudy décor; the frilly lilac drapes around the four-poster bed that had been shoved to one side of the room, the huge twirly silver-framed mirror that would suit a ballroom better, and the wallpaper patterned with a flock of birds, damaged by the storm. Then there was the hastily covered-over hole in the brickwork.

'I presume a Disney princess is coming to stay.'

'Lark's responsible for the furnishing,' Seth sighed. 'To make her feel involved. Mina seems to have been a kindly sort like that.' He first double checked that the lock on that door really had been busted when Rendleton had shouldered his way through.

'Perhaps it's Lark who should have been murdered,' said Angelique, her gaze sweeping the room and lingering over an untidy dressing table and its litter of opened bottles, face cream and lotions; powder spilled across the top. Valuable-looking rings and bracelets had been haphazardly discarded.

Seth was already in the bathroom, picking up each of the expensive glass bottles of bath foam and luxurious hair conditioner, unscrewing each lid and taking a sniff. He was disappointed that all of them seemed regular scents – cherry blossom and straw-berry – because he was remembering that sour smell. Did that mean it hadn't been the bath foam?

'She was strangled, Seth, not poisoned.'

'But how could she have been? There was a smell in here yesterday, like a strong citrusy tang. Nothing like these expensive products.'

'I don't think a smell is going to tell us how she was strangled.'

Angelique had been drawn to one of the huge windows that gave out on to the mesmerizing view.

'It is spectacular, isn't it?' said Seth. 'You should have seen the waves and the sky in the storm last night. It was better than watching a movie. Until we actually got struck by lightning, of course.'

'And one of the family died.'

'Yes. There is that.'

'A very unlucky family. What's your feeling, Seth?'

'There is definitely something weird about the whole place,' he responded eagerly. 'You can explain accidents, things moving about, electrics failing. But Soul Snakesmouth was a sinister sorcerer who disappeared about eight years ago, presumed dead.'

He knew the way Angelique worked. Her silver-topped red cane was a magical instrument. He'd seen her flip up the top and poke in corners and zap everything with a crackle of blue light and then take readings. Apparently, magic left invisible ripples that disturbed the air, and that's how she knew if magic had been used recently.

He stopped, because Angelique barely seemed to be listening, but also, she wasn't zapping everything.

Were there traces of magic in this room? Pewter had told him S3 knew about Soul Snakesmouth and the lighthouse had been cleaned. But might the magic have returned – if magic returned – or been brought back somehow? And then there was the ghost . . .

'You seem to have got very friendly with that girl in a short time,' said Angelique. 'Celeste is a suspect, you know.'

Seth looked at her in disbelief. 'Celeste was with me when Mina Mintencress died. They were more like best friends than anything.'

'Mina was an incredibly rich heiress. I'd say this is less likely to be about magic and more about the fact that she's got squillions of cash. I wonder, does Celeste get anything in her will?'

It was a good question. Seth knew Celeste had been with Mina for years. Lark had been left something; it seemed obvious Celeste would have been too. Seth hesitated, as Angelique seemed to have too much curiosity about the maid, and he wanted to ask all about the cleaning.

'Can't you just zap the room with your divinoscope and check if magic has been used recently?' he suggested. 'It was home to a sorcerer. I know it was cleaned, but there could be some magic left here. She died in a locked room, but was strangled. Could that have been done by magic?'

'Really sophisticated magic, maybe.' Angelique shrugged. Then wrinkled her nose. 'I've never been into somewhere already cleaned before.'

'And there's something wrong about it?' he asked hopefully

'It just doesn't have the feel I'd expect . . .' She shook her head. 'But you are imagining a big plot, Seth. Before you go running away with too many ideas, remember – you think that magic is much cleverer and more powerful than it is. Magic is limited to the skill and power of the sorcerer using it. Killing someone like you described, alone at the top of the lighthouse . . .' She gave her head a little shake and turned from the windows and the glorious view. 'One of our really experienced agents, Copious Bladderwrack, cleaned this, Seth. I think we might be looking for a more regular explanation.'

'You think there's really a ghost?'

Angelique threw him a scornful look. 'Not entirely what I meant by regular. I mean, all those disturbances are much more likely down to someone deliberately playing games. Although, it's interesting . . . You are always very observant. Anything else strike you?'

She was waiting, and Seth considered. She might be right about the ghosts being someone deliberately setting out to jinx the project. That was pretty much what Mina had suspected. If someone had staged those accidents – could they also have found a way to cause Mina's death?

He was thinking about magic and knew it could be the most ordinary things being out of place that you needed to pay attention to, so he thought hard. 'There were quite a lot of dead gulls when I got here,' he said, knowing how lame it sounded.

He felt she was fighting an urge to laugh. But all she said was: 'I'm sure there are dead seabirds on many islands, especially after a storm.'

'This was before the storm,' he said. 'Oh, and a couple of times I think I see things moving, scuttling in the corners – but when you look, there's nothing there.'

'Spiders and dead gulls. Hmm.' She had started wandering the room, pausing to look into the deep tub in the middle.

Seth remembered something else. 'And Brockler

has this weird carving he turned into a pendant, as Mina wanted to wear it. She thought it would bring her luck. It's shaped like a dragon eating the lighthouse. He seemed secretive when he showed it to me.'

'Sinister jewellery. Hmmm.'

He longed to start tapping the floor. If it wasn't down to magic, then what? Someone must have got in here. There might be a secret entrance or a trapdoor he could find. A way someone could have reached Mina and strangled her. But he feared Angelique would just laugh at him.

He looked up at the ceiling and, once again, out of the corner of his eye he thought he saw a dark shape move, but it was so quick it was easy to believe he'd only imagined it.

'Have you asked yourself why someone from the magical world would even want to kill Mina Mintencress?' said Angelique. 'And then there is the question of who here is likely to have that level of magic. Seth, you have much to learn about magic.'

'And whose fault is that?' He kept his voice to a low grumble, trying to conceal how upset he felt. 'I want to learn and train to be magic – I thought you were going to help me!'

'I wanted to get in touch,' said Angelique in a

small voice, 'but things were so complicated.'

'Oh really. What was stopping you – abroad on holiday? Held prisoner? Or just too busy flashing about with your fantastic magic and your great job and your new charming friend McStormface.'

He opened the window, breathed the sea air. He stared out at the glorious view, blue sea dotted with furls of white and a sky above with clouds scudding across it like they were in a race. 'This was once the home of a sinister sorcerer. It has to be connected.'

He looked at how far up they were and found himself remembering how strong Rendleton must be to go for a daily swim, even in those churning waves after a storm. Could he have climbed up? Was that the answer?

No, that was stupid.

Angelique came and stood alongside him at the big picture window and seemed equally captivated by the extraordinary view. She stared at him, pushing back her glossy hair with its one dramatic stripe of red. 'Why don't you tell me your theories before someone comes and finds us sneaking about?'

'My theory is that someone here knows this was the home of a sorcerer. Somehow the magic has come back and someone has found a way to use it.'

'And she died in this bath?'

Angelique casually lifted her red cane, flipped the silver top and sent a gentle cascade of soft blue light slowly around the room, peering into the end of the cane to take a reading. Her nose crinkled in concentration, a small frown appearing.

She unexpectedly sent a fierce jet of blue into the bath, making the white enamel shine with a shimmering cornflower-coloured haze.

She perched on the edge and took another reading.

'The trouble is, Seth, magic doesn't just reappear. This place was cleaned. Magic doesn't turn up again. Magic doesn't work like that. Someone would have needed to bring that magic back – and the things you are talking about would be powerful magic.'

It took Seth a second to notice something was happening behind her.

Black dots were starting to appear on the wall. Not just flitting shadows this time – there was no mistaking that these dark shapes were real, and getting larger.

Seth found himself staring for a moment, and before he could even lift his hand to point or speak, the dots were multiplying. Suddenly there were hundreds of them. He wanted to shout a warning, but looking at the dark swarming made the warning cry die in his throat.

Before he could do anything, there was a cloud of them. They lifted from the wall and started swarming like bees, but silently, and they were coming together and forming a thick cloud that was heading straight for Angelique.

22. EXPECT SOMETHING HORRIBLE

The swarm gathered unbelievably quickly, grew and got darker in seconds. Before Seth could move or cry out the swarm of dots had formed to attack. And the nearest thing was Angelique. She was right in the firing line, but her attention was concentrated on the end of her cane. And it was all happening in silence.

Angelique's cane gave a couple of short flashes of blue. She stared at it and her mouth formed a wide 'oh' of surprise. Only then did she begin looking wildly about her and Seth guessed that warning flash had told her something was horribly wrong, but not that a swarm of shadow bees were about to strike.

Then, instead of swarming around their target, the dark dots formed into a long thick rope that whipped and coiled itself around her neck. It was clear that the shadows had become real; no longer just a shade, or darkness, but had turned into something physical, something that was strangling her.

She put up her hands to try to grab at the thick coil. Her fingers clawed and grappled to free herself from the tightening rope of shadows, her eyes round with terror, while Seth was frozen in horror, wasting valuable seconds. He was desperate to think of something to do, but knew she was fighting with magic. How could he fight against magic?

Angelique was trying to grope for her divinoscope. She'd dropped it to clutch both hands at the snake-like rope around her throat. Her struggle upended a small wooden table next to the bath and a range of beautiful bottles smashed on to the tiles, filling the room with a gorgeous scent of herbal perfume.

Seth had to snap out of his paralysis. *Do something*. Angelique's face was turning crimson as the rope cut in tighter.

He looked at the fallen divinoscope. He had no idea how to use it or whether it would even work for him, but he snatched it up anyway, then he felt a beating in his chest and he remembered he had a magical object of his own he always carried with him.

He dropped the divinoscope and snatched instead his black book from inside his tunic and raced towards the black snake, the book lifted in the air like a club.

The shadow snake must have sensed an imminent attack, as it shot out a tendril to try to grab him too.

Seth dodged his head out of the way, took a step backwards and spun around, taking back his arm and swiping at the shadow creature as hard as he could. He sent the black book right into the middle of the loose tendril flying towards him. It felt like it had connected with nothing, but it sent the dark rope of shadow bees flying and splattering like silent rain against the wall.

There was a pause. The snake momentarily lost its rope-like look and seemed to dissolve back into thousands of dots as it decided what to do. As if it realized things were no longer quite all going its way.

The loosened hold was enough for Angelique's hands to successfully wrench the rope from around her neck and she grabbed at the divinoscope that Seth thrust at her.

Then the shadow bees rushed towards Seth in a terrifying swarm.

Seth's instinct was to run. But he stood his ground, even as the swarm grew into a vast black shape. He lifted his arm and swiped at it again and again with his black book. For a moment he thought he'd left it too late and the shape would engulf him, but he battered on, swinging with all his might until the swarm started to back away.

Angelique was choking and coughing, but still managed to flip open the top of her cane and flash the shadows.

Seth didn't let up; he was winning, he was moving forwards. The shadows were backing away. The shape was beginning to loosen and dissolve from the thick black rope to an unformed misty cloud, but even this Seth clubbed, hitting it again and again and forcing it towards the open window, even though it felt like he was connecting with nothing.

Angelique joined him, sending piercingly fierce sapphire jets into the creature as the shape got looser and looser.

Seth kept forcing it towards the window, until he felt all the black shapes had gone through. Then he slammed the window closed, breathing hard and fast. He looked at Angelique. She slumped next to the mess of broken bottles floating in a channel of gooey lather.

She rubbed around her neck, lifted her divinoscope and looked at the end of cane in deep concentration, breathing in fast gulps.

They both stared out of the window, but not even the faintest wisp of a shadow could be seen. A sharp, unpleasant citrus tang in the air the only remaining evidence there had ever been one at all.

23. Closer To Solving The Mystery

They were crouched, clearing up the evidence, when a voice took them completely by surprise.

'You two have been having fun.'

They both started guiltily. Dexter Stormforce's face peered at the sticky, frothy muddle of broken glass and indulgent bath products as Seth and Angelique scooped the mess into the bin.

'More fun than me anyway. That Rendleton really is the dullest man I've ever come across,' went on Dex. 'Talked for a full fifteen minutes about ductwork. Anyone even a clue what ductwork might be? Wow, I must say, when you make a mess you guys really do it properly. Smells like a perfume factory in here.' He frowned as he sniffed the air.

Angelique looked up from where she was smearing and scooping something once ultra-expensive across the floor. 'Not having fun, Dex – investigating. We are closer to solving some of the mystery of how Mina Mintencress was strangled alone in a locked bathroom.'

'And such an imaginative way of going about it. You've invented the world's most expensive cleaning product on the side. Let me guess – killed by perfume fumes?'

While he was talking, Dex took something out of this pocket. It looked like a small silver letter opener. It had a red hilt encrusted with small sparkling jewels, and a very thin, very lethal blade. Seth wasn't sure if it was a letter opener, or the thinnest of daggers.

'We know exactly how she died,' said Seth quietly.

'Er, actually, we don't.' Angelique was shaking her head.

'Don't tell me,' groaned Seth, 'magic isn't as simple as that.'

With a flick of the wrist, Dex pointed the blade

towards the bath, but Angelique quickly grabbed his arm and cried: 'No! I just used my divinoscope and almost got strangled by a shadow rope. Something magical must have set it off when Mina was in here.'

Dex took a sly glance at Seth.

'It's OK, Seth is one of us,' said Angelique.

A feeling of warmth rushed through Seth's body as she said *One of us*. She meant someone who knew of the existence of magic. The warmth didn't even subside when Dex looked at him as if he'd be less surprised if she'd been referring to one of the gulls.

'You are telling me you were actually attacked by shadows?' Dex said, starting to examine the walls. 'That is incredible. I don't think I've ever . . . what happened exactly? And what did you do with the little fellas?'

'We forced them all out of the window,' said Seth.

'No!' cried Dex, his long hair falling into his eyes crossly as he dashed to the window and looked down to the ground far below. 'What you do that for? You've ruined any chance of examining it!'

'It seemed a better alternative than leaving it to choke the life out of Angelique.'

'I think,' said Angelique calmly, 'we need to talk to Inspector Pewter.'

*

They found Pewter in the dining room. He looked up guiltily and moved quickly, but not before Seth had seen he'd been again studying that same map covered in crosses.

'Ah, just clearing up,' he said, hurriedly folding away the map, taking a mouthful of toast and dusting his fingers of crumbs.

'Looks like you are stuffing your face with the last of the breakfast,' said Dex, seizing a slice of bacon. 'Finally got myself a break. Rendleton's tied up showing the doctor about the place. She's not visited since the changes.'

'Perhaps Dr Malinger is enjoying the fresh air and is more impressed than she expected,' said Pewter. 'This place really is bracing. Mina Mintencress might have been on to something you know. I think folk might just flock here. Well, I'm pleased to see you three are getting along and having fun,' he added, helping pile together all the plates and cups.

'I think first they might need to get rid of the shadows,' said Angelique stiffly. She rubbed at where there was a red welt on her smooth neck. 'We need to talk.'

'Yes,' began Dex, 'because I guess you have probably all been wondering the big question. What brings a totally awesome dude like Dexter Stormforce to a minor death at a remote lighthouse?'

'I *was* wondering why they didn't send Copious,' said Pewter, as they headed for the kitchen.

Dex took a seat at the kitchen table and put his smartly booted feet up on a chair. He reached to sandwich together two leftover slices of bacon between two thick slices of toast.

'Well, I can tell you exactly why I'm here.' His green eyes glittered. 'You will be pleased to know that I am quite possibly *the* expert in darkwitching. Plus Copious, unfortunately, is away on a walking holiday in the Gascoigne Mountains. But hey – I almost got to see some darkwitching in practice. I envy you two.'

'What's going on?' Angelique spluttered, sounding shocked. 'Why was someone allowed to buy this place if there are darkwitching elements loose? I thought this place was cleaned?'

'Well, of course, there aren't *supposed* to be any elements of any kind of magic left after a cleaning,' said Dex soothingly.

Seth spoke up nervously. 'Inspector, you mentioned darkwitching yesterday. I still don't really know anything about it. What exactly is it?

'Shadow sorcery,' said Pewter. 'Controlling the darkness, the shadows, the shapes that every object can cast. It's very rare to find a darkwitch. One of the trickier lines of magic.'

'Soul Snakesmouth was one?' asked Angelique.

Seth regarded her curiously. He hadn't expected her to anticipate his own question. 'But you'll know all about the MFE you're trying to track down,' he said to her. 'You'll have researched this place before taking the job here, no?'

Angelique rolled her eyes. 'You are utterly terrible at believing people. I told you – it's *Dex's* case. I asked him to bring me along. I didn't have time to research anything. I came to see you, Seth. I wanted to apologize.'

'Apologize?'

She took a deep breath and looked at him with her dark eyes. 'I wanted to have something good to tell you about Tiffany and the firefly cage. I wanted to wait until all the news I had wasn't bad. But it's all dead ends and false alarms and I'm really sorry. I know our best chance of finding her was before she'd had chance to get very far. I couldn't face being the one to tell you.'

Seth let this sink in, while Angelique brought Dex up to speed with who Tiffany was.

'You mean she's completely escaped. She could be anywhere?' said Seth finally.

'The search continues,' said Pewter, slathering several slices of toast with butter and marmalade.

'But she—'

'Shall we focus?' interrupted Dex. 'I guess, Seth, that if you've lived all your life in a former home of a sorcerer before the place was cleaned, you'll know all about stumbling upon a grimoire. Or discovering someone's left a nice ramiteb and is using it to light fires or keep flowers in,' said Dex, helping himself to the top slice of Pewter's pile of toast. 'All fun stuff. Until people discover their grandparents have turned into white mice. That's the sort of accident me and Angelique try to stop happening.'

Seth signed. 'I understand what you and Angelique do. But I don't know what a grimoire or a ramiteb is. I really don't know all that much about magic.'

Dex looked at him curiously over his slice of toast as if trying to work him out. 'A grimoire is a spellbook.'

At his words, Seth felt again that beating next to his chest. His black book seemed more alive than ever. It had a special name in the magical world. Was that what it was – a grimoire?

'And a ramiteb is a device some sorcerers use to channel their magic. Sometimes it's a ring, or – you know about Angelique's divinoscope? Not everyone has the sheer marvellousness to conjure magic just by using their bare hands.' Dex nodded deferentially at Pewter.

'Does takes a little more practice,' said Pewter quietly.

'Hey, explaining magic is fun,' said Dex. 'I should consider taking on an apprentice.'

Seth ignored him. 'Let me get this right. This place was cleaned – so someone else has brought *new* darkwitching magic here to the lighthouse?'

He saw Dex, Pewter and Angelique exchange a glance that, as always, simply shut Seth out. He couldn't help but let a sigh escape him.

'I don't think that's likely,' said Angelique.

'Darkwitching magic is powerful and rare,' said Pewter. 'And a sorcerer who practised it lived here, so that would be too much of a coincidence. Yes. The darkwitching surely must be connected to Soul Snakesmouth.' He looked thoughtful.

'I do have something else exciting to share that might explain a lot,' said Dex. 'It'll be quicker than me explaining if I can show you.'

With a flourish, he opened the palm of his hand to reveal a drab-looking stone.

Seth stared for a moment, feeling underwhelmed.

Then he recognized it. 'It's a wordstone!' he exclaimed.

'It's a way of experiencing a book, like being plunged right into the pages,' explained Dex to Seth. 'They are a bit difficult to get used to, you might not get much out of it at first. I can talk you through it.'

'Seth's used them and he's pretty good at it,' said Angelique. 'But where's the book this has come from? There must have been a book if there's a wordstone.'

Dex nodded. 'Copious discovered the wordstone here when he cleaned. But no book. Mysterious, huh? That's the bad news. And there is more bad news—'

'Now would also be a time for any good news,' said Pewter. 'I'm hoping there is some?'

'Almost none. Snakesmouth was incredibly secretive about all the work that went on here and we know almost nothing. But the good news is that he couldn't quite resist showing off how clever he was. He wrote a book called *The Deadly Secrets of Dark-witching*. That has to be the book connected to the wordstone. It was offered to the Elysee library, but they would only consider it for the Problem section and Snakesmouth was enraged.'

'What's the Problem section?' asked Seth.

'Prohibited, Radical, Objectionable, Banned, Ludicrously-unlikely, Extremely-iffy and May-cause-people-to-react-with-violence. The Problem books,' said Angelique, wrapping her long stripe of red hair around her finger.

'From what I've seen of the sorcerers in the magical world,' muttered Seth, 'I'd say most of the books they are likely to write would come under one of those headings.'

'Guess we're ready, then,' said Stormforce, with a grin that lifted one side of his mouth more than the other.

Seth knew he meant to take them into the word-stone and felt far from ready as Dex led them out of the back door, where the wind welcomed them excitedly. Dex extended his hand and Seth watched, fascinated, as he saw the dull stone start to glow like it had a heart of fire. Then it moved, turned smooth, became a vivid green like lush grass and then reformed so it was sharp as a dagger.

Angelique reached her hand forward and so did Pewter. Seth was the last to tentatively extend his hand and all he could think as his fingers touched the wordstone was the first time he'd done this, he'd thought he was going to be torched and eaten by a dragon.

Now he was going to be plunged into a magical book written by a sorcerer who practised banned and dangerous darkwitching.

He had a feeling this was going to be even worse.

24. WHAT IS THIS PLACE?

The next thing Seth knew, they were all standing together in a small, dark room that started slowly to take shape around them. He blinked to adjust his eyes to the gloom, and was more than a little afraid. When he'd used a wordstone to travel into a book before, he'd been disturbed by seeing unexpected things so vividly. He'd even met someone he knew was dead.

The lighthouse faded to nothing, his skin prickling as he waited for what would appear out of the darkness. Before he knew it, they were in a circular, shelf-lined room. Along the centre a long, clinical metal table was set up with flasks and test tubes, as if waiting for a complicated experiment to begin.

Seth didn't dare move in case he sent something flying, but Angelique had no such hesitation and bent to peer at the books and bottles that lined the shelves. Some were filled with coloured liquids. There were larger jars packed and with strange substances or pallid creatures suspended in slimy-looking fluid. The largest looked like it might contain a whole cauliflower ... unless that was a brain? Seth shivered.

'Some extraordinary titles here – I wonder if Ethylene Despair even knows of the existence of some of these,' said Angelique, tilting her head to one side as she read the titles of a cluster of books propped next to a silver-topped flask filled with a dark-red viscous substance.

'Who is Ethylene Despair?' muttered Seth.

'Head librarian at the Elysee library,' explained Pewter. He appeared to be more interested in looking at the ceiling than the cluttered shelves or the long table of experiments. 'Fun character. A reformed sinister sorcerer,' he continued, taking out a magnifying glass to examine the floor. 'Very intuitive librarian.'

'Hate to think of what was dreamt up in here,' said Angelique, scribbling furiously in the red notebook she carried with her.

Seth found himself eye to eye with a staring creature suspended in purple slime. It had two huge eyes on stalks and Seth was convinced it was alive and looking right at him. 'What is this place?' he said, turning to Dex.

Dex was pacing the room slowly, peering at every shelf, bending to the low ones, walking along every inch of the walls. He spread his arms wide. 'This is the secret laboratory of one of the cleverest and most powerful sorcerers in history. The laboratory of Soul Snakesmouth.'

Seth couldn't help but think that, like Pewter, Dex was in awe of the sort who practised evil magic.

'He could make shadows do unbelievable things,' went on Dex.

'This laboratory was in the lighthouse?' said Angelique, moving further along a shelf and making more notes. 'Why are you showing us the version that still exists in the wordstone? What can we learn here?'

Seth reached out to touch the creature in the purple slime, but his hand went straight through it. That's when he remembered that he need not have worried about knocking anything over. Of course, all of it was only an image. None of them could actually touch any of it. None of this was real.

Angelique turned to look accusingly at Dex. 'Please tell me all of this was cleaned?'

'If this room was in the lighthouse,' said Pewter slowly, 'it would have been cleaned by Copious.'

Dex was grinning. 'Absolutely spot on. Discovering the laboratory of a notorious sinister sorcerer would have meant utter joy for Copious Bladderwrack, and his future fortune and career.'

'"Would have"?' said Angelique. 'I am not liking the sound of that.'

Dex carried on explaining as he wandered the room. 'I may be a fabulous S3 agent, but I only got your call last night, so I haven't managed to read all of Copious's notes. But I can tell you what I know. After the Unpleasant, Soul Snakesmouth was pretty much the shiny big apple at the top of the tree when it came to tracking down those Missing Feared Exploded.'

'So Snakesmouth was involved in the Unpleasant?' said Pewter.

'Around that time two things happened; he disappeared and there was a local disaster where they lost a chunk of coast to the sea, almost as if he was somehow offering magical protection to the village, which left with him. Who knows what he was really up to. He was a real paranoid kind of a guy, lived alone on this isolated rock. He was married for a short time, but she disappeared to the other end of the earth. Probably discovered how he really spent his days out here. Doing his research alone in a building not even connected to the mainland wasn't secret enough; he went further than that. He actually hid his laboratory.'

'He doesn't sound like the sort of person who wanted to open up the magical world to more people from outside and take on apprentices to pass on all this knowledge,' muttered Seth, wishing they could find a way to add smells to what you see with a wordstone. He relied on his nose so much and it was telling him nothing.

'Nope – didn't really want to share his magic with anyone,' agreed Dex.

Seth was reminded of the words Brockler had used when he'd talking about going into the history of the lighthouse: *A really fascinating man, Soul Snakesmouth. A man full of secrets.* When Seth had asked what he'd meant, he'd only answered: 'If I told you, they wouldn't be secrets.' Brockler had given a little chuckle and had looked more furtive than ever.

Seth was convinced the lawyer had uncovered at least some of the truth about Soul Snakesmouth.

'I still don't understand, where is this, exactly?' Angelique wrinkled her nose. 'I'm confused. This secret laboratory – Copious would have looked for it. Are you saying it wasn't cleaned because it isn't in the lighthouse?'

Dex gave a small bow. 'The answer to your question is – I have no idea.' He paced once more around the room. 'It would have been a main target for cleaning. Unfortunately, the truth is more bad news. This room was never cleaned because it was never even found.'

'Not found!' Angelique turned, startled. 'You mean all this stuff is just lying around somewhere?' She gestured at the creature that was still leering at Seth.

Dex nodded. 'It is somewhere so secret, even Bladderwrack couldn't find it. He was forced to give up.'

'So are you two concluding that the fact that Snakesmouth's darkwitching shadow magic seems to have come back,' mused Pewter, 'is down to faulty cleaning?'

'It certainly means I suggest we rather urgently look again.' Dex flashed his white teeth. 'I don't know how, exactly. But this laboratory is where I guess the shadow magic is coming from. If we could find it, that would be a great start.'

Dex was busy again, inching his way about the room, peering at every shelf. Seth felt that if he could have moved all the books and jars aside, he would have done, but of course, they were only images, he couldn't physically touch any of it.

'And Copious concluded it wasn't in the light-house?' said Pewter.

'He did.' Dex shrugged. 'But I reckon he was wrong. Those rampaging shadows prove pretty conclusively that all of the darkwitching power has just been lying here, dormant, waiting for someone to kick it all off again. Someone or something powerful has got all this working. Not only have the shadows come back, but . . . check out the walls, people.' Dex took out his dagger and flashed a jet of blue light from the end.

The image around them became clearer.

'Notice what's different about them?' said Dex, sounding cocky.

Angelique paused in her note-taking. 'All right. I was being slow. The walls are curved, I get it. And you don't get curved walls in many buildings.'

'And there is something important missing.' Dex

again covered every inch of the shelves, looking at the mad jumble of equipment and books stuffed into this room. 'There isn't a door. There has to be a secret way in and out.'

'So it *is* here,' said Pewter. 'This secret laboratory, the heart of darkwitching, is somewhere in this lighthouse.'

'Yep,' finished Dex. 'Now all we have to do is find it. Before someone else dies.'

PART FOUR

25. SERIOUSLY IMPRESSIVE MAGIC

'I guess we have a couple of possibilities.' Pewter considered for a moment. 'Maybe three,' he said, taking a seat at the long kitchen table once the four of them had emerged from the wordstone and were back in the lighthouse kitchen.

Seth made tea, slowly readjusting to reality.

'The shadows attacked you,' said Pewter to Angelique. 'That's very helpful.'

'That was very painful.'

'You stirred them up again just with a few short

flashes from your divinoscope?'

Angelique nodded. 'That's all I did, and what happened, well . . . no one could have missed those shadows,' she said, rubbing her neck.

'Then I think we can safely presume that did not happen when Copious was here,' mused Pewter. 'When Bladderwrack was here the magic must have been completely dormant, otherwise he would never have given up trying to discover that secret laboratory. He would never have passed the Snakesmouth Lighthouse cleaned and safe for the unfortunate Mintencress party to buy. So the real puzzle is – what's changed?'

'We should go over all Bladderwrack's notes,' said Angelique as Seth handed them each a mug of tea.

'That may take some time. We've already had one death,' said Pewter, deep in thought.

'The magic has managed to return?' said Seth. 'So – how can that happen?'

He was thinking of his own home. Angelique had been on a secret S3 mission to investigate his mother and whether the Last Chance Hotel needed cleaning. But since learning of the existence of magic, Seth had begun to suspect that there had always been magic lurking there, even in the fabric of the building, even in the walls. It hadn't come back, it had just never completely gone away.

But when Copious had checked this place out, the magic hadn't been here. And Angelique had already told him that magic didn't return all by itself.

'Yes, what has stirred up this very powerful hidden magic?' Dex's eyes glinted.

'Seriously impressive magic,' said Pewter, steepling his fingers, then reaching absent-mindedly for a biscuit. 'Getting those shadows to form and strangle like that...'

'I know Brockler has got interested in the history of this place,' said Seth tentatively, recalling again that furtive look when the lawyer talked about secrets. 'I wonder if he could have...'

'I think what we saw was too powerful for someone who discovered magic for the first time when they arrived here, Seth,' said Angelique, wrapping her strand of red hair around a finger again.

Seth thought back to his own disastrous attempts at magic and could see she had a point. If someone had been trying to tap into Soul Snakesmouth's magic and kickstart it, how could they have done that without leaving a trail of destruction? Unless, of course, whoever was controlling those shadows possessed more than just a spark of magic – perhaps a magic that was much, much stronger?

'It's difficult to believe that Brockler could have taught himself to grow a wart on the end of his nose since he's been at the lighthouse, let alone master the sinister art of darkwitching,' said Dex.

'But it has to be one of the Mintencress party,' said Seth carefully, thinking of everyone who had been here when Mina died.

'And I thought you were going to say the ghost of Soul Snakesmouth has come back and is responsible,' grinned Dex.

Seth was about to ask if anyone thought that was even possible, but Pewter was moving on.

'Your thoughts and suggestions are always very insightful, Seth,' said Pewter. 'What made you think straight away of Brockler?'

It was so easy to get things wrong where magic was concerned. So easy to say things that made him look a complete fool, but Seth could imagine Brockler being the sort who would stop at nothing if he'd found out that Snakesmouth was a sorcerer and that the possibility of magic might be within his grasp.

He hesitated. 'Disturbing things have been happening. Ladders moving, problems with the electrics. I think Brockler might have been trying to spook everyone to get Mina to give up the project and leave.' Seth tried to think things through logically. 'Is it possible he accidentally triggered something? He was definitely interested in the history,' he added cautiously. 'And I think he must have been poking around Snakesmouth village, as he told me he picked up a few things there *and* he mentioned knowing about Snakesmouth's secrets.' It all sounded a bit lame, even to him. 'Was the village cleaned? Do the records show if Copious Bladderwrack checked it out at all?'

Angelique was looking at him with her dark eyes. 'That's a really good idea.'

'Well, there's no harm in checking,' said Dex. 'Bladderwrack ran out of ideas and leads and gave up. Angelique, you get on that boat, go and check out the locals and the scenery. I'm going to see if I can't get a fix on these shadows that terrified you and Seth, although I know you did your best to mess up any chance of me finding out anything useful.' Dex's green eyes gleamed. 'I plan to finish what Bladderwrack started and find that laboratory. There's a whole island here Snakesmouth might have played with. Did Copious search the whole island? What if the entrance is concealed somewhere?'

'There's an old boathouse down in Gull Cove,' offered Seth.

'OK. A place to start.' Dex waved his dagger with

a flourish. 'Soul Snakesmouth's darkwitching laboratory has to be here. I will find it – and find out who else knows about the power of darkwitching. Unless you two are planning to beat me to it?'

He threw out a challenging look, which Seth could tell didn't include him.

'I wouldn't rate your chances of doing anything if Rendleton's determined to get a proper assessment of the storm damage,' said Pewter dryly, as the sound of footsteps approaching from outside could be heard. 'He'll keep you busy, once he's finished giving Dr Malinger the grand tour. Which I don't think will take very long.'

'That sounds like a challenge.' Dex's eyes shone and he gave a big smile. 'First one to the laboratory wins. Well, let's get at it. Someone has picked up what Snakesmouth started. We are on the trail of a darkwitch and I am very excited.'

26. IS THAT EVEN POSSIBLE?

The back door flapped open, but it was Jo, not Rendleton, who stepped through. The handle was wrenched out of her hand by the wind, and it was with difficulty that she closed it firmly behind her, shutting out the roar. 'Boat's ready whenever you are. The wind's still up, but there's no rush. Is that coffee I can smell? And perhaps a biscuit? Could manage a slice of cake?'

She slid into a chair and Seth poured her coffee and cut her a slice of the apple cake. Celeste had said how Jo was the one who was always telling the local stories. Well, Seth would love to hear what she had to say about the Snakesmouth Lighthouse.

'Oh, Mr Stormforce,' cooed a soft voice from the top of the steps down into the kitchen. It was Lark, her hair loose and flowing. She was wearing a tight-fitting lilac dress along with black leggings. 'Oh, there you are, I just wondered, would you mind looking at my wardrobe door. It seems to have come a little loose. I know it's rather a small job for a builder, but if you could just take a look?'

There was a short beat where Dex cleared his throat. 'A wardrobe door you say? No job too small, Miss Sunrise. Be there soon.'

Lark looked at Dex from under her dark lashes. 'Now would be wonderful.'

Seth couldn't help but think that Pewter was spot on in not rating Dex's chances of getting much free time. He'd be lucky to make any progress in discovering what Copious Bladderwrack had failed to. Seth turned to share a smile with Angelique, but she'd somehow managed to sidle out without anyone noticing. And that meant Seth was determined to follow.

As Lark led Dex to the dodgy door, Seth hovered in the entrance hall at the bottom of the central spiral staircase, wondering which way Angelique had gone. Surely it was only seconds since she had slipped out of the kitchen, but the space was already deserted. He poked his head into the lounge, but saw no sign of her.

Where could she have gone? Taking another look at the scene of the crime, perhaps? Seth sprinted to the top floor. Sure enough, someone was crouched down, methodically but messily going through the contents of Mina Mintencress's wardrobe.

'Are you looking for something?' Seth said, moving closer to the figure partially concealed by one of the open doors. 'What are you after?'

It was difficult to tell who was the more shocked; Seth, or Brockler, who looked up, his face startled, guiltily eyeing the terrible mess of discarded clothes behind him.

The lawyer stood up, his knees creaking slightly, giving away the fact that he must have been crouched there for some time. He dropped the high-heeled pink shoe he was holding as if it was a hot potato.

Then he recovered himself and took a step nearer to Seth and grabbed him by the collar. 'I don't answer to the kitchen boy!'

'You just looked like you needed a hand,' said Seth

as mildly as he could. 'Perhaps it's something I can help you with, sir. That's what I'm here for.' Brockler released him.

Seth straightened his tunic and began to slowly gather the hurriedly discarded clothes, placing coats and trousers back on hangers and tidying them back inside the wardrobe. His curiosity was soaring, but his mind was also working furiously.

'Yes, I suppose you might be able to help me,' said Brockler, with a small cough. 'After all, I suppose you work for me now. If you want to keep your job.'

Seth began to fold an array of jumpers in a whole rainbow of colours.

'Of course, sir.' He kept his voice very even and respectful, but he was already asking himself questions and wondering how he could get answers.

Brockler leant against the wall and said easily: 'I have to take charge of things now.' He examined his perfect nails. 'All this work half-finished. No builders. There is a lot of money at stake,' he drawled. 'You won't understand any of that. Business. Difficult decisions. I am mostly thinking of young master Alfie's future, of course. Someone needs to face up to the responsibilities.'

'Of course, sir.' Seth could have asked how any of that had led to him ransacking Mina's wardrobe, but he carried on folding. 'What is it you'd like me to do, sir?'

'Pleased to see Mina made such a very good choice when she employed you, young man.' Brockler gave a smile that made his mouth look over-full of teeth. 'I might need someone I can trust. Can I rely on you?'

'Of course, sir.' Seth waited. He'd overheard the lawyer and Lark arguing over who would take charge of Mina's business affairs. Hadn't Lark said Mina had secretly made a new will? As her lawyer, Brockler hadn't liked that news at all. Seth could understand if Brockler wanted to see a copy of that will urgently. Was that what he was searching for? But what Brockler said next took him completely by surprise.

'I'm on the hunt for a small portrait. It was mine, but Mina took a fancy to it, so of course, I gave it to her.' The shrug he gave was accompanied by his wolfish smile. 'But I would rather like it back.'

Seth's thoughts echoed Lark's words from earlier. What on earth was Brockler up to?

'If you see it, bring it straight to me,' Brockler said smoothly 'Don't mention this to anyone and we'll see about you keeping this job of yours. Now, off you go.'

Seth was glad of the chance to leave and sped back

downstairs, not forgetting he was on the hunt for Angelique. As he passed Lark's room he heard Dex and Lark chatting and slowed.

'. . . Do you want to know the funniest thing, Dex? Mina was so pleased when she found this place had gone up for sale. But you know, the actual light she used to watch from our dreary boarding school wasn't from here at all. They moved the light years ago to a better place along the coast. I mean, you think she could have worked it out – there isn't even a light at the top of this place any more . . .'

Seth dashed on. If Angelique had an idea that would give her a head start on locating Soul Snakesmouth's laboratory, then he wanted to be in on it too. He tracked her down in the dining room. She was huddled over something she was holding in the flat of her hand and didn't even glance up at him as he bounded in.

As Seth drew closer, he recognized instantly what was in her hand and was confused. It was her Elysee library card – a card that gave you access to the secret library of magical texts. Studying books from the library was how sorcerers improved their magic, once they'd passed the Prospect and were invited to join the magical world.

'Angelique, why do you need a book right now?'

he asked, closing the door quietly behind him.

'Because it's the quickest way I can think of finding out more about that book the wordstone came from: *The Deadly Secrets of Darkwitching*. I think Dex believes he's going to get there first—'

'You're trying to beat Dex to finding Soul Snakesmouth's book?!'

'I'm not worried about beating Dex at all. Tracking down the book that Copious Bladderwrack failed to find is important. Copious had the wordstone and still he failed to locate the laboratory. There's a possibility there might be more clues if we could see the actual book. Doing it before Dex is just . . .' She allowed herself a small smile as the card continued to grow. 'Thought I'd just see if the library might have a copy.'

Seth had watched her do this once before, when he'd continually pestered her for details of the magical world and she'd actually been kind enough to check out him a book for him.

But it was still astonishing and beautiful to watch as the card grew into a miniature room, and then that grew bigger in her hand until you could see the detail of the magnificent old library – vast, seemingly endless, with an arched ceiling, full of shafts of daylight that highlighted ancient maps and globes and shelves and shelves of books, towering upwards.

He tried to ignore the ache inside that told him how much he longed to be part of this – to be invited to join the magical world and to be able to walk in that library – as he watched, utterly enthralled. She grew the room even bigger and began to walk her fingers along one of the long, book-lined stacks.

'The trouble is that I don't think I'm going to find the book quickly without help, and I've visited Ethylene Despair rather a lot recently and I hardly dare ask another favour. But I think it's the only way.'

'Ethylene Despair? The head librarian at the Elysee library has been helping you recently? With what?'

Angelique hesitated.

'You're not going to tell me, are you? Why can't you just trust me?'

'Maybe because if I tell you the truth you have a terrible habit of not believing me anyway. And what I am trying to find out is incredibly complicated.'

'You don't think I'd understand?' Seth snapped, noting the small sigh that accompanied her words.

'No. It's more than . . . well, all right, what I've been getting help with involves you.'

'Me?'

'What's been worrying me is . . . well, it's the possibilities of rescue from a firefly cage. And that is not easy to find out. Almost impossible, I've discovered.' Angelique turned from the image of the room for a moment to raise her dark eyes to Seth's. She fixed him with a long look. 'I knew you'd have questions. I told you that's why I didn't want to get in touch. And there are almost no books on the subject. Now, I need to concentrate on this. That is the honest truth.'

'I don't think I understand what you're talking about.'

'To be honest, I don't understand it either, which is far worse. Now, I won't be a moment.' She turned back to peer at the magical image in her hand. 'I'm not simply borrowing a library book.' Her long, tilted nose was pressed into the room. 'I need to access the Problem section of the library. If the book is there, maybe Ethylene will let me have a quick look.'

'We are actually going to visit the library now? Is that even possible?'

'Most things are possible, Seth, just not very easy.' As she talked, her eyes didn't lift from where she was still walking her fingers through the library stacks, and she gave a small tsk of annoyance. 'This is so difficult to find. And, just to be clear – Seth, you do not have a library card. So *we* are not doing anything – you can wait for me here, I'll be as quick as I can.'

'OK, I'll just wait here then.'

Angelique took a step back and glanced at him, suspicion creeping into her expression. 'Really? Thank you.' She gave him a quick, nervous smile before she was again fixedly peering into the image of the room and muttering: 'Just need to find – ah! It's not the easiest thing to use if I'm honest. But it should pick me up.'

Seth waited until the air around her started to shimmer, readied himself, then at the last possible second he leapt right beside her and grasped her around the shoulders.

27. SKYSCRAPERS OF BOOKS

This time he was much better prepared for the white noise of the teleport and not knowing which way was up. He concentrated on staying upright and not crash-landing.

And he was nowhere near breaking his ankle this time when he landed. He was *so* getting better at this magic stuff.

The sunlight streamed in through high-up windows and gleamed on warm polished wood. Seth looked at the serene room, with shelves that seemed to stretch as far as the eye could see – where on earth would anyone start? It was so impressive.

Not that Angelique was impressed when she turned to him, fury written in her face. 'What do you think you are doing,' she spluttered, barely able to speak. 'You cannot be here.'

Even in the face of Angelique's anger, all Seth could feel was complete joy that he was finally in that room with its skyscrapers of books.

He shrugged as nonchalantly as he could manage. 'I'm here now, Angelique. Tell me what I can do to help.'

'I can tell you exactly,' she hissed, earning herself a reproachful look from a woman dressed from head to toe in green tweeds, including a matching tie and shoes.

'Don't touch anything. Do not move. Do not talk to anyone and do not even watch what I am going to do. Got that?'

He could easily spend a happy hour browsing in this beautiful, welcoming room. If someone put up a hammock he could happily move in here permanently. But he didn't have long, he had only a few snatched moments, and he had an angry Angelique to deal with.

She marched off in the direction of another stack

of books, her face furious. She turned back quickly to see if he was spying on her. But Seth was studiously avoiding looking at her. The second she had gone, he carefully removed a couple of books from a shelf so that he could peer through the gap and watch exactly what she was up to.

She took a quick glance over her shoulder, then approached a really higgledy stack of books that looked as if they were awaiting sorting. Some had their spines turned inwards so you couldn't read the titles, big books on top of small, and others looked as if someone had started sorting them according to colour – the pink ones were grouped together, anyway.

She walked up to the stack, lifted her left hand and placed it on the collection of pink books, palm flat, fingers splayed. Seth watched, entranced, as she reached with her other hand and dipped it into a sort of ancient leather bucket attached to the wall. She removed a pinch of some kind of powder and made a sprinkling movement, then opened her mouth to breathe hard and long into the dust she had released into the air, which formed into writing. It spelled out her name. *Angelique Squerr*.

The shambolic shelf of books started to shift, one by one, and formed a doorway just big enough for

Angelique to step through, and then the shelf closed behind her.

Seth was now alone, illicitly, inside the Elysee library of magical texts. Where should he start? He thought of what Angelique had said – where would he find anything that mentioned a firefly cage?

Famous Sorcerers and Their Even More Famous Cats.
The Houses of the Family of Pod.
Style Secrets of the Siegfried Sorcerers.

Seth began to feel more urgently that his aimless wandering along, reading the titles of shelves, was not going to get him anywhere.

He looked up and found himself face to face with another figure. He hadn't even seen anyone coming. He remembered all Angelique's warnings, put his head down and carried on along the row. If he was discovered, thrown out and tossed out of the Elysee library, he might never be allowed in officially. Banned before he started. Would Angelique be banned too?

He tried to look busy and relaxed, as if he came here every day, trying not to sigh with relief as the person passed him. But when he turned sharply after the next stack, the same figure was in front of him.

A tall person, with very short swept-back dark

hair, wearing a violet-coloured close-fitting suit and a navy shirt. A sorcerer? He looked more like a businessman who had stumbled in here by mistake on the way to a meeting. Apart from the violet. When Seth noticed the stranger's features, there was something about the soft line of the jaw and the narrow forehead that made him look twice, not quite sure if he was looking at a man or a woman.

Seth tried hard to focus on the shelf in front of him. A section on witches through the ages. He felt himself the object of scrutiny and couldn't help but look up. The figure had come much nearer, and Seth now felt sure he was looking at a man. The face was smiling kindly, with a pair of friendly light brown eyes.

'Big place this is, isn't it?' the suited businessman said in a surprisingly deep voice, waving to the vast room.

'Huge,' agreed Seth. He'd promised not to talk to anyone, but a one-word answer couldn't possibly count.

'Can be tricky to find what you are looking for,' said the man. 'Sometimes we can all do with a bit of help.' He stood there expectantly, hands behind his back.

And it was on the tip of Seth's tongue just to say

exactly what he wanted. He had to almost force himself not to speak.

He made a sideways move and grabbed the nearest book off a shelf, pretending he'd finally spotted what he was looking for.

When he opened the rose-coloured cover, music started playing; violins and sweet piano. He glanced at the title. *Love Potions for the Hopeful Yet Inexperienced.* He quickly shoved the book back on the shelf and was relieved when the music immediately shut itself off.

The man hadn't moved. He was looking at Seth even more intently – suspiciously? The man could hardly know just by looking that Seth had no right to be here. Sweat started to prickle his palms nonetheless.

'My job is not to make rules. My job is simply to advise,' he said.

Seth didn't know what to do. What did he mean by rules? Was he going to demand to see Seth's library card? Whatever happened, he would have to keep Angelique out of it.

'And my advice is that love potions are not at all the best place to start for the inexperienced,' said the man. 'Fraught with trouble when things go wrong. And when things go wrong, people lose heart.' He seemed to be looking so intently at Seth, so deep into his eyes, that it was as if he was trying to peer right into Seth's mind. Seth wanted to look away, but couldn't. 'Was it love potions you were looking for?' The man cocked his head on one side. 'Or something else?'

Seth took a step backwards.

'I thought not. I know I shouldn't really. But I can't help myself. As I say, my job is not to make rules. I just want people to have the right books.' He gave a little smile and thrust a book towards Seth. 'Keep it for when you are ready.'

Seth found himself with little choice but to accept the small book, bound in neat green leather. *Curology: Herbal Essences and Their Magical Uses.*

It seemed to smell of the woods and leafy places and plunged Seth back into the kitchen of the Last Chance Hotel, in among all the herbs and brews he had experimented with alongside his father. All those days and evenings spent side by side as his father had taught him his love of cooking. And everything he had learnt as they had foraged and collected in the woods. He grasped the book firmly, feeling a desperate longing to find a quiet corner and read it.

He didn't know what he should say, but the man

moved his face even closer to Seth's, his nostrils quivering.

'An affinity with curology, I'd hazard. Good at cooking, are you?'

'Erm . . .'

'Your affinity. You'll discover most sorcerers have a type of magic they find comes much easier to them. I expect yours will be potions. Perhaps because of your father.'

'Sorcerers have an affinity?' began Seth. 'But I'm not—' He broke off as the man's last words fully registered.

The man was turning the corner at the end of the aisle, Seth just catching his words as he headed for the next stack.

'Haven't heard from your father for a while, you know. Hope he's well?'

'You know my father?' Seth stepped after him. '*My* father? But you can't – he's not part of the magical world. Don't you mean my mother?'

He turned where the man had turned, desperate to talk to him, arriving in the next stack only seconds after him, but it was too late. He had completely vanished.

Seth felt a firm grip on his arm from behind. He swung around and was faced with Angelique's angriest face yet.

'I thought I told you not to wander off. And –' she pointed furiously to the book he was clutching – 'I definitely told you not to touch anything! You didn't speak to anyone in the library, did you?'

Seth coloured as she gave him a very piercing stare. 'Sorry – I – er – Did you find what you were looking for?'

'That book . . . where did you get it?'

She jabbed it, and even her finger managed to look angry.

'I . . . Someone might have . . . spoken to me. Thought at first he was a businessman in a suit. But he handed me a book.'

'Businessmen in suits don't just happen to recommend the perfect book for you, not even in the middle of a magical library.'

'No, I suppose not.'

She insisted Seth describe the man in detail and Angelique groaned and closed her eyes as if in pain. 'No, no, no, no, no! You know who that was? That was the head of the library.'

'That was Ethylene Despair? Well, he didn't look much like a sorcerer – I thought Pewter said the head of the Elysee library was a reformed sinister sorcerer?'

'Well, I'd be pleased if you'd describe exactly what you think he's supposed to look like. Should he go around with a cloak and an evil sneer?'

She tried to take the book from him, but Seth pulled it out of her way.

'He really wanted me to have this. So I can't see what harm it'll do. It's his library.'

'This is not good, Seth.'

'But how did you get on?'

'We're doomed.'

'Did you find Soul Snakesmouth's problem book?'

'No I did not. Mostly because I couldn't find Ethylene anywhere. Now I find that's because you were having a cosy chat with him.' Her eyes were flashing. 'He didn't know I'd brought you, did he?' She loomed in closer to him. '*You* should be locked away in the Problem section, Seth Seppi.'

She had a book too, but before Seth could read the title, she had shoved it into the red handbag she carried everywhere with her.

'Erm, Ethylene really wanted me to have this book, only—'

'Only what, Seth?'

'I don't have a library card.' He pointed to the one in her hand. 'Would you mind awfully, perhaps . . . taking this out on yours?'

28. You May Never See Her Again

By the time they'd teleported back to the lighthouse, Dex had somehow managed to slip away from Lark and was lurking in a corner of the kitchen quickly downing a coffee and eating a fresh round of toast. Angelique sat down at the table and started going through her notebook, studiously ignoring both of them.

'Going to get a quick squint about, Seth, before that Rendleton grabs me,' said Dex.

He shrank deeply into his jacket as the back door

was flung open.

'Boat leaves in ten, right,' Jo announced, 'Just time for a couple more biscuits.' She filled her pockets from the tin and headed back outside.

'So are you here working with Inspector Pewter?' Dexter asked, sidling up to Seth. 'What's that like? Must be great.'

'Not work exactly. He's more of a friend.' Seth heartily wished he could say that he was here working with Pewter. He didn't want to admit to Dex that he was only here as the kitchen boy.

'I've never worked with him,' said Dex, sounding wistful. 'But he's supposed to be one of the best rudiments.'

'Ah. Is he?'

'I'm guessing you've not passed the Prospect yet? Just in case you didn't know, a rudiment is someone whose magic comes from the elements. Some rudiments have an affinity with one element, but those at the top of their game can control everything – water, air, fire, earth. I'd love to see Pewter at work.'

Celeste had crept into the kitchen, once again wearing the dark glasses. Probably trying to cover up the purple smudges beneath her eyes telling stories about whether she was managing to sleep no matter how many times Seth sent her to her room to rest.

Dex strode over to where she was sliding out a kitchen chair, treating her to a close-up of his white teeth. 'Don't think we've met. I'm Dexter Stormforce, here to shed light on these strange mysteries of ghosts and flickering electrics.' His eyes sparkled.

'Oh, yes, good,' said Celeste uncertainly, reaching to see if there was any coffee left.

'What I mean is,' said Dex, with his charmingly off-centre smile. 'I'm the new builder.'

Celeste pushed up her dark glasses. 'Brilliant. I'm Celeste Crackling. I was maid to Miss Mintencress,' she whispered, fiddling with her hair, which was completely hidden under the old-fashioned cap she insisted on wearing.

Celeste's face did look exhausted, despite the snores he'd heard. He told himself that when he got the chance he'd ask her if she'd seen any of them – Brockler, Lark, Rendleton or possibly even Alfie, he supposed – doing anything strange. Something that could have fired up the magic.

Magic, Pewter repeatedly told him, was mostly hard work. If someone had been trying to do really sinister magic, magic that led to someone dying, surely there would be signs? If someone had been practising with those shadow snakes you might at least expect to find scorch marks, the smell of burning. He wouldn't be surprised if you found bodies. Seth sighed as he thought of trying to boil milk and the mess he'd made. It couldn't be that everyone found magic easier than him.

'Amazing what the smell of coffee drags out,' muttered Nightshade, leaping on to the kitchen countertop.

'Nightshade, please keep your voice down,' Seth breathed into her ear. 'I'm never sure who can hear you, but the last thing I want to have to do is explain to anyone why my cat talks. Life is complicated enough. And –' Seth scooped her on to the floor – 'please stay off the worktop. You're too fluffy and unhygienic to be in a hotel kitchen.'

'How rude. Huh. I have come to talk to you – you're always too busy yabbering with everyone except me. Why bother coming to see how *I'm* doing? I haven't even had any breakfast.'

'Last time I saw you, you were fast asleep,' said Seth, sliding a look at an empty plate on the kitchen table, where not long ago there had definitely been a few rashers of bacon. 'And I guess it wasn't you that helped yourself to a little bit of bacon?'

'What's a cat supposed to do? I'd starve around

here if I left it to you.'

'Seth, we should catch a lift on the boat,' called Angelique as she headed towards the back door.

'Catch the boat? Me?' said Seth.

'The new cook is leaving already?' said Celeste sharply.

'Getting in supplies,' said Angelique unconvincingly and let slip a short puff of annoyance. 'Seth,' she said quietly as he joined her by the door. 'I think it is a great idea to see if Snakesmouth village was ever cleaned, and if Bladderwrack missed anything there. Despite your disgraceful behaviour at the library, it *was* your idea. So, you coming?'

Seth was thrilled. Angelique had asked him along to hunt for magical texts and devices – she was cleaning and Seth was helping.

'And I suppose you're leaving me to do dinner?' snapped Celeste.

Pewter arrived at just the right time to step in. 'Maybe we can rustle up something together. Might be fun. Maybe one of those things with pastry – what do you call them, Seth?'

'A pie?' Seth offered cautiously.

'Seth, hurry, I'm not going to miss the boat,' snapped Angelique. 'I'm off,' she warned, and headed outside without any further hesitation.

Nightshade was busy with the last bit of bacon under the table. Seth gave her a cuddle then sidled up to Inspector Pewter.

'I've got it all covered.' Pewter clapped Seth on the back. 'You know you can trust me completely.'

'Are you going to help Dex find the darkwitching laboratory?'

'The mysteries are piling up, aren't they? I have questions about shoes. I would very much like to solve the Mystery of the Apple Cake. That was the one you baked last night? Or was that a chocolate cake? I think the fruit cake was from the night before.' He rubbed his chin thoughtfully. 'Perhaps it doesn't matter. But I should have plenty of time to do dinner.' Pewter beamed. 'First, and most important, I would really love to find a dead seagull.'

Seth found himself staring, as he often did with Pewter. Just for a moment, it felt as if the inspector was deliberately getting rid of him. And the thing with the gulls was worrying. 'Er – you weren't thinking of using a gull in the pie, were you?' asked Seth warily.

'Hadn't even crossed my mind, young Seth. But now that you've mentioned it . . .' Pewter's eyes twinkled.

Seth scrambled to follow Angelique down to the boat. He wished he could make sure that Inspector Pewter was joking. But he was too busy being excited. He was on his way to investigate magic.

29. Serious Doubts About That Story

The little boat danced low in the water, with Dr Malinger, Angelique, Lark and Alfie already loaded in as Seth raced along the beach, desperate not to be left behind.

As he reached the boat, he caught the drift of the conversation between Angelique and Jo. Seth was surprised to hear Angelique was quizzing her about Celeste.

'Dunno. If you really pushed me, I'd have to say she's ordinaryish. Sort of shortish. Brownish hair?

Can't says as I particularly noticed the maid.' Jo puffed out her cheeks, struggling to remember.

It wasn't a helpful description. But why was Angelique asking?

'Has she been with the Mintencress family long?'

'Well, maybe, although no, I don't think so. I'm not sure.'

Seth shuffled into his place at the back. The boat sank a little lower.

'Is Dex not coming?' asked Lark mournfully. 'They do a very nice tea along the coast in Merricove. I'm sure he'd have fun.'

'Oh, he finds concrete and cracks great fun. You can't tear him away from peering at rendering and roof tiles,' said Angelique. 'Most of his conversation is usually about drainpipes. And ductwork. He's very keen on ductwork.'

The moment they were away from the shelter of Gull Cove, the boat dipped and rose with every wave, spray dousing the travellers, their stomachs left somewhere above the foam. The stormy weather hadn't quite abated yet.

'It's a bit like being on a roller coaster,' cried Jo joyfully.

It was too exciting for Alfie to want to stay stuck with Lark tucked in at the back of the boat. He moved right up to join Jo, his face alive with joy at the exhilarating pace of the waves, and he beamed even more when she gave him a go at steering.

Seth glanced at the boy and couldn't help but worry what would happen to him. Celeste had been right when she'd said how much fun the boy had on the island, learning to be a strong swimmer, poking about in rockpools and learning about the birds. And it was great to see how everyone had swooped in to keep him from having time to dwell on his sister's death. Who would be the boy's guardian now? Had Brockler been serious about staying on here and trying to finish what Mina had started?

Seth remembered Lark asking the lawyer what he was up to and questions rose in his mind now. Brockler claiming he wanted to stay; Brockler hunting desperately for a painting, of all things.

But they were questions he hoped he might find more answers to in Snakesmouth. He was keen for his first clear view of the village, the nearest point on the mainland. The place he'd heard so much about. From this distance, buildings were still indistinguishable, but he could make out a row of white blobs lining the waterfront.

Angelique spent the journey huddled towards the back of the boat, gripping one side, pasty-faced as the waves hissed and heaved them up and crashed them down again.

Dr Malinger sat right at the back, her tightly curled hair neatly tied in a bun, but she put her face right to the wind, as if drinking in the breeze. Seth could hear Angelique attempting to draw her into a conversation about what she'd thought of the changes to the lighthouse. Seth guessed any second now she'd probably steer it towards talking about Mina Mintencress's death.

That left Seth clear to shuffle in and chat to Jo, who was at the wheel, steering confidently through the waves.

'You live in Snakesmouth, don't you?' he asked, now able to make out a cluster of tired-looking cottages surrounding a larger central building as the village of Snakesmouth began to come into clearer focus.

'This place?' said Jo, indicating ahead with her thumb. 'Me? Nah, no one lives there. Haven't you heard the story? You must have heard how the same night Soul Snakesmouth vanished, a whole slice of the coast fell into the sea. Practically cut off the whole village and made the cliffs unstable. Everyone moved out. It was as if he'd somehow been protecting the village and it collapsed when he died. But then,' Jo warmed to her tale enthusiastically, 'there were plenty of stories about that old Soul Snakesmouth.' She lowered her voice, even though Seth doubted even Alfie could hear them above the wind and the throb of the engine. 'They say he used to do these experiments. Bad things. He didn't always live alone, you know? But one night, he did something so dreadful, it terrified his wife so much, she ran off to the other end of the earth. Some,' whispered Jo, clearly enjoying herself, 'as reckoned his experiments were with magic.' She paused.

'That is a great story,' said Seth.

Jo turned from steering the boat. 'That Mr Brockler loved it too. You believe it?'

Seth tried to remember Brockler's words. 'I think there's a lot that people can't simply explain.'

Jo nodded enthusiastically. 'Too right. But, nah, I live over at Merricove, just along the coast a bit. Nice place, Merricove. Great tea room. Best scones for miles. Are you sure you want to stop off here at Snakesmouth? Everyone stays as far away as possible.'

As they drew closer, Seth could see cottages that had once been bright colours now just looking drab, paint dried out and peeling in the stinging, salty air. Brockler had told Seth that strange carving of a lighthouse being eaten by a dragon had come from here, and that had pricked Seth's curiosity. Brockler had been so keen to rescue it from the bottom of the bath. Mina had worn it as a pendant for good luck, he'd said.

But as they approached the harbour and Seth saw the village close up, he had serious doubts that Brockler had been telling the truth about where that dragon carving had come from. Yet everything associated with the lighthouse should have been taken away when Copious Bladderwrack had done the cleaning. So where had it really come from?

Seth had an uneasy feeling as they landed at a short, broken jetty.

This was going to be a waste of Angelique's time. And he was the one who had persuaded her to come.

The quay was dominated by a once white-painted hotel, now smeared with a green slime that was taking over. He could see a weather-beaten front door was battened down with boards. The hotel had an impressive veranda, but tables and chairs were just stacked against the wall, leaving an expanse of crumbling concrete, nibbled by lichen and home to hundreds of those same small, tough flowers Seth had seen clinging on in every nook and cranny on the island.

'Why on earth do you want to visit a completely deserted village?' said Dr Malinger unexpectedly. 'There is really nothing to see.'

Seth's instincts were telling him she had a point. He did seem to have a habit of believing the wrong people and watching his careful theories blowing away.

Jo was pointing to the far side of the semi-circular harbour, where a gate was half off its hinges, battering against its post in the wind. Beyond it, a path wound up the cliff. 'Up there is where the star fell from the sky. I did tell you about that, didn't I? Just a short while ago folk saw a bright light up there right where the rift is. They took it as a sign change was coming.'

Alfie scrambled out of the boat to help Jo tie a rope to a rotten-looking post.

Angelique leapt gladly from the rocking boat.

'Mind yourselves, it's not very safe,' said Jo. 'You really sure you want to stop here? Much nicer to travel with us along the coast.'

'Oh, we'll be fine,' said Angelique, striding off down the jetty.

As she stepped on to the shore at the deserted village of Snakesmouth, the deeper Seth's certainty became that, once again, he was on the wrong track.

And he'd dragged Angelique here for no reason. He felt doubly bad, after being responsible for her failing to talk to Ethylene Despair in the library.

Wherever Brockler had got that carving from, it wasn't here. Seth could see the air of sad neglect, the shuttered, mournful windows on all the buildings. It was as Seth went to clamber out of the boat that he caught sight of the brand-new drill Jo had pinched from the Sunrise Wing. It had been poorly concealed, but seeing it made some things fall into place. He had a fresh idea, and wondered why it hadn't occurred to him before.

He took Jo to one side so that Dr Malinger, Lark and Alfie wouldn't overhear and spoke in a low voice.

'It wasn't just stories Mr Brockler was interested in, was it? Mr Brockler showed me a strange carving. He told me he got it when he came here. But looking around I don't think that was true.' Seth looked right into Jo's eyes. 'But you seem to know everything. I bet you know where he got it from really?'

Jo's eyes refused to meet Seth's. 'No idea.' She could not have looked more guilty and Seth felt sure this time he had finally guessed right.

'I bet you loved sharing all your stories with Mr Brockler,' he pressed on, determined to get the truth.

'I bet he asked you lots about the history because you know so much about it? Didn't he? I bet he believed you when you said Soul Snakesmouth lived in a remote lighthouse because he was experimenting with magic. I bet not many people believe you. But I think Mr Brockler believed it and I believe you too.'

This time, after barely a pause, Jo nodded eagerly. 'Most people don't believe it. But, yes. He really did do magic.'

'When they put the lighthouse up for sale and you heard someone was going to come clear it all out, if I'd been you, I'd have gone and had a look around. All that stuff was about to go. No one wanted it. Bet you thought it'd all be thrown away.'

Seth waited, trying not to hold his breath. It took a little longer for the girl to nod, as if she'd been weighing up if she was going to be in trouble. 'I might have saved a few bits and pieces. Well, as you say, thought they'd be chucked away. And when Mr Brockler asked me, I brought them and showed him. He was really interested. He believed in the stories. He believed in the magic.'

So, Brockler had learnt of the prospect of magic, and Seth knew exactly how exciting that could be.

The chance of somehow being able to do magic was almost irresistible. Hadn't Tiffany tricked everyone

238

and schemed to run away with the firefly cage once she knew it could give her access to powerful magic? Had Brockler been trying to find a way to gain access to the magical world too?

'Was there a book?' asked Seth urgently.

There had been that wordstone that Copious had found, but he had never found the actual book when he'd cleaned. *The Deadly Secrets of Darkwitching*.

Disappointingly, Jo shrugged. 'I can't say as I remember. It was all bits and pieces. But . . . there might have been.' Jo was scratching her head. 'There was that carving. It was made from a real dragon's tooth, don't you know. And this small painting.' She looked challengingly into Seth's eyes. 'He gave me money for them. Am I in trouble? Am I going to have to give the money back? Because I already spent it.'

Seth tried to give a reassuring smile. 'I think it will help that you've told the truth.'

Jo suddenly started peering at the way the water was lapping at the jetty, then stared up at the sky. 'You know, I'm not sure as I should leave you here. The water shouldn't be this high. It happens sometimes after a storm. You get a freak high tide. I think you should come with me now. Come and see Merricove. It's worth a visit.'

Angelique had finally drifted back and heard

what she said: 'I'm sure it'll be fine.'

'But I can't promise I can get back. Not in time to pick you up and get you safely back to the light-house. High tides can be unpredictable and dangerous here, and the currents change.'

'No, we certainly wouldn't want to leave you stranded here, not knowing what might happen to you,' said Dr Malinger at Seth's shoulder. He started – she'd appeared right behind him without him noticing she'd even got out of the boat.

Seth looked at the desolate boarded-up village and was expecting Angelique to nod. But he recognized that particular look of determination. Her long nose was pointed in the air.

'Oh, don't worry about us, we'll be absolutely fine.'

'As it is, 'fraid it'll only be a short trip to Merri-cove,' announced Jo, starting to untie the boat quickly. 'Tide is already higher than it should be. Want to make sure I get everyone safely back to Snakesmouth Island. Sure you two is all right?'

'But you still can still walk around to Merricove? We aren't entirely cut off here, are we?' persisted Angelique.

Jo looked doubtful and scratched under her orange oilskin. 'Would take you a while.'

'Good, I fancy a walk. We'll see you there.'

Seth could only hope Angelique was right as he watched Jo leap into the little boat, and their best means to leave the deserted village and get back to the lighthouse sailed away.

30. A STAR DROPPED OUT OF THE SKY

Angelique strode up to the first of the short row of houses, flipped open the silver top of her cane. She hardly waited until Jo's little boat disappeared from view to send a jet of blue light from the end of her divinoscope and bathe the largest building, right in the centre, in a shimmering wash of cornflower.

She took a reading and then pressed her hands flat against the boarded-up door. Seth was torn between just watching her fascinating work and undoing the anxious knot in his stomach by telling her they'd made the wrong decision. He should also tell her everything he'd learnt from Jo. He should have done it before the boat left. She was going to be angry.

'No one's been here in ages, have they?' stuttered Seth, trying to think of a way to tell her.

Angelique was sending a flurry of sparks into one of the blank windows. 'It was you who said Brockler got some interesting objects from here.'

'Er. Yes. Well. Actually . . . about that.'

She fixed him with her dark eyes, and, haltingly, he told her how Jo had confessed to lifting a few bits and pieces from the lighthouse before Bladderwrack visited – and then selling them back to Brockler.

'So there were artefacts belonging to Soul Snakesmouth that wouldn't have been there for Bladderwrack to find and take away when he cleaned. But they've found their way back there now – that's bad, isn't it? They might be magical devices. I'm sorry, I should have told you the minute she told me and got you back on the boat. But I was too busy thinking and, besides, I didn't want to blow our cover.'

Angelique nodded.

He waited for her to be really cross. He thought she might want to find some way to get Jo back here right away so they could return to the lighthouse.

But she kept zapping everything. She kept taking readings. She sent larger swathes of the blue light across the hotel, bathing it in a shimmering unreal light. Then she did the same with neighbouring buildings.

Eventually, she sighed. 'There's really nothing here, Seth. Only – did Jo say there was a book among these little *trinkets* she kept hold of?'

'She wasn't sure.'

'And you believed this little friend of yours? The one who had just admitted to being a thief and also selling on stolen goods? Seth – have I ever mentioned before that you have a bad habit of trusting all the wrong people.'

Seth knew she was still sore about him messing up her chance to speak to Ethylene Despair and of tracking down a copy of Soul Snakesmouth's book. But there wasn't anything he could do about it right now. To distract her, he suggested they take the path that led through the clackety gate.

'Did you hear Jo say how some sort of star fell from the sky about the time the Mintencresses moved in?' Seth puffed as they climbed the path.

Angelique's hair was being whipped around and she started to have to lean into the wind as they neared the top of the cliff. She darted him an annoyed glance. 'At one time I thought you might have started to believe in the murderous ghost, Seth, and now falling stars? Forgive me if I keep looking for facts.'

They'd reached the end of the footpath, which stopped suddenly at the highest point of the cliff. A huge yellow and black barrier and a gigantic warning sign reading 'STOP! TURN BACK' barred their way. Someone had also crudely graffitied in a picture of a person screaming as they fell off a cliff.

'Nice,' said Angelique.

'No wonder everyone stopped visiting Snakes-mouth,' said Seth. He was looking at an inlet right in front of them that stretched into the distance, as if someone had cut a long, thin slice from the land. The sea was plunging and foaming a long way below.

In the distance, to their right, Seth could see the lighthouse. How were they going to get back there? Jo had said it might take a good while to walk around to Merricove.

'I suppose you're going to tell me Merricove is that way?' Angelique pointed to where the path plunged into the sea, only carrying on again on the other side of the channel.

Seth scratched his head. 'There's no way across to pick up the path, is there? We can still reach it, we just have to walk all the way around this channel.' He pointed way into the distance. 'Wanna start walking? Sorry, Angelique.'

Angelique was still frowning into her divinoscope. What was it telling her? She sent another jet of blue light, as if she suspected there was something magical to detect here.

Seth was curious about Jo's story of the bright light and began to look about. His nose was telling him there was some underlying smell over what had already become the everyday smells of sea, salt, sand and seaweed. Something like scorching.

Over the lip of the chasm he could see some intriguing black streaks, wide and deep.

'Do they look like scorch marks to you?'

'So now we *are* believing the locals, not just with their stories of ghosts, but also their mysterious mystical stars in the sky?' scoffed Angelique, her words almost whipped away in the wind. 'How come you believe all of that, but you find it so difficult to believe me. I mean,' she gave a little laugh, 'when we first met you wouldn't trust me one bit.'

'That might be because you pretty much lied to me from the start.'

Seth started to look for a way down. He scrambled a little further to get a closer look, clutching on to some flimsy tufts of grass, the only thing in some places to stop him plummeting into the water.

'I don't feel that's entirely fair,' Angelique was continuing, although still too absorbed in her divinoscope to worry about what Seth was doing. 'And it is particularly not smart to let one of the suspects get you wrapped around her finger. Anyway, those black marks are probably just some different rock, or a harmless seaweed.'

'You're talking about Celeste, aren't you?'

Seth carried on down a little further, fixed on the tracks of those deep, dark black gouges in the side of the cliff, and trying not to look at the huge waves below. Something about the way they chased into the narrow inlet meant he was getting wet, despite the sea being a long way below.

'She was Mina Mintencress's personal maid, really,' he went on. 'I don't think she's even realized that she could easily lose her job now. I don't think she's got any other family. She needs someone to look out for her.'

'She says.'

'What do you mean?'

'You are not always the best judge of character, Seth, if you don't mind my saying. And I haven't brought a rope, so if you are thinking of climbing down any further and you pitch into the sea I won't be coming in to save you.'

'Not seaweed!' he called. 'Can you smell sort of a bonfirey smell?' It wasn't a smell of the sea, but of woods and forests. A smell that, strangely, reminded him of home. 'You'll need to come closer.'

She flipped the silver top of her red cane, flashed the edge of the chasm and took a reading.

'When you are in the middle of a murder enquiry, Seth, everyone is either a suspect or not a suspect.'

Seth could only just hear her. Typical Angelique, to pick an argument when they were on a windy cliff face.

'Well, you seem to be wrapped around Storm-force's little finger,' he called.

'The difference being he is not a murder suspect,' drifted back Angelique's voice.

'No. He's a talented S3 agent. And doesn't he know it,' Seth yelled back. 'Celeste is going to be totally on her own now and I know how that feels.'

'If that's your way of asking me to apologize, I did say sorry, Seth. I did try to explain the moment I arrived, only Celeste interrupted. There is a reason, you know, she's totally incompetent as a maid—'

'Incompetent?' Seth wanted to rush to Celeste's defence, but he stopped, remembering the delicate shoes and wonky slices of bread. He was also distracted by the realization that all the tufts of grass were concealing something. 'There's a cave here! I've never seen a cave before. Have you been inside a cave? Angelique, come on down here and take a look!'

31. MULTIPLE UNEXPLAINED DEATHS

'You do know Celeste only got the job a couple of weeks ago?' Angelique was still muttering as she climbed down towards him.

'That is so not true! Just shows you don't know what you are talking about,' said Seth, too excited by his find to be cross.

'I can't believe you made me climb down here to look at a hole in the hillside,' grumbled Angelique as she joined him on the ledge a few moments later, wiping a splodge of mud from the side of her hand. 'I

250

have been in loads of caves, loads of times.'

The sea seemed to have crept up even nearer. The wind had not died down. Seth could taste salt on his lips and was still getting that hint of bonfires as he showed her the dark space.

'Do you get a smell, like a dying fire when it's just the embers? It's stronger when you poke your head inside.'

'Nope.'

He fished his trusty torch out of one of his pockets, and shone it on the sandy floor just inside, out of the wind. 'Any interesting readings? Any traces of what caused that bright light in the sky? Something magical? One of Jo's stories suggested it was the ghost of Soul Snakesmouth returning. What's your divinoscope telling you?' asked Seth eagerly.

Angelique was poking around in the plants that clung to the sides of the cliff. She lifted the cane and set a low crackle of cornflower light into the hillside. Then she did the same deep inside the cave.

He shone his torch further, but the light didn't penetrate far. 'Wonder how far back this cave goes. Maybe this isn't a cave. But an entrance to a tunnel.' Seth pointed to a mess of flattened sand. 'What d'you reckon? An alien landing?' he grinned, trying to get Angelique to take a closer look.

Seth shone the torchlight further in where there was more flattened sand and found himself staring in disbelief. 'Actually, I don't think it was caused by anything very mystical. Guess what I've found – footprints. Footprints, here? How is that even possible? Someone has been down here before us.'

'Footprints? *Are* those footprints?' said Angelique, drawing alongside him. 'Well, maybe. Whoever was down here was probably someone like you who believes too many stories. Probably Jo. That girl gets into far too many places she's really no business being.'

She frowned again at the end of her cane. Was he imagining it, or did she look worried? Was it telling her someone or something magical had come this way?

'This isn't just a cave you know, it's a tunnel,' she said.

'I think I was trying to tell you that,' muttered Seth. He'd found a clear footprint and put his own boot alongside it. It was smaller than his. Perhaps it really was Jo's.

Angelique was hesitating just where the tunnel narrowed. It looked low and dark and not at all inviting. 'Smugglers used to make great use of these coastal caves. Sometimes they were left over from abandoned quarries and mines; those went on for miles,' she said hesitantly.

Seth plunged on into the darkness. 'Let's see where it goes.'

Even with the torchlight, going from sunlight to the complete black of the tunnel meant it took a good few minutes before he could make out much at all.

He felt Angelique's breath on his neck and knew she was beside him.

'Just before we plunge any further into a dark tunnel when we have no idea where it goes, I think I should tell you something,' she whispered into his ear. She gripped his arm hard. 'It's not just traces of magic I've detected. It's worse than that – it's sinister magic, Seth.'

Seth heard himself swallow. 'So at the end of this tunnel, we could meet up with a dark sorcerer?'

'Still want to go on?'

'Come on,' he said, more loudly than he meant to, trying to boost his own courage. 'Let's find this sinister sorcerer before he finds us.'

In the torchlight he could see Angelique's determined face as she followed.

The tunnel went swiftly downwards and the sand beneath their feet quickly gave way to rock. As they went further, they had to walk more slowly as the rock became slippery underfoot. There was a dank stench that owed a lot to the shimmering slime on the walls.

Seth stopped and focused the torch beam on the floor.

'New fascination with epic slime, Seth?'

'I think we're still following those footsteps.'

Angelique shivered. 'Great. You've made me feel so much better about this underground, dark, long slimy tunnel adventure you've brought me on.'

It was narrower, the roof lower, and soon they were walking almost at a crouch, hardly making progress at all, the torchlight looking eerie and green.

'Let's hope Jo wasn't serious about a freak high tide.' Angelique bent further to touch the slippery rocks beneath their feet, then reached up and tugged at a spider's web up by the ceiling. 'Because we're walking under the sea. Do you think this tunnel fills with water at high tide?'

'She was just putting the pressure on to get us back in the boat,' reassured Seth, but he couldn't help remembering how the waves had been churning really close to the entrance to the cave.

'You shouldn't be here at all,' Angelique said

unexpectedly. 'All this getting involved in the Mintencress trouble, it's not really . . . You should be focusing on joining the Elysee, you know. Passing your Prospect. Perfecting a spell. That's not going to happen overnight.'

Seth might have argued, but he had a horrid feeling Angelique might have a point, even though it was typical that she'd decided an awkward, slimy tunnel was the place to talk about it. He didn't fancy this being the place he confessed he was never going to get into the Elysee. Magic was about hard work and practice, he knew that, but he also understood that, crucially, it all depended on you having that spark of magic inside of you in the first place. And magic didn't always get passed on in families.

They both were silent for a while, their footsteps echoing rhythmically on the uneven floor. When Angelique spoke again, it was as if she was thinking out loud, because he really couldn't catch her drift.

'I've been dreading news, you know. But also expecting it. Multiple unexplained deaths or a disaster, a freak bridge collapse, something terrible. I've been looking for signs, Seth.'

'Angelique, I know I complain that you don't tell me things. Well, I'd also like to complain that sometimes you tell me things and . . . *I have no idea what you are talking about*. You do have a habit of launching into things. Like, what did you mean earlier about a rescue from a firefly cage? Just before we meet the ghost of a dark sorcerer in a slime-filled underground tunnel, can you please, for once, explain?'

She sighed. 'I'm just seriously worried. I know what a device of enormous sinister power could do in the wrong hands.'

Seth stopped and held up his hand for silence, thinking he'd heard a noise. Was it the sea coming in behind them? He'd been listening out for that. Or was it more of a scratching sound from up ahead?

Seth's back was aching from being bent almost double. He convinced himself the sound was just his imagination and pressed on, but something cleared in his mind.

'I do get it! You're talking about Tiffany?'

'Of course I am talking about Tiffany Bunn! She really is the very last person who should be in control of a device of such immense power as a firefly cage. It is just about as dangerous as magic can get.'

'You really don't have to tell me. I have been practising my magic and I do totally intend to get on her trail.' He hadn't completely given up hope, not yet. Talking about Tiffany reminded Seth how crucial it was that he worked at it and found a way to get admitted into the Elysee.

Angelique was right. How exactly had he ended up walking in a tunnel under the sea on the possible trail of a dark sorcerer when he should be concentrating on gaining an ability to do some sort of useful magic.

'I need answers to so many questions,' he admitted, knowing those answers lay within the magical world. 'Like – how did she do magic with the firefly cage? It traps a sorcerer, doesn't it, so someone else can use their magic – isn't that how it works?'

He could just about make out Angelique nodding in the eerie darkness.

'Pewter tells me they have the best people on it. You said all the leads came to dead ends. But no one understands as well as I do that we can't just leave Tiffany out there. Tiffany's smart,' he said, all the frustration returning, knowing that he could do nothing about it. 'She knew exactly how to make my life difficult because she thinks ahead. She has loads of patience. I bet before she even decided to leave the Last Chance Hotel she'd have had a plan. She'll cause problems wherever she goes.'

'We will get her, Seth.'

Then it came again. Unmistakeable this time.

That scratching sound. He snapped off his torch and listened in the dripping darkness, then he nudged Angelique and put his finger to his lips.

This time a noise up ahead told him they were definitely not alone in the tunnel.

32. I DIDN'T COME HERE FOR A PICNIC

'Should we go back?' hissed Angelique, gripping Seth's arm so tightly he felt her nails bite in.

Seth groped his way forwards in the darkness, reaching out slowly and carefully, feeling the sharp rocky walls, inching forwards as silently as he could, so he could see whoever was ahead without being seen himself.

Then his fingers were touching nothing. The tunnel was suddenly opening out. He groped for the reassurance of a wall, sliding sideways in the blackness, grateful to again feel the slime beneath his fingers. A dim bit of daylight penetrated from high up.

'Maybe it's just a rat,' muttered Angelique nervously.

But Seth was staring right at the source of the scratching.

'Nightshade!'

'Did you just say rat?' the cat grumbled. 'Did you mean me? Charming,' she growled, slipping over to him and rubbing around his legs. 'Well, wasn't expecting you to be down here. Nice of you to drop in. So, where's the way out? Been here bloomin' ages. What brings you into this dark, slimy and smelly tunnel?'

'I was about to ask you the same question.'

'Well, I didn't come here for a picnic. It was your bloomin' inspector's doing. Would I like to do some detecting? he says. I'd much rather catch up on a little snooze time, I says. Next thing I knew, he had me chasing around on an endless hunt for dead seagulls. I fell down this hole.'

She looked up and Seth could see sky far above them. 'Lucky cats always land on their feet. Anyone less nimble than me is sure to have broken a toe at the very least.'

Angelique grabbed the torch from Seth, switched it back on and started shining it around the walls. 'Is this the end of the tunnel, Nightshade?' Something about her voice made it clear what she was really asking was, *Are we trapped down here?*

'No idea. Didn't fancy heading off down a nasty, dark, damp-looking place on my own; never know what you might find. Maybe some dirty big rat,' Nightshade answered with a shiver.

'Nightshade, you are a cat,' said Seth.

'Oh, so that means I have to actually like rats, do I? I mean, would you want to meet one unexpectedly in the dark? And have you ever tasted one?'

Angelique's shining of the torchlight revealed there was absolutely no chance of scrabbling up the walls to reach that patch of daylight. It would be like trying to climb a chimney. Nightshade's green eyes glowed with reflected light.

Seth carried on feeling his way around.

If Nightshade had fallen in, it had to mean they were really close to the lighthouse. The tunnel had to end somewhere they could get out. Seth was suddenly convinced he'd hit on where it was leading – were they about to discover the secret laboratory?

He reached an almost invisible, narrow cleft in the rock. It had to be a way forward, and soon the three of them were squeezing through, disappointingly into yet another passage. Seth decided not to share his thoughts that he was starting to feel they were somehow being lured even further away from daylight. That somehow, from beyond the grave, Soul Snakesmouth was playing tricks on them.

He felt completely trapped between the vague unease that there might be a rising tide behind and quite possibly a dark sorcerer ahead. But still he kept pressing on.

'Checking out apple cake,' he said. 'Peering at maps,' Nightshade grumbled on.

'Inspector Pewter?' Despite Dex's obvious admiration, Seth wondered, uneasily and not for the first time, just how good Pewter was as an inspector. 'He's not been looking for the laboratory or any signs of darkwitching?'

'Had me and Celeste out on the hunt. Wanted a gull to give to Dr Malinger.'

'Did he say why?'

'Wanted to find out exactly how one of them died.'

'He's one of the best MagiCon inspectors,' reassured Angelique, reading Seth's look.

'You mean a bit like Copious Bladderwrack was one of the best cleaners?'

'You have no idea how complicated investigating magic is,' said Angelique, as they carried trudging on. Then she stopped. 'Is it me, or does the sea suddenly sound much louder?'

They all stopped and listened.

'Great!' said Nightshade, shaking out her paws. 'I wonder where we'll come out.'

'What makes you think we're going to come out?' asked Angelique.

'Er – because we can hear the sea, that must mean we're nearing the end of the tunnel. We must be near a beach.'

Angelique glanced at Seth and sent a jet of blue light along the tunnel. 'Unfortunately, that's not the only reason we may be able to hear water.'

Seth feared she was right. This was not the gentle slap of waves from somewhere just ahead, it was coming from behind them.

'Is it me, or does that sound more like a torrent travelling very, very fast along an enclosed space?' said Nightshade.

'Run!' yelled Seth.

He grabbed Nightshade and followed Angelique down the tunnel, feeling his feet slide on the slime as he picked up the pace, still not sure they weren't simply running into a dead end.

'Can you get out your library card and zap us back to the library?' he suggested breathlessly.

'No time,' replied Angelique crisply. 'But I think there's something giving off a magical signal right up ahead. Let's hope it's a way out. And not a dark sorcerer.'

At least the ceiling was higher here. Seth kept on running, not daring to turn, but it only needed his ears to tell him that a huge cascade of water was following them and was moving fast. Then, abruptly, the tunnel stopped. They couldn't run any further. They faced a blank wall of rock.

'This can't be it, we must have gone wrong,' cried Nightshade.

Angelique was desperately swinging the torch from side to side and floor to ceiling, but all it was showing was blank rock.

'Any minute now this whole tunnel is going to be filled with seawater, and I am not a fish,' said Nightshade, wriggling.

'Shut up, Nightshade,' snapped Angelique.

Seth could only fearfully stare at the rock in front of them and think of that wall of water approaching fast. 'Surely someone wouldn't have built a tunnel without a way out,' he said, trying to be practical and not panic, even as his ears latched on to the roar of water, making it difficult to think of anything other than just how close it was.

Angelique lifted her divinoscope, flipped the silver lid, cried 'Duck!' and flashed a zap of blue light right into the rock. The light fizzed and ricocheted off the walls. Angelique let out a sharp cry. Seth really hoped she'd seen what he thought he'd seen. Just a glimpse of a small wooden door revealed by the sparkling blue light, blending into the rock itself. But it vanished again the second the blue light faded.

Angelique planted herself right in front of where it had appeared, running her fingers along the rock. Seth put down Nightshade and helped, scrabbling with his fingernails, feeling for anything that might be a handle. A way out. An edge, anything to show there really was a door.

Angelique held the torch in her teeth and used both hands to frantically go over every inch of the dark rock in front of them.

'Sea's getting closer,' said Nightshade.

'Shut up, Nightshade,' said Angelique and Seth together.

If it really was a door, there was no light coming through. Seth put his shoulder to the rock and shoved and his shoulder crashed painfully. Nothing.

The door didn't give an inch.

'I can feel my life flashing in front of me. It happens when you are about to die,' said Nightshade, her green eyes closing.

Angelique sent out another jet of light. This time, instead of sparking and rebounding off rock, the light hovered for a moment, sending blue shivers across the surface, and out of nowhere appeared an iron handle. Seth grabbed it before it could disappear, then he risked a look back and saw a wall of water racing towards them.

He put all his weight into making the rusty old handle turn, but it started to give and the latch lifted, just seconds before the shock wave of cold water caught him.

'I think I can smell kippers,' said Nightshade.

They all threw themselves against the door and fell through on to a solid flagstone floor.

Seth turned and slammed the door shut behind them. He heard water hitting the other side like someone was practising knife-throwing. But the door held, and appeared to be watertight.

Only then did Seth look up and see where they had come out.

Not in the laboratory. In the kitchen of Snakesmouth Lighthouse.

33. Do Not Alert Your Suspect

As Seth and Angelique flopped on to the floor, grateful to no longer feel only impenetrable rock beneath their fingers and gasping the air gratefully, Inspector Pewter turned from where he was peering into a large saucepan. Seth caught a whiff of something spicy.

'Ah, was that you knocking? And I was beginning to think you wouldn't be back in time for dinner,' said the inspector, as if they weren't breathless and smelling like creatures of the deep.

He took a small spoon, tasted a tiny mouthful of whatever was cooking in the saucepan, and winced.

Celeste was staring at them in astonishment. 'Were you . . . ? Where did you . . . ? I didn't realize you were on the boat too. The others have been back a while.' She looked confused, but as Pewter didn't ask questions, she returned to prodding the bottom of the large saucepan with a wooden spoon.

Seth turned back to the tunnel door. Now it was a blank wall. But it was exactly the place where, a couple of times, he had thought he'd seen something move out of the corner of his eye. As if the door only existed in shadows. He felt the wall all over, but it was completely smooth, with nothing to give away the fact that there was a door there, a secret passage that led to the coast path at the top of the deserted village on the mainland.

Angelique's hair and clothes were a soggy mess. She extracted a small glob of tunnel slime from her hair. Nightshade ate it in a single bite, sat down and started washing herself. They had brought bits of sand and seaweed on to the kitchen floor, which Seth swept up, avoiding looking too closely at what might be lurking in the saucepan.

'Thought you were doing a pie.' He gingerly lifted the lid and peered at a brown sludge.

'Miss Celeste here decided to put together something a little more adventurous and surprising. Our own recipe. Did we come up with a name?'

'Turnip curry!' cried Celeste. 'At least, we think that's what they were. We found a pile of small round vegetables in a corner. And some other bits and pieces. We just threw it together. It's a totally new recipe!'

'Sounds delicious.'

Celeste was frowning into the saucepan. She had forgotten again to put on her work shoes and was wearing her delicate little blue pumps, but she still had on that white cap that covered her hair.

Pewter rubbed his hands together. 'This is great, Seth; I do the cooking while you've been off investigating.'

Angelique dashed out, muttering about how long hair and seaweed do not mix as she unthreaded tendrils of it from her locks.

'Is it meant to be quite such a revolting brown colour?' Celeste poked doubtfully at the dinner again. 'I can't believe how long it took. We seem to have been standing here for ever. Would anyone miss me, do you think, if I went for a lie-down?'

With Angelique out of the way, Seth seized the chance to say: 'First, Celeste, can I ask you something?'

'Uh-huh.'

'Now we know Mina Mintencress was murdered, there will be questions. Like – have you really been working for her for years?'

She eyed him sharply. 'Oh?' She tugged down her cap. 'I don't know what you mean, Seth. Are you accusing me of something?'

Seth could almost hear Angelique's sharp words in his ear, telling him this was not the way to go about investigating. *You do not alert your suspect.* 'What I mean is,' he carried on awkwardly, 'you didn't really just start working for her, did you? Like, a couple of weeks ago?'

Celeste moved closer to him. Her eyes, open very wide, were fixed directly on his. 'Believe me, Seth, I have known her for absolutely ages.'

Then she marched down the corridor to her room, looking really offended.

Seth suggested that Pewter should lay the table in the dining room, and once the inspector was gone he started to try and salvage something edible from the mess in the saucepan.

'Has anyone seen Brockler?' said Lark, stepping into the kitchen, accompanied by Alfie. 'Alfie wants to go beachcombing after the storm. I wondered if he wanted to come. We can't find him.'

Alfie looked unusually tense and tight-lipped, not at all as if he was desperate to go beachcombing.

'Might he have gone beachcombing by himself?' said Seth, but he was thinking of Brockler's tailored trousers, perfect hair and starched white shirts, and couldn't see him taking off by himself to the beach.

Lark was biting her nails and Seth realized she was seriously worried. She hadn't even asked how they'd managed to get back.

'I think we should look for him,' she whispered. 'After what happened to Mina.'

'Right. Let's get Inspector Pewter and organize a search.'

Inspector Pewter was nearly done laying the table in the dining room and agreed immediately. 'Missing, hmm? On an island as small as this one?'

Lark hovered anxiously over by the door, out of earshot, with a strangely quiet Alfie.

'How did you get on today, sir?' Seth asked in a low tone as he watched the inspector rearrange all the knives and forks the wrong way around. 'Did you solve the puzzle of the dead seagulls?'

'Could not find a single blasted one. I fed your cat, though.'

'Thank you. She's used to living in a forest, where there's plenty of food about.'

'And you, young Seth, how did you get on? Find anything except a fascinating new route from the mainland?'

'I was hoping,' Seth replied in an even lower tone, 'to find out if Brockler is the one who has been investigating darkwitching, sir. But . . .'

'Tricky to prove, huh? You will learn that one of the most important things in any investigation is correctly seeing what you actually find. Far too easy to see what you want to and to disregard the rest. Takes years of experience to tell the difference between the two. I'm only a beginner myself.'

'So, were the dead seagulls important, sir?'

'That is what I failed to find out.'

Pewter pressed the tips of his fingers together and approached Lark. 'Now, Miss Sunrise, have you thought of anywhere Mr Brockler might like to go if he fancies a little quiet time alone.'

She shook her head. 'His room was the first place I looked.'

Pewter asked Seth for ideas. He had his suspicions of Brockler, but didn't like to say much in front of Lark. He suspected Brockler of being behind Mina Mintencress dying and somehow using magic to make it look like an accident and gain control of the family fortune. But it was all guesswork. What evidence did he really have that the lawyer was up to something? And why would he now vanish?

'I did find out that Brockler lied about where he got the dragon's tooth pendant from,' Seth said quietly enough that only the inspector would hear.

Pewter leant forward. 'Dragon's tooth pendant?'

'The one Brockler took from the bottom of the bath.'

There was something in Pewter's face that told Seth this was news to Pewter and he explained quickly that he'd discovered it was something that had belonged to Soul Snakesmouth, and why it hadn't been here when Copious Bladderwrack cleaned the lighthouse. How Jo had pinched some objects and sold them to Brockler.

'Mina took a fancy to the carving and he made it into a pendant so she could wear it. And there was a painting he was looking for. I'm pretty sure,' Seth finished in a low voice, 'that Brockler believed Snakesmouth was a sorcerer.'

'When I said a moment ago about working out what is important . . . you didn't think to mention this to me earlier?' said Pewter. 'It's the kind of small detail, Seth, that might have been good to know straight away.'

'Er – well, I only just found it all out. Sorry.' There

was no point in adding he felt he only ever seemed to say things that made him look an idiot whose understanding of magic was wrong. But there was no chance to explain anything. Pewter had already flown towards the back door.

'Brockler is wearing a pendant that belonged to a sinister sorcerer. And he removed it from the bath where Mina Mintencress died? Why do people never, ever tell me anything?' he muttered. 'I'll get Dex and Rendleton to organize a search outside,' he said more loudly, over his shoulder. 'Do the same inside. Seth – let's find him, and quickly.'

34. WHAT'S FRIGHTENING YOU?

'Let's start at the top,' Seth called to Lark as they darted for the staircase. The last time he'd seen Hari Brockler he'd been searching Mina Mintencress's room. It seemed a good place to begin.

'Where could he possibly have gone?' said Lark, biting her nails and following. 'You really think something has happened to him?'

Seth went into the room and first took in that almost completely circular view of the sea and sky, thinking he might have a chance of spotting the lawyer if he was outside. He scoured for signs of a figure, but from here you just mostly got the never-ending blue and simply could not see all the island's coves and inlets. He'd have to leave that to Dex and Rendleton.

'I looked in every room in the lighthouse, except the staff rooms, because I didn't think it was likely Brockler would be there,' said Lark.

'We should check,' said Seth

Angelique had just arrived, looking concerned but far less damp. She heard, gave a quick nod and disappeared again at a run.

Alfie was hovering uncertainly in the middle of the room, playing with his catapult. Seth hit on an idea. 'Brockler's playing that game – hide and seek. Have you played that here? What do you think, Alfie?' said Seth encouragingly. 'I bet you know all the best places. Where would you hide?'

Alfie simply shrugged. He didn't seem the least bit interested, just kept flexing the catapult.

'It's a game we can all play,' joined in Lark encouragingly. 'You always have the best idea of places to hide.'

'I don't know where he is. I didn't see him do anything strange.'

'You didn't see him do anything strange?' echoed

Seth, moving closer to the boy, convinced this meant entirely the opposite.

Lark had the same idea as she crouched next to the small boy, whose bottom lip wobbled. 'What is it?' urged Lark. 'Do you know something?'

Alfie turned huge, frightened eyes on her but said nothing. Lark caught him by the hand. 'Alfie, no one will be cross, but if you've seen Mr Brockler, if you know anything, you really should tell us.'

But Alfie stubbornly shook his head. Lark drew in an impatient puff of breath. Seth was convinced the boy knew something. He'd noticed Alfie had become silent and withdrawn. That might be under-standable after the death of his sister, yet when swimming with Rendleton and on the boat trip, he'd appeared to be coping well. Something had happened. Seth remembered how Alfie was convinced he had seen the ghost – even though he'd called it some-thing else.

Seth had a feeling the boy knew things, and some-thing about Brockler's disappearance was troubling him. How could they convince him to talk?

Angelique returned, shaking her head. 'He's not in the staff rooms and it's getting dark. Rendleton and Stormforce are still outside. Let's hope they've seen him about somewhere.'

'Lark's checked the lighthouse, you've checked the staff rooms. What about the Sunrise Wing?' said Seth.

'No!' Alfie leapt in. 'Not there!'

Lark looked startled and spluttered: 'But it's always locked. It's mostly still just a building site. I don't think Brockler would go there.'

Pewter arrived and Seth was surprised to see he was holding a small, framed picture.

'You told me Brockler had a picture that belonged to Snakesmouth,' he said to Seth. 'And what did I happen to find but this – on the stairs.'

The painting was of a happy and confident young man with blond hair and a big smile who was standing in the centre of the lighthouse, immediately recognizable even without the thick carpet and the shimmering wallpaper.

'I think this is a picture of Soul Snakesmouth,' said Pewter.

Seth was intrigued to see that the sinister sorcerer was so much younger, so much happier-looking than he'd imagined him. Seth had always pictured him as sallow, thin and glowering.

Looking more closely at the picture, Seth was immediately intrigued by something else.

'What's he doing?'

Rather than looking straight at the artist, Snakesmouth had been painted facing out of the picture, with one hand lifted above his head.

'That is a really strange way to pose for a picture,' said Angelique, putting her long nose so close to the portrait that it almost touched it.

Seth went over to Alfie and crouched in front of him, showing him the picture. 'When you say you didn't see Brockler doing anything odd – did you mean you didn't see him doing anything odd with this picture?'

Alfie was puzzled by the question. 'Er, yes.'

'Then he did do something odd with this picture?'

Alfie hesitated then nodded, just once.

'Perhaps, Alfie, you could show us where you were and tell us what strange thing happened. Take your time,' said Pewter.

Everyone turned to Alfie. He hesitated for just a moment and then set off down the spiral stairs until they were halfway between the ground and the first floors. Then he stopped. They had all followed and now Pewter turned to the boy.

'I've seen some extraordinary things in my time,' Pewter said to Alfie. 'Whatever you tell me, no matter how mad it sounds, I'll believe you because I particularly love stories like that. See if you can surprise me, but I bet you can't.'

Alfie looked at him for the longest time, then gave a short nod. 'I saw him disappear.'

'Disappear?' snapped Lark. 'If this is your idea of a joke, Alfie, I will kill you.' She stood over him, hands on hips. 'You little monster, you're just making this up.'

'Miss Sunrise, might I suggest you leave this to me,' said Pewter.

Rendleton and Dex arrived from outside, looking breathless and windswept. Dex went straight over to the picture, seizing it from Seth.

'Wow. This is the guy? Where'd this come from? Wondered what old Snakesmouth looked like. Not that old, actually.' He turned and gave his lopsided grin at Rendleton. 'Surprisingly like you.'

Dex grinned, but Rendleton only frowned.

This surprised Seth, who had rarely seen Rendleton anything other than cheerful and positive.

'Alfie is about to show us how Mr Brockler disappeared,' said Angelique.

They all looked at Alfie, apart from Dex, who was scrutinizing every detail in the picture.

'Exactly where?' asked Pewter. 'Are we in the right place?'

Alfie turned and looked in silent anguish at Pewter.

'Here?' asked Rendleton, his voice full of disbelief.

'He disappeared from here?' said Dex, beginning to run his hands lightly over every surface.

'Alfie, you are a lying little toerag. This is serious,' snapped Lark. 'How could he possibly have disappeared from here?'

She was right. You couldn't access any of the rooms from this point, only continue up or down. How on earth was it possible that Brockler could disappear?

Seth examined the portrait again as he tried to work out the exact spot where Snakesmouth had been. The sinister sorcerer was raising his right hand and was holding something that had been painted in great detail. Seth peered in closer and could make out a small wooden object he recognized – of a snake devouring a lighthouse with small red jewels for eyes. 'He's holding that carving that's supposed to be made from a dragon's tooth,' he said in a low voice. Dex kept glancing from the picture to the walls.

Lark was still looking furious. 'This story gets more ridiculous. Why on earth would anyone want to look at a picture on the stairs and then disappear?'

'He stopped right here.' Alfie sounded mulish. 'He did.'

'And what did he do next?' asked Pewter.

'I told you, he disappeared.'

The only thing that was just a little odd was that at this point the stairs widened slightly. In fact, they seemed to go slightly off being right in the centre of the lighthouse. From here, Seth realized, you could reach out and touch one of the walls.

'Sorry, what exactly is this?' said Dex, pointing to Snakesmouth's hand in the picture. 'What's he holding?'

'The dragon's tooth pendant,' said Seth, and explained again about Jo's thieving and why the pendant and the picture had never been discovered during Copious Bladderwrack's cleaning.

Dexter nodded enthusiastically and went about trying to recreate the exact pose Soul Snakesmouth was striking in the picture, running his fingers over the smooth banisters and reaching for the wall.

Pewter tried again with Alfie. 'OK, young man. Remember everything you can. Close your eyes if you need to. Be as precise as possible.'

'He was feeling about. Then he walked right down that wall over there and disappeared.'

'Oh please!' snapped Lark.

Nightshade padded softly up the stairs. Until now she had kept herself pretty well hidden and everyone might not have even known she was here.

Seth quickly scooped her up and whispered in her ear to please remember not to talk.

'But you'll want to hear what I've got to say,' she purred, very softly in his ear. 'You're not the only one who can play detective, you know. I watched him earlier. He was pacing about, walking up and down the stairs, just like the boy says, holding that picture. He was here for ages. I guess he must have come back and tried again. Whatever he was looking for, I'm guessing he found it, which might not be altogether good.'

She wriggled out of Seth's arms and went and rubbed against Alfie's legs and the boy bent to envelop her in a big hug.

Seth joined Dex in reaching to one of the wooden beams that criss-crossed the inside of the lighthouse. The wood felt bumpy and grained, and his fingers brushing over something that felt like a deeper indent than the other knots and grooves of the wood. He beckoned Dex.

Dex checked the picture again. This had to be exactly the same place where Snakesmouth was lifting aloft the hand holding the carving.

Dex smoothed the beam with his fingers, frowning, rubbing it, then pressing hard. Pewter joined them and did exactly the same. The inspector fumbled in a pocket and brought out a small grey ball of what looked like putty. He warmed it in his hand for a moment, then squished it into the deeper dent in the beam.

'What's that?' asked Seth in a low voice. 'Some kind of substance that detects magical doorways?'

'No, it's a small grey ball of putty,' said Pewter, carefully removing it again. He held it in his palm, revealing that the putty had now taken on the shape of the indent. It had a familiar twisting form.

'That's it,' cried Seth. 'That's the carving that Mina Mintencress started wearing as a pendant.'

'It's not a pendant, it's a key,' said Dex.

'What are you talking about, mate?' asked Rendleton.

Dex was hesitating, but with everything that had happened, the truth that Snakesmouth really had been a sorcerer was bound to leak out anyway. He explained about the hidden laboratory and how the entrance was so secret, not even an expert had been able to find it. 'But what really worries me is that Brockler is wearing this key,' he finished.

Angelique sent a sharp crackle of blue light from

her divinoscope into the indent, making Alfie, Lark and Rendleton gasp.

Then everyone waited for something to happen. The room got darker. Seth wasn't sure if he imagined it, but he felt the shadows had begun to creep in.

The atmosphere had changed.

Something dark flitted in the corner of his eye and he tried to turn quickly.

Where the wall had been completely blank before, something was coming into focus. The shadows were forming a dusky image that was gradually becoming clearer.

It was a set of steps, leading down into darkness.

35. Darkwitching Magic

'This is where Brockler went?' said Rendleton, sounding incredulous and looking uncertainly at the shadow steps.

'Can we, like, actually walk on these?' asked Lark giddily, as everyone stared and tried to take in what they were seeing.

'I expect you'll find you can,' said Pewter, gingerly extending one of his long legs and putting it on the top step. 'Although maybe not that you should.'

Pewter took another step down and Angelique

leapt in behind him, closely followed by Dex. Seth took a step forward too, his brain having difficulty registering that the black shadow felt firm under his boot, and cautiously walked into a dark space. A space that took them, step by step, beneath the lighthouse.

Seth saw with relief that Pewter was now cradling a spark of light in the palm of his hand, so they weren't simply walking into blackness.

Behind him, he was aware that Rendleton, Lark and Alfie were following curiously too.

They reached a circular room lined with shelves. Everything was covered with a layer of dust; the long, stainless-steel table with its combination of test tubes, clamps and Bunsen burners was almost exactly as they had seen in the wordstone. Seth found himself face to face with the container and the bug-eyed creature that looked like it was staring right at you. He reached out and, this time, was able to touch it. Soul Snakesmouth's secret laboratory. The room Copious Bladderwrack had failed to find when he'd cleaned the lighthouse, here all the time, but buried within the shadows of darkwitching magic.

He could smell the room this time too. A sort of citrusy tang.

There was the sound of something soft stubbing against something hard and immovable, and a curse.

'We could do with a bit more light,' grumbled Rendleton.

Dex tried a lamp on the table. He flicked a switch and a light gradually buzzed into life, filling the room and bringing the edges into focus.

It showed that, beneath the long laboratory table, on the floor of the shadow study, was the sprawled body of Hari Brockler and, alongside him, the dragon's tooth carving.

PART FIVE

36. STILL A LONG WAY FROM THE TRUTH

'Is he dead?' asked Rendleton, as Pewter crouched to examine the body.

Pewter looked up. 'Strangled.'

Lark quickly drew Alfie to her.

Pewter prodded the dragon carving gingerly with his toe. 'He was wearing the pendant, just like poor Mina Mintencress in her bath. It's unwise to wear something so absorbed by darkwitching magic, and those shadow snakes. Looks like Brockler fought to take it off, but the magic was too strong for him.'

That citrusy tang should have warned Seth, and he thought back to the battle he and Angelique had had in the room where Mina died.

He was taking it all in, but his mind was reeling at the same time.

He'd been so convinced it was Brockler who had been responsible for Mina's death. Seth had thought he'd got it all worked out, thought Brockler had planned how, by becoming Alfie's guardian, he could pretty much seize complete control of the family's vast fortune.

He'd been trying to find evidence that Brockler had learnt about magic, believed in the magic and had been experimenting with trying to become magical himself. Seth had been convinced that all the answers lay in the fact that the lawyer had learnt enough shadow sorcery to arrange Mina's death and make it look like an accident.

But now Brockler was dead and nothing added up any more. As he looked at the body of the lawyer, he knew that he was still a long way from the truth.

'Well, we've found the laboratory, largely thanks to Mr Brockler,' began Dex. 'Guess that is one mystery solved.'

From above them came a scream.

Silhouetted at the top of the steps and staring

down at them was Celeste. Her hands were clapped to her face.

Seth rushed back up the steps to steady her. She was gasping for breath between sobs.

'He's dead. Another death? He can't be dead,' she wailed as Seth steered her away.

'You? But how?' he heard Lark say in a puzzled voice, looking up from where she was comforting Alfie.

Celeste clung to Seth and didn't protest as he led her down the stairs, through the kitchen and to her room. He wanted to go and make some strong sweet tea. But Celeste held on to him and he sat on her hard bed and let her sob.

'What was that room? Was he really dead? What is happening?'

Seth found it really difficult to know what he could say that was going to make this any easier. 'Perhaps you need to talk to Inspector Pewter. Let's get everyone tea.'

Celeste wiped her eyes, pinched her cheeks and said she would help.

Seth was still trying to puzzle through the big questions. Who had killed Mina Mintencress if it wasn't Brockler? And who had killed Hari Brockler? Who had woken those shadows?

Seth puzzled through what he'd learnt from Pewter and Angelique about how magic worked. Magic didn't work by itself. That darkwitching magic had to be controlled by someone – and that had to mean a powerful sorcerer – here. But it still made no sense. Who could be a powerful sorcerer? Brockler had been his best bet.

'Brockler started to go on about a bad sorcerer having lived here,' said Celeste as they made tea. 'I thought he was just believing too many tales. Then I wasn't sure. Then I thought he was using the ridiculous stories and doing those things to make us think there was something supernatural going on here. When Mina died, I thought . . .' Celeste blew her nose and sat down at the kitchen table.

'Did you think he killed Mina?' said Seth quietly.

'I thought he must have done. Now Brockler's dead so I guess he didn't?' Celeste looked questioningly at Seth. 'Or did he? But then who killed him? And who killed Mina?'

Seth turned at a sound.

Angelique's eyes flashed dangerously as she faced Celeste, standing right in the maid's line of vision across the kitchen table.

'Tea, Angelique?' said Seth.

'Seth, Celeste has urgent questions to answer.'

The maid looked up at her over the rim of her mug, her eyes narrow. 'I'm far too upset. My – my employer is dead.' She looked pleadingly at Seth, doing her best to ignore Angelique.

'Do we have to do this now?' he asked.

'I rather think we do.'

Then Celeste surprised Seth by saying coolly: 'All right. Ask me anything you like.'

'What are you really doing here?' Angelique tilted her nose into the air.

'You know that. I work here. I'm the maid.'

'I think not. It's over. You might as well tell us everything. You're going to be arrested anyway.'

Seth waited for her to defend herself, but Celeste said nothing. The longer the silence went on, the more Seth had an uncomfortable feeling that he knew what Angelique was going to say.

But Celeste couldn't be responsible for all this, could she?

He mentally went over everything he'd learnt – everything he'd assumed. What he'd got wrong – the little he'd got right; dreading what Angelique would say next.

Someone here was a sorcerer. Had to be. Angelique had kept warning him not to trust Celeste. But Celeste had seemed so genuinely fond of Mina. Seth couldn't think it through any more.

Angelique dipped into her red handbag and placed something on the table right in front of Celeste. It was a card, like a small playing card, showing a picture of a wild red flower.

Seth recognized that card with a jolt. He'd seen it before and he knew exactly where. It was from when they had worked together at the Last Chance Hotel. It was a card carried by followers of the sinister sorcerer behind many deaths of magical people: the sinister sorcerer behind the plot to recover the firefly cage from the Last Chance Hotel. The one ultimately responsible for the death of the kindly Dr Thallomius.

That card being here could only mean one thing.

Red Valerian, the most-wanted sinister sorcerer, was somehow involved here.

Angelique took a step closer to Celeste, who shrank back. She picked up the card and held it up in front of the maid's face.

'I am waiting to hear if you can explain why you have got the calling card of the most notorious sinister sorcerer hidden in your room.' Angelique's eyes never left Celeste's as she finished: 'I'm sorry to have to be the one to tell you the truth, Seth. She's working for Red Valerian.'

37. A Notorious Sinister Sorcerer

Seth really could not take this in.

Angelique did not take her eyes from the maid, who sipped her tea.

'I've never even heard of this Red – whatever that is,' said Celeste, defending herself stoutly. She snatched the card out of Angelique's hand. Her eyes narrowed. 'Have you been snooping in my room?' Celeste leapt up, slopping her tea. 'I'm not working for anyone.'

'Interesting.' Angelique paused. 'Yet you claim to

be working for the Mintencresses.'

'Oh, that's not fair! That's different.' Celeste gave an annoyed frown.

Seth waited for Celeste to carry on defending herself, but instead, she let out a sob and ran off to her room.

'Angelique,' said Seth, 'it doesn't make any sense. Perhaps that card got there, I don't know, by accident. She knew Mina so well. She's really not pretending.' He softly laid a hand on Angelique's arm, but she shrugged it off and followed Celeste.

Seth followed too.

'I'm sorry, but Mina Mintencress took on a new maid only a few weeks ago. Celeste appeared to know her so well because she must have been re-searching her. It's the only way. You've been taken in.'

Seth was dumbfounded. Could it be true? He was piecing things together. Angelique had told him there was a reason she was such a terrible maid. How had he not realized she couldn't possibly be a maid at all? Sheepishly, he knew she was right. Why hadn't he seen it?

Inspector Pewter had only been telling him a short while ago what made a good detective – seeing things as they were and not as you wanted to see them, an ability to work out what was important. He felt incredibly stupid, particularly because Angelique had kept trying to warn him and each time he'd only got cross.

'You really aren't Mina Mintencress's maid, are you?' said Seth slowly, as they entered Celeste's room.

Celeste shook her head. 'Afraid not. I'm sorry, Seth. I had no choice but to lie to you. Thanks for all you've done for me.'

She wasn't sitting sobbing on the bed. She was going through the narrow wardrobe in her room, flinging things on to the floor. She swung around to look at Angelique. 'You really are foul, aren't you? This was working out so well.'

'Just looking for the truth.'

'Oh, that?' Celeste threw off her white cap and her long, dark curly hair cascaded out. She removed the dark glasses she had taken to wearing, revealing light-brown eyes. She didn't look the least bit cowed and caught out. She gave a spiteful little laugh. 'The truth? Are you really here as a cook?'

'That's hardly relevant.'

'Poking your nose in. Undercover, just like me.'

'The main difference being, I haven't killed anyone.'

'Same,' replied Celeste. Soon everything from the

bedside cabinet was in a pile on the floor. 'If you found that card in this room – what else might be here? What was that little witch up to?'

The door was flung open again and Lark swept in and faced the woman defiantly rummaging under the thin mattress.

'How dare you – how dare you make me think you were dead!' She rushed towards Celeste, burst into tears and threw her arms around her.

And then Seth could finally see one thing for what it really was.

He looked at Angelique. 'OK, you were right. This isn't Celeste, Mina Mintencress's maid. But she's not working for Red Valerian either.' The way Lark was hugging her told him the real story. 'This *is* Mina Mintencress.'

38. Cover Blown

Angelique stared at the pair clinging to each other. 'The woman we thought died in the bath?'

'The body in the cellar must be of the real maid,' concluded Seth. 'The one who was working for Red Valerian.'

Celeste looked at him.

'And I just thought you were too upset to face speaking to any of the family, when all the time you were just worried about being seen,' Seth went on. 'No wonder you wore that ridiculous cap to hide your hair. I thought your dark glasses were to hide the fact that you'd been crying!'

Every single time anyone who might recognize her had entered a room, Celeste had scurried off. 'That's how you got away with it – none of the family have actually been in the same room as you since you've been pretending to be Celeste.'

The tall figure of Pewter strode into the room. 'Ah.' He spotted Mina and Lark in a close hug. 'Cover blown?'

Mina nodded.

Mina, not Celeste, thought Seth. That would take a bit of getting used to.

'You knew!' said Angelique, looking furiously at Pewter.

Pewter shrugged. 'Someone tried to kill her. Not a bad plan to keep her safe by letting everyone believe she was already dead. Hoped that would give us enough time to work out what was going on. Now, Dex is under instruction to keep Alfie and Rendleton away from here just to give us enough time for a little plan.'

'Great,' said Angelique expectantly.

'So who's got one? A plan, that is,' said Pewter.

'Putting Mina in danger like that!' screeched Lark.

'Keeping her from danger,' assured Pewter.

'I had to do it, Lark. I didn't ever believe there were ghosts at the hotel. I was convinced someone was playing tricks but I just wasn't quite sure who,' Mina began to explain. 'I got the idea when I realized how similar I looked to the new maid. I thought if we swapped clothes and I put my hair under a cap, as long as no one got a good look at me, they'd just think it was her. It was easy enough to arrange an argument and lock everyone out. Far easier for me to sneak around for a bit and keep an eye on everyone when they thought "Mina" wasn't watching. People just don't notice maids so much.'

'It was a good plan,' agreed Seth.

'I thought if everyone believed I was out of the way, they might try one of their tricks. I might see what was going on. I wanted to catch them at it. I only meant to switch places with her for a couple of hours. She seemed happy to go along with it.' Mina shook her head. 'But I don't get it. Who is this Red Valerian? What was Celeste really doing here?'

'That, I fear, we can only guess,' said Pewter.

'Oh my goodness! Wait until Alfie hears you're not dead!' cried Lark.

'No. Not yet, you can't tell anyone yet. I still haven't a clue what's going on. I thought Brockler was up to something and I'd catch him at it. But turns out the maid was up to something. But she died. And now Brockler's dead. What's going on?' Mina finished in a whisper. 'Who killed me?'

39. I Didn't Expect Her To Die

Lark still had her arms around Mina, as if afraid that if she stopped clinging to her she might disappear. 'You need to sort this out!' she snapped at Pewter. 'You need to end this. You've got until tomorrow morning, then we leave here for good.'

Angelique threw the card with the red flower on it down on the bedside table like a challenge. 'Until tomorrow to discover who has killed twice. Where do we start?'

'I didn't expect her to die,' wailed Mina.

'It's not your fault!' cried Lark.

Mina turned to Angelique. 'You've no idea how terrified I've been. If I hadn't decided to swap places with that new maid – it really would be me dead in the bathtub upstairs.'

Seth thought there was little point in not coming clean. He told her Brockler had been right when he'd believed this had once been the home of a sorcerer.

'Red Valerian is behind a lot of criminal activity among magical folk. No one knows who he is – he gets his followers to do his dirty work for him.'

Determination to get his hand on the means to powerful dark magic was what had led one of Red Valerian's followers to the Last Chance Hotel. Seth guessed it was the same story here. Red Valerian must have guessed there might be a way to access Soul Snakesmouth's darkwitching magic, but the Mintencress party moving in had made it much more difficult.

'What do you do now?' asked Mina. 'Am I safe? Who would want to kill me?'

'Well, I guess we know it wasn't Brockler who stirred up those shadow snakes. But does that mean he also wasn't behind all those strange happenings that spooked the builders and had everyone believing in ghosts?' said Seth.

'We all tried to pretend the builders were making stuff up,' said Lark. 'But I never wanted to go near the place. There were definitely noises. Things definitely moved. You know, I think Brockler had truly convinced himself it was the ghost of Soul Snakesmouth.'

There was a long pause. Seth's mind whirled with everything he'd heard about the haunted rooms and those shadow snakes. After all that had happened, was it actually possible it was all the work of a ghost? And all that focused on the Sunrise Wing.

'I guess that's our next step. It's time to search the Sunrise Wing.' He looked about him. 'Er – anyone want to come with me?'

'You're suggesting the ghost of Soul Snakesmouth is actually at the bottom of this?' scoffed Angelique.

'Well, it isn't Brockler, is it?'

'But only the builders have been in there,' said Lark. 'It's always locked. It's not used for anything yet. And – well, I noticed when we were looking for Hari – the key has gone missing.'

Angelique led the way out of the staff room, into the kitchen and to the closed door everyone shrank from opening. 'Not a problem.' She muttered something under her breath, took out her cane and, with a blinding flash of blue light, the door blasted open.

'Ready when you are, Seth.'

His instincts told him to step as noisily as he could, scare away whatever might be lurking. But they needed to find whatever might be in here. So Seth followed Angelique's slow and noiseless footsteps as they crept through the door that separated the Sunrise Wing from the rest of the lighthouse. Pewter joined them.

It was evening now, and although Dex might have fixed the lights, no one switched them on. Seth was pleased to find the torch he always carried was safely in a pocket. It sent a narrow beam on to the floor just ahead of them.

The noises are quite probably just mice, Seth tried to reassure himself. He told himself he didn't believe in ghosts.

The long windowless corridor, with its white-washed walls and tiled floor, was much colder than the light-filled lighthouse with its thick carpets. But Seth was convinced there was a particularly icy chill in the air now, and that dampness was starting to creep down the back of his neck.

He tried not to imagine invisible fingers stretching out and feeling for him.

The corridor stretched ahead of them, doors on each side. They had come this way before and he had seen inside each room, strewn with rubble and bags of cement. They had seen nothing extraordinary, apart from Jo cramming her pockets with any tools the builders might have left behind.

Seth saw the stairs halfway down on the right. Again, he thought he heard a soft footstep behind him, the brush of breath approaching.

A soft, warm breath right on the back of his neck.

'Pretty big mice,' said Dex's voice right in Seth's ear.

Angelique punched him hard on the arm. 'Don't creep up on us like that. Thought you were the ghost.'

Hadn't Angelique said she didn't believe in the ghost?

'Can't believe you're ghost-hunting and you didn't wait for me,' smiled Dex.

Seth shone his torch at the staircase. On the bottom stair, in the chalky dust of plaster, was a clear footprint.

'Well, that could just be the builders,' whispered Angelique.

'Small feet for builders,' said Dex. 'And most builders tend to wear boots – that's not a bootprint.'

'The noise we all heard before came from upstairs,' said Seth.

'Well then, let's go,' said Dex.

Seth put his own boot alongside the footprint. The print was slightly smaller, just like the one he had found in the sand of the cave back at Snakesmouth village at the entrance to the tunnel that led right up to the lighthouse.

'Alfie?' suggested Angelique.

'He's terrified of this place. Why would he have come here?'

Dex took the lead as they crept up the stairs, still using only the light from Seth's torch, now moving so silently Seth felt none of them were even breathing.

Every sense was alert, his mind spiralling around everything, all the odd things that had happened in the lighthouse since the Mintencresses had bought it. He felt ready for anything. Even Soul Snakesmouth's ghost.

40. PRETTY BIG MICE

But a ghost didn't make that footprint. Seth was busy trying to puzzle it through, trying to make sense of everything. That footstep reminded him that someone had been down that tunnel under the sea recently. And what about that light in the sky?

Seth was trying hard to be a good detective. Concentrate on the facts. Find a way to make it all fit.

He tried to think of the things Pewter had focused on. Things Seth had totally disregarded because they seemed too random. Small mysteries –

food disappearing in the night. Dead gulls. Then there was the map Pewter had spread across the dining-room table, covered with tiny crosses, as though Pewter was on a treasure hunt.

'Last time you were here, there was a noise. Where from?' said Pewter in a low voice as they reached the top of the stairs.

Seth pointed with his torch to the far left of the corridor. All the doors were closed. Dex took his sharp-looking letter opener out from a hidden pocket in his jacket, unsheathed it and sent a low blue light shooting over the first door. There was no crackle, just a silent shimmer, but he quickly gave a nod.

'Something magical has been this way recently,' he said.

He moved to the first door and, with a quick movement, flung it back.

But it revealed nothing but a furnished room with a double bed, a chest of drawers, a desk and a lamp. Rendleton had been right when he'd said some rooms were all ready and waiting for visitors. There was nothing in the bathroom.

The next rooms were exactly the same. The three of them halted by the final door. Dex did exactly the same as he had each time, and flung the door open.

But as he was about to step through, this door was

flung right back and slammed shut in their faces.

Angelique stepped forward again with Dex, flipping the top of her divinoscope, and two flares of blue light flashed simultaneously.

'I've got this,' snapped Dex.

Angelique ignored him and looked deep into the end of her cane. 'No, I really don't think you have. I have a very bad feeling—'

She didn't have chance to finish, as the door was jerked inwards, taking them all completely by surprise. But not nearly as surprised as they were by what happened next.

Seth had convinced himself to expect a tall, grey spectral figure. But the figure that came flying out was small, not at all ghostly.

It was a girl.

Seth registered the girl's long blonde hair, her face in an ugly grimace, her teeth bared as she flew past them while they stood in a stunned, helpless, slow-motion silence. In Seth's mind things had fallen, all too slowly, into place. But now he got it. In fact, he really should have been expecting it, with everything he knew. If only he'd thought everything through correctly. This was the only thing that made every-thing add up and make sense.

'What the hell was that?' said Dex, the first to

recover and start the sprint after her.

'You mean *who* the hell was that,' said Angelique, already after him. 'That was Tiffany Bunn!'

41. Causing Chaos The Whole Time

'Who the heck is she?' said Dex. 'Where did she come from?'

Seth was the last to move, stunned to see the daughter of his former employers run out of the room. He'd warred with Tiffany for as long as he could remember. It was like a recurring nightmare he couldn't escape. Now she was here.

He'd known what she was capable of. Now he thought about it, this was the only answer – only Tiffany could be at the bottom of all of this. Only

Tiffany Bunn being here made everything suddenly make complete sense.

Tiffany had run away from the Last Chance Hotel, having first grabbed the firefly cage, a magical invention of enormous power that had been hidden for years. She'd escaped via a teleport, double-crossing her accomplice who'd helped steal it. But Tiffany would only have risked such a daring escape if she'd already had a good plan to get away. Tiffany must have known exactly where she was headed.

That map covered with crosses Pewter had been examining wasn't about some mad treasure hunt Pewter was engaged in. Of course, they were the places he'd searched. Pewter must have got a trace of her being somewhere near here. That meant he had been searching, probably since the moment she had left the Last Chance Hotel. And Seth had accused him of giving up.

And Tiffany had actually been holed up here at the Snakesmouth Lighthouse causing chaos the whole time. She must have arrived by teleport, and even known she could get to the lighthouse using the tunnel under the sea. What a great place to escape to; an empty and secluded secret hideout, and former home of a sorcerer probably well known to Red Valerian.

The plan had only gone wrong because the Mintencress party had moved in.

Angelique, Dex and Pewter had all started to chase after Tiffany, but shock rendered Seth unable to move.

He looked at the rumpled bed sheets, the dirty plates and cups littering the desk.

But what really terrified him was that around the room were blasted patches and dark scorch marks. Places where the newly plastered walls were charred back to the brick. Exactly the same sort of marks he'd caused himself at the Last Chance Hotel. Marks from his attempts at magic.

With a terrifying swirling sensation in his gut, he knew, with certainty, that in the time Tiffany had spent here she had been perfecting how to use the power of the firefly cage. She had been practising magic. It was Tiffany who had managed powerful enough magic to get Soul Snakesmouth's darkwitching sorcery to start up again.

Seth started to run.

But his mind hadn't stopped making connections. The light in the sky the locals had seen must have been Tiffany – crashing through the teleport carrying the powerful magical light of the firefly cage. The doors slamming, the food going missing, the builders' accidents – Tiffany, trying to scare everyone away from her hideout by playing on all the rumours and local superstition about this place.

She had got away with it while the work was focused on the main lighthouse. But then the builders moved to the Sunrise Wing. By then, Seth guessed, she had found some irresistible success at using the power of the firefly cage, and had tapped into the existing hidden magic. Stirring up the shadows. Seth could even imagine she had thoroughly enjoyed herself with the accidents, fear and havoc she had caused, using her new-found powers to scare off the family.

And she almost succeeded in completely driving everyone away. The builders had fled. Lark and Brockler had pretty much agreed to talk Mina into getting out. But Tiffany hadn't reckoned on someone quite so determined as Mina.

He arrived in the kitchen to be met by Lark, her eyes blazing in a deathly pale face. Her hands were clenched by her sides. 'She's taken Alfie.'

Mina whispered, 'I hadn't even had a chance to tell him I'm alive. Rendleton went straight after her and told us we had to wait here. The others followed. Outside.'

42. WHAT IF HE WAS WRONG?

The wind whipped at Seth as he plunged outside. He was shocked to see the sky was already midnight blue. All he could hear in his ears was the roar of the wind. Which way had they gone?

Using his torchlight to guide him, Seth headed up to the cliffs and down the paths making towards Gull Cove – the best way on and off the island. But Jo wasn't there in her boat. Surely Tiffany had no way of escape – they knew she hadn't used the tunnel – but she did have Alfie.

'Pssst, over here, Seth.' It was Dex, crouched among some rocks with Pewter and Angelique where the paths went in different directions. Seth hurried over to join them.

'First rule of war – know your enemy,' said Pewter. 'Seth, what would she do?'

'She'll have a plan. She's smart. She'll use Alfie to force us to help her. And she's got a dark device of really sinister and immensely powerful magic that she won't hesitate to use on him or us. She's been practising magic. She's got the shadows working for her. She's become powerful and she's responsible for those two deaths.'

'I was thinking of something more positive.'

'Believe me, there is nothing positive about having Tiffany as your enemy.'

'And she's been hiding at this lighthouse?' said Dex.

'Not so much lying low as spreading a little mayhem and murder,' muttered Pewter. 'I never dreamt she'd get so far with working out how to get the power out of that device.'

'Everyone always underestimates Tiffany,' said Seth.

He knew his panic was growing, but he had to think. What would she be planning? Could they get one step ahead?

'Why not wait for her to come to us? She needs us to get off this island,' said Dex.

Seth cried: 'The boathouse! There's an old rowing boat there. Leaving after dark in some sort of rickety boat would be exactly Tiffany's plan – and we don't have another boat to follow her.'

'And she's got the firefly cage to help her,' finished Angelique.

'You keep saying that,' said Dex. 'Are those things even real?'

'Real, and deathly dangerous,' said Seth.

He'd barely got his words out before Angelique was flying through the darkness, heading for Gull Cove.

The going was difficult in the dark, and there was no sign of Rendleton, Tiffany, or Alfie. Were they ahead? Or had Seth guessed Tiffany's plan wrong? Was she hiding, ready to leap out and take them by surprise?

They all hesitated at the top of at the ridge overlooking Gull Cove. From here there was a good view of the beach below.

'Do we go down?' wavered Angelique, as they crouched in the shadow of a large rock.

The wind was sending clouds scudding across the starry sky. Every now and again they'd get a helpful slip of moonlight. Seth scoured the beach below, desperate for any sign of movement that told them they weren't too late, that he had guessed correctly. The waiting was awful.

Which way would Tiffany come? Or was she here, already in that boathouse, about to make good her escape? Seth tried to slow his breathing, afraid she would be able to hear him, imagining that in the dark she was right behind him. And she'd know how terrified he was.

But he also couldn't stop thinking about the tunnel. She knew about the tunnel, he was sure of it. What if she was planning to use that instead? What if she'd lured them all outside and then doubled back to the entrance in the kitchen?

'You've been looking for her, haven't you? Since you left the Last Chance Hotel?' he said in a low voice to Pewter.

'We've been searching places she might be hiding, yes. Never thought of the lighthouse, because she wouldn't have a boat. Such a brave and dangerous game she's played.' Pewter sounded almost in awe.

'Red Valerian must have still been after the firefly cage,' said Angelique. 'And knew where it was after Tiffany took it from the Last Chance Hotel – he'd had a hand in setting up the teleport she escaped in after all, and he'll know all about Soul Snakesmouth. But he also knew about the Mintencress party moving in to the lighthouse. So he sent in that undercover maid to find the firefly cage and bring it back to him.'

'But Tiffany has stayed one step ahead of Red Valerian – that isn't something most people could do,' said Dex, also sounding impressed.

If they didn't catch her she'd disappear. And she'd take the firefly cage with her. She'd get away completely. Seth pictured Tiffany, running free, a smile on her face. Only then did he think again of something else that had been increasingly bothering him. He always listened to how magic worked, tried to learn it all. And he'd thought for some time that there might be a sorcerer trapped inside that firefly cage.

There was so much at stake. Tiffany still had Alfie. What if he was wrong? Should he go and check the tunnel? He couldn't believe there was just silence, that nothing was happening.

'We have to go down,' he said, unable to bear just watching and waiting any longer.

'Let's plan a little surprise,' said Dex, nodding.

But Seth could only feel, as they moved cautiously down the cliff and the steep steps hewn in the rock, that any surprises were going to come from Tiffany.

It was difficult to approach silently on shingle. Seth kept imagining Tiffany listening to their approach from the boathouse, already hauling out the boat, forcing a terrified Alfie to help her. And where was Rendleton?

Pewter spoke quietly. 'Just to be clear, our priority is Alfie. I'm afraid capturing Miss Bunn comes second.'

Seth nodded in the darkness, but he hated that that meant there was a chance they'd have to let Tiffany get away.

He was straining his ears, his eyes, his keen nose, but was only aware of the soft swooshing of waves trundling up the beach and the gentle crunch of shingle under their feet.

Then the thinnest slip of moonlight broke cover from the clouds – it was enough, because they could make out two figures on the opposite side of the beach, already near the boathouse.

There was a soft whimper and Seth could see a small shape being dragged by a larger one: Tiffany, holding an unwilling Alfie. She must have scrambled further along the clifftop than they had, knowing that the most dangerous part of her journey was crossing the beach.

Dex's thin blade glinted in the moonlight as they all crept closer. Seth spotted another figure close on Tiffany's tail. Rendleton. And he really had no idea what he was dealing with.

'Idiot, he's going to get himself killed,' said Dex, extending his dagger arm, but Rendleton was already between him and Tiffany.

'Remember – we make sure Alfie is safe,' said Pewter.

The moonlight must have given Rendleton the same idea – that now was the best time to break cover. He launched into a sprint.

But Tiffany was on to him. Seth watched in horror as she swung around and lifted aloft a tiny cage, gripped in the hand that wasn't clutching Alfie's arm. The firefly cage.

A mesmerizing golden light spilled from between its intricate bars. Now Seth knew for sure how much Tiffany had been practising. The light was responding to her. It blasted out from the magical device in her hand, showing her face in all its gleaming triumph.

The beam flew out of the cage and struck Rendleton right in the chest. Seth watched him collapse on to the shingle without even the chance to let out a cry. He dropped like a stone, and was no longer moving.

Dex had lifted his dagger, but even he had paused after seeing how effortlessly Tiffany had dealt with Rendleton.

But she didn't pause; she was at the boathouse door and bundled Alfie inside.

Dex sped past Rendleton's prone body and on towards the boathouse. Seth pelted across the beach behind him with Pewter and Angelique, all three of them splashing through the incoming tide.

Pewter was the first to reach Rendleton, and knelt to check for life-signs.

He looked up. 'Not dead, not quite, not yet. But we're going to have to get him some magical medical attention as quickly as possible.' He threw an anxious look at Dex's running figure, and was already cupping a ball of pink light in his hand. 'Seth, Angelique – help Dex. But don't forget – the priority is that boy. Don't let her hurt him.'

Seth nodded and set off at a sprint, but by the time he and Angelique reached the small wooden building, all they found was Dex standing outside, looking furiously out from the empty boathouse into the inky darkness beyond, where Seth could just make out a boat pushing on into the cover of the night.

43. A DANGEROUS MIX OF MAGIC

'I couldn't stop her. Not with Alfie there,' Dex muttered in agitation, pushing a hand through hair already dishevelled by the wind. 'We can't let her get away. She took the boy with her.'

Seth helplessly listened to the splash of oars from the retreating boat. Before he could even think of his next course of action, he saw the firefly cage being raised and dragged Dex out of its path.

A jet of golden light flashed and they threw themselves on the ground. At the last second, the golden light turned to a bolt of white and made a direct hit on the cliff right behind them. There was an explosion and a section of rock behind them disintegrated, dust and debris raining down on them.

Seth covered his head with his hands in a futile attempt to ward off the torrent of rocks and tried to scramble to his feet. A spray of grit flew right into his face, sending him into a fit of choking.

He struggled to see. He knew Tiffany would be using these precious few seconds to pull away strongly in the boat, beyond their reach. He turned and, realizing there was no longer a need for secrecy, flicked on his torch. Its faint beam revealed Angelique's dark hair laced with a covering of rock dust, and a trickle of red blood running down her hand. Dex's face had lost its usual grin. He had come off the worst. Blood was pouring down his arm and there was a gash in his leather jacket.

Another bolt shot over their heads, they ducked, there was an almighty crack and this time a huge shard of cliff dislodged. A massive boulder was falling towards them, fast.

Then Pewter was there, and Seth felt a wave of air move past him, strong enough to nearly knock him off his feet. It deflected the boulder away from them at the last second, sending it bouncing effortlessly into the sea like a giant stone being skimmed.

'Alfie?' asked Pewter.

Dex shook his head.

Seth now had only one idea. He cupped his hands around his mouth and yelled.

'Alfie! Jump! Swim! You can swim, Alfie, it's not far. You can do it! You can get away. She can't stop you.'

He knew Alfie would be terrified. But he also knew how strongly the boy could swim, and with Tiffany distracted by sending bolts of lightning after them, she couldn't yet be so very far out. They were going to have to rely on the boy taking his chance. And if they could get Alfie to safety, they might stand a chance of capturing Tiffany.

Another helpful shift in the clouds revealed exactly what Seth had thought – Tiffany was not yet far from the beach.

'Now, Alfie – please, just jump!' yelled Seth. 'Swim to the shore!'

He could see that the firefly cage was no longer being held aloft. Tiffany was making a huge effort to row away. But Alfie was rigid with fear.

Seth remembered one thing that might make a difference.

'Mina is alive! She's waiting for you. Alfie, you can

do this – you can swim. Mina is desperate to see you. She's waiting back at the lighthouse.' As he said the words he hoped she was keeping a safe distance and that she wouldn't, like Rendleton, decide to blunder in, thinking she could help.

Tiffany was rapidly putting clear water between herself and the shore. Pewter, Dex and Angelique were simply standing there. None of them could do a thing as long as Tiffany had Alfie. And then the fire-fly cage was lifted and swayed in her hand again.

There was a rumble behind them. Pewter swung around, curling his arms and fingers and making a movement as if he was throwing something towards the cliff. But the rumbling continued, and rocks began to tumble towards them.

Seth felt helpless. But then he was convinced he'd heard a splash. He dashed up to his knees in water, scouring the dark sea, trying to make out what was happening, searching for the shape and movement of the boy swimming towards him. Pewter was working hard to counteract the rockfall, bringing the largest boulders to land gently on the beach. Angelique and Dex were helping him.

Seth waded further out, trying to find Alfie in the darkness.

The boy was fully clothed. It was dark and cold.

Had Seth done completely the wrong thing telling him to jump overboard?

'I think Alfie's jumped!' screamed Seth. 'But I can't see him!'

Dex turned and sent an exploratory jet of fierce blue from his dagger flashing out towards the boat.

Tiffany intercepted the shot with the firefly cage. She waved it, swaying it from side to side, until the sea around her started to bubble and boil, the waves rising.

Alfie would be in the middle of that.

And it was no longer just water. The waves were forming themselves into ice, becoming a torrent of sharp spears hurtling their way to the shore, right towards them.

'Get down!' yelled Dex, only feebly able to deflect a couple of spears with the light of his dagger. He and Seth hurled themselves flat on to the shingle and could only watch as the ice spears flew up the beach to where Pewter and Angelique were deflecting the last of the boulders safely.

'Get down!' yelled Dex again.

Pewter turned just in time to sidestep the first spear. There were dozens coming at him and he and Angelique threw themselves behind one of the huge boulders. Ice spears smashed into the boulder and splintered into thousands of tiny shards.

The inspector, dodging oncoming ice spears, ran right down to the edge of the waves, and gestured with his arms again. Seth watched as a bubble of magic scooped deep into the water and lifted a spluttering Alfie safely to shore, where he lay gulping like a fish.

Dex threw the boy over his shoulder and tore back up the beach as fast as he could.

Angelique was sending out jets of blue light across the water, but they were falling a long way from the boat. Any bolts Tiffany was sending out of the firefly cage were also now feeble and badly directed.

Alfie was safe, but the moonlight showed that Tiffany wasn't even bothering to fight any more. She had picked up the oars again. She was nearly out of the cove and on her way to freedom. She was going to get away.

44. WE DO WHAT ALL SORCERERS DO

'We can't just let her go. We have to do something!' yelled Seth.

'We've no boat,' said Angelique, sounding equally helpless, small glistening rocks scattered in her hair like diamonds. 'No way of catching her.'

Seth looked from Pewter to Angelique, hoping desperately to hear an idea, hardly able to watch as the determined figure in the small boat left the trivial waves of Gull Cove behind and hit the sea that surrounded Snakesmouth Island.

'You two must be able to do something.'

'We do what all sorcerers always do,' said Pewter, softly. 'We work with what we have. Don't forget, she's only using someone else's magic – she has no power of her own, whereas we are four talented sorcerers. Come on, the game is not over yet.'

Pewter started off up the beach. He might not yet have a plan, but he hadn't given up. And *four* sorcerers? That meant Pewter was including Seth.

Dex met them at the top of the cliff; Alfie must already be back at the lighthouse. The agent kept darting looks out to sea, and it didn't take more than the sliver of moonlight they had to show he was tasting bitter defeat and not liking it one bit.

'I must get Rendleton off the beach,' said Pewter. 'You three go on. If you go over the top of the island, I think we might still have surprise on our side. Work together. I'm counting on you. I will join you as soon as I have made Rendleton comfortable.'

Seth didn't need telling twice and started to run. They would be up high and in a good position to see Tiffany round the spur of Gull Cove. They must get in a good position before she rounded the point.

The three of them stood there in the moonlight, buffeted by the wind. It was back to waiting.

Dex and Angelique were poised at the top of the

cliff, Angelique's glossy hair blowing wild. They waited until, finally, the prow of the rowing boat came around the farthest rocky outcrop. Tiffany surely must be struggling and growing tired now, even though she was drawing most of her strength and power from the firefly cage.

'She thinks she's away. She already thinks she's won,' said Dex. He took out his dagger. 'This is not over yet.' This time, as he held his silver dagger aloft, it grew until it became a shining sword. Definitely not a letter opener.

Angelique lifted her red cane.

Out in the boat, Seth could see Tiffany put down the oars and lift the firefly cage in reply.

As Dex gripped his sword in readiness, Angelique dropped her cane. 'It's too dangerous to mix too many different kinds of magic,' she said. 'We daren't bring in too much, we'll have no proper control over it, anything could happen.'

Dex nodded, and waited not a second longer to blast Tiffany with a jet of pure blue. Seth watched her knocked backwards as the spear of light collided with the boat.

The waves around Tiffany were pulling and tugging against her rickety boat. Her face, illuminated by another blast from Dex and mixed with the moonlight, showed a flash of fear. But that was quickly replaced with one of determination, as she once more lifted the firefly cage. A golden light started to build inside it. Seth sensed she was going to call on something new.

There was an eerie silence, as though something was muffling even the sound of the wind and the waves. At the same time, they lost the light of the moon. A silent darkness was upon them, like a thick blanket thrown over everything.

Seth realized with fear what it was, and the citrusy tang in the air confirmed it. 'She's been learning how to control the remnants of shadow magic on this island,' he said in a warning voice. 'Look out!' he cried, spinning to try to see what was approaching, but he could see only darkness.

He shouldn't even have been able to notice the shadows arriving, but there was some peculiar quality to their darkness – they didn't just blank out the light, but seemed to absorb it – that meant Seth knew that they were swarming.

'We'll need to hit the shadows with everything we've got, and we'll barely see them coming.'

But they could feel those dark shadows, cloying in the air, making it seem thicker and more dangerous.

Seth braced himself and was suddenly struck

again by Pewter's words. *Four sorcerers*. He was a sorcerer too. And as the first tendril of shadow reached him, he had just enough time to remember his battle with them in the lighthouse. He slipped out the black book from under his tunic, and smacked it as hard as he could into the darkening air around him, hitting out again and again.

Seth could just make out that Pewter had joined them. His hands were moving rapidly through the air. Seth wasn't sure what he was doing, but unless he was imagining it, as Pewter's hands moulded the air, the waves below were getting bigger.

The inspector was concentrating on bringing Tiffany in to shore, and Seth knew he had to protect him from the shadows while he did so. Swiping the silently deadly air, he moved closer to Pewter. The inspector was standing firm on the clifftop, his long silver hair curling around him, his fingers flexed forward, making Seth think that he was standing side by side with the wizard Merlin, back in a time when everyone had known of and believed in the existence of magic.

A shadow rope lashed out at Pewter, snaking itself around his neck, forcing him to grasp to free himself from the strangling rope. The waves dropped, the inspector's hold on them broken.

Angelique flipped the top of her red cane and zapped with a fierce blue light, narrowly missing Seth's head as he battled on, using his black book as a cross between a club and a sword, ignoring anything coming for him and just hitting and hitting at the snake that was attacking Pewter.

Dex tried to grab the shadows with his bare hands.

'Use your dagger!' Seth heard Angelique yell.

'You said . . . too much magic about,' Dex yelled back, wrestling with a shadow snake that was inching him backwards to the edge of the cliff.

'I know what I said!' growled Angelique. 'Forget that!'

Dex lifted his dagger, now shrunk back to its original size, and an intense light began to glow around him. It expanded to take in all four of them as they battled and blasted the shadow ropes.

Dex then began to twist his dagger, and Seth could feel there was a loosening of the bonding power of the shadows. Dex started to draw them together, to control them. It was as if they were growing sticky and thick, less sure and slower-moving, as if the air was growing sluggish.

The shadows were growing weaker, Seth could feel it as he struck out again.

Finally Dex twisted, shook himself free and began to use his dagger to guide the shadows to him. He started to wind them around and around, waving the dagger through the air, twirling it again and again, gathering all the loosely bonded shapes together so the ball of darkness grew. The shadows started to look as innocent as candy floss.

Then, as the shadow attack subsided, Dex put his hands around the ball and compressed it down and down. Soon it was so small that he was able to reach into his pocket, pull out a bottle and shove the whole lot inside, before sticking a stopper in the neck.

He heaved a sigh of relief. 'Told you I was pretty expert in darkwitching!'

But they'd all taken their eyes off the boat. Seth looked out to sea, expecting Tiffany to be no more than a dark speck distant in the water, a determined figure drifting further and further from their reach, picked out by a channel of the palest moonlight. But he couldn't even see her.

45. FORGET THE RULES

Seth's insides clutched in crushing disappointment.

He scoured the horizon. Pewter was at his side, his hands gesturing again to the waves. Seth could tell the inspector hadn't stopped using his own magic; gentle, yet strong. He kept at it, but he'd never turn that tide. Tiffany would be far out to sea.

Then the moon seemed once more on their side, and Seth was suddenly able to pick out the boat. The reason he hadn't seen her was because he'd been looking in completely the wrong place. She must have been so busy using the firefly cage to control those shadows that she hadn't had a chance to row. She wasn't any further out at all; if anything, Pewter's magic had brought her closer to the island. Was she still within their reach?

'Forget the rules.' Angelique said. She raised her cane, Dex his dagger alongside, and Angelique gave a short nod. 'Just blast her with everything we've got.'

Angelique rained bolt after bolt of blue light on the boat. The sea boiled. Dex's dagger once again reformed to a silver sword and Seth could see, in the weird mix of moonlight and competing magical flashes, that the waves looked just like they had during the storm – angry, and as they wanted to hurt someone.

Seth watched, wanting to do more than will his friends on, wishing more than ever that he had a spark of magic to offer. He clung to his black book, and suddenly it felt like someone was whispering. The words came to him and he yelled them into the wind at the top of his voice.

'*Yma nam-well!*'

The capturing spell from his mother's book had come back to him like a thunderbolt.

He did exactly as Pewter was doing; kept his arms

outstretched, flexed his fingers, as if beckoning something to him. He raised his arms and said the words, repeating them over and over, yelling them out to sea.

He felt his hands jerk.

They seemed to snag, as if he had something on a hook. He felt something tugging back on his hands, getting stronger and stronger, and he had to lean backwards to control it. But he didn't care. He didn't care who was watching and if this ended in scorch marks and blasting and disaster.

Then, just when it seemed as if they must be winning, that Tiffany was running out of anything to throw at them, there was another blast of light from the firefly cage and a shower of ice spears flew towards them.

Seth was so focused on the tugging feeling in his hands that he didn't want to move. He didn't see the spear hurtling towards him, the pointed blade as sharp as a rapier.

He did feel the impact a second later. Something had slammed into him from the side – Dex had flung himself at Seth, and they were both now sprawled on the ground. Seth sat up, winded. He tried to make out the tiny boat in the huge waves, tried to tell whether Tiffany was going to win, but then he saw that Dex hadn't moved. He just lying flat out on the ground, blood on his face, his eyes closed.

'We're nearly there!' yelled Angelique.

Seth leaned over Dex, feeling for any signs he was still alive.

He felt a pulse, enough for now. Seth stood, lifted his arms and it was as if the words of the summoning spell were ripped out of him again. He was barely aware of Pewter and Angelique, lost in a dark whirlwind that blinded his eyes and clouded his mind. *Yma nam-well.*

The boat was moving towards them, seemingly carried on the crest of a wave that grew quickly, draining all the water from the sea around it as it sucked and spewed and lifted the boat higher and higher, all to the sound of Tiffany's terrified screams.

The crest was level with the clifftop now, and Seth could see Tiffany was clutching the boat with both hands as the vast wave began crashing down on to the beach below them, water cascading in every direction.

Pewter was running down the path to the beach now, but Seth was still repeating the words again and again, over and over – he couldn't stop.

The last of the waves splashed down on him, soaking him and Dex like a bucket of cold water.

Seth finally stopped reciting the spell, and turned to see Dex shaking the water from his hair and getting to his feet.

Seth staggered to the cliff edge and looked down. The tidal wave had gone. There was a spent flatness now about the water. The waves had subsided to a gentle ripple and there was a darkness to them that seemed bottomless.

Of the boat there was no sign. Had it been swallowed by the endlessly dark and greedy sea?

And there was no sign of Tiffany. They might have stopped her, but they hadn't captured her. And that meant they had lost the firefly cage. It would be sinking to the bottom, past the fish and the weeds and heading slowly for the sand and the rocks.

Seth ran down the path and edged nearer the water, picturing the firefly cage sinking slowly on its final journey. It was lost for ever among the creatures of the sea, taking with it his last hope of ever finding out if anything of the sorcerer's spirit trapped inside it remained, any chance of freeing that poor soul whose power Tiffany had been stealing.

'Get it, Seth,' instructed Angelique's voice sharply, right alongside his ear. 'Get it.'

'It's gone.'

'You're close to it. You can get it.'

'It'll be at the bottom of the sea.'

'Only you can do it.'

Seth raised his hands again. He felt a faint tug, as if he had fish on the end of a line with one fight left in it.

He stared at his fingers and reacted instinctively, moving his hands, lifting, reeling in, bringing the sea and the waves closer.

And then, as if it truly was caught on a line, the firefly cage erupted from the water in a jet of white foam and flew into his hand. Pewter immediately sent out another bubble of magic and, just as expertly as he had done with Alfie, he scooped up a bubble containing Tiffany and brought her dripping and coughing on to the beach.

46. CASE OVER

It was tiny. So very small, even smaller than Seth remembered. Far too small to contain a whole human being. Perhaps he was wrong.

Seth clung to the cage, still not quite able to believe it was in his hands and not at the bottom of the sea. But as he clasped it to him, there was no trace of warmth, of light, of anything that might give a sign that it was anything other than an empty cage made of flimsy twisted wire. It did not look the least bit powerful.

He wasn't sure how long he stood there, lost in the howling wind and the rioting waves – the sea was once again its own master, and seemed furious at having been manipulated. He was numb with cold, exhausted to his bones, and barely moved until he became aware of Angelique speaking in a low voice and trying to prise the firefly cage from him.

He swiped it away from her, clutching it more fiercely – he would have started to run, but he could no longer feel his legs.

He felt a warmth flood through him and it seemed to unfreeze his mind as well as his body. He could see Angelique, her face a picture of concern, putting out a hand to steer him along the path.

When they reached the clifftop Dex was on his feet, grinning, despite his leather jacket bearing a significant scorch mark and a trickle of drying blood spoiling the side of his face. He was clearly dazed, and not fully aware of what had happened. 'Well, that didn't go quite as expected. Did we win?' He scoured the raging sea, swaying a little.

Pewter pointed to where Tiffany floated behind him, tugged along by a piece of twine, like a balloon. Her face looked serene, her cloud of blonde hair making her look like an angel, hovering above them. It was almost unbelievable that someone who looked so sweet could have such a rotten core.

Alfie had described the ghost as an angel. Had he caught sight of her, perhaps sneaking down to steal food from the kitchen?

'She's under magical arrest,' explained Pewter. 'Keeps prisoners very quiet and easy to manoeuvre. Tricky one for the Elysee; they're going to hate me bringing in someone non-magical for questioning. Nothing I ever do leads to a promotion.'

'Non-magical?' repeated Dex, wiping away the blood that still flowed from his forehead. 'Could have fooled me.'

'All down to this little trinket,' said Pewter. He'd taken the firefly cage out of Seth's hands before he could even realize.

Seth stood awkwardly in front of Dex. 'Thanks, Stormforce. You . . . thanks.'

Dex wiped another smear of blood from his handsome face. 'Hey, blood spilled . . . does that make us like brothers now?'

He grinned, and Seth shook his freezing hand.

They made a silent procession back to the lighthouse. Seth's heart felt like someone had put a hand inside his chest and was squeezing it.

He felt sure that the power Tiffany had tapped into must belong to some poor sorcerer who had been trapped in the firefly cage. Now they'd got it back, what would they find? Would the sorcerer still be alive? Would there be even a spirit remaining?

Ever since he'd understood that the evil magical device had been kept at the Last Chance Hotel, he'd felt a connection to it, a responsibility. He'd wanted to find Tiffany, get his revenge, make sure she was not able to seize the power of the firefly cage and wreak havoc. But he'd also wondered about that poor trapped soul.

He kept his eyes locked on the cage, desperate to know if there was any chance of releasing someone alive from such a prison. The cage itself no longer looked alive.

Seth didn't know where the chair or the cup of tea appeared from. He vaguely remembered being guided into the kitchen and Pewter talking in a low voice, assuring Mina and Lark that Alfie was OK and that Rendleton would recover. He clasped the cup, feeling its heat between his fingers.

Then he felt a comforting lump throw itself on to his lap, and a purring noise start up like a kettle boiling, and all he really wanted to do was put his head on Nightshade's soft fur and sleep.

'Well, five of you set off after Tiffany and only

four came back. Rendleton didn't make it?'

Seth stroked her soft fur, the feeling bringing life back to his weary limbs, blood flowing to his fingertips. He reached for his scalding tea. 'Think Rendleton has been taken to some sort of magical doctor by Pewter already.'

'And Tiffany?'

'Tiffany's magical power had grown unbelievably – she'd tapped into the firefly cage. But we won.'

'Off to MagiCon HQ for her, then,' said Night-shade, shifting her claws like needles into Seth's legs. 'Hope they don't let her out in a hurry. Then there's Brockler and the maid's bodies to be shifted some-where. And I guess an S3 team will come in and clean this place again and make it properly tidy. Case over.'

Seth was aware of Dex and Angelique talking in low voices. He could make out Angelique telling the story of how the firefly cage had ended up in Tiffany's hands. A story that Seth had been part of, but that already seemed like a long time ago.

'Its inventor, Dr Thallomius, had been trying to locate it for years. Only it was snatched by Tiffany.'

Dex lifted a cloth out of an inner pocket of his leather jacket and unwrapped it to reveal the dragon's tooth carving.

Angelique sucked in a hesitant breath. 'You should be careful with that.'

'Oh, I intend to be. I certainly don't want to be hanging on to it longer than I need to. Celeste Crackling and Hari Brockler were both wearing this when they died.

'So –' he fixed Angelique with his lop-sided smile – 'Tiffany. What do you think? Did she manipulate the shadows, or was the carving somehow programmed to get the shadows to attack? What I'm saying is – did she mean to kill Mina or the maid or Brockler?'

Angelique was shaking her head and frowning. 'Magic is so complicated,' she sighed. 'It's possible we'll never know how much harm she actually intended. Perhaps she really didn't know what she was doing.'

If Seth wasn't so weary he'd have spoken up and said he thought differently. He knew Tiffany. Those scorch marks in the room where she'd been hiding out told how hard she'd been working to discover the power of the firefly cage. She wouldn't have wanted to use that power for anything good. He could easily believe everything bad about Tiffany, but he also knew it would be almost impossible to prove.

'I guess that will be the focus of the magical interrogation,' said Pewter, strolling in and snatching up one of the chocolate digestive biscuits Angelique had put in front of Seth. 'Hope it'll put a stop to her having any magical ambitions. But actually, somehow, I doubt it.'

He went on cheerily. 'So, Rendleton's in a better place. Tiffany probably in a worse one. Who or what is next?'

Angelique slid a book alongside the biscuits. Seth glanced at the cover. *The Shocking Secrets of the Firefly Cage*.

'You've been working out what to do with it once you tracked it down?' said Dex, helping himself to three biscuits, taking the seat next to Seth and flicking through the book.

Angelique nodded, but sighed. 'But there is so little we know. That is about the only book I could find on the subject and it doesn't really tell us anything.'

Pewter placed the tiny, intricately carved cage in the centre of the table so they could all study it closely. It was only the size of a tin of beans, but beautifully crafted. The difference now was that it had lost its magical light.

'I guess the best thing is just to have a little go

ourselves and hope for the best,' said Pewter.

It was hardly reassuring.

Seth knew that for everyone else, today might be just another job, another few dangerous magical artefacts taken out of circulation. But Seth stroked Nightshade and waited. For him it felt so much more personal than that.

He felt Pewter looking at him earnestly. 'Now, Seth, you need to understand. Miss Squerr and I have tried to research this. But a firefly cage is a rare thing. I have to be honest here, no one knows what'll happen if we open it. So maybe we shouldn't.'

'You can open it?' asked Seth, stroking Night-shade more rapidly.

'I think we can, yes. But, really, it's up to you.'

'Me? I don't know anything.'

The firefly cage looked dark, with none of that flowing golden light. Had the sorcerer inside been alive up until tonight? It didn't look anything more than a piece of fancy metalwork. Had they recovered it only to fail at the last minute?

'Seems not to be glowing now. But it's been used a lot today,' said Dex.

'And it ended up at the bottom of the sea,' muttered Seth.

Pewter put his hands in the pockets of his shiny

suit. 'I guess the sensible thing would be to deliver it to the Elysee. Put it in the hands of the best people.'

'Like the ones who cleaned this place?' added Seth.

'There are a lot of risks if we just open it,' said Angelique.

Nightshade leapt from Seth's lap on to the table and nudged it with her pink nose. 'Of course he wants it open,' she said.

'Or,' said Angelique timidly, 'we could wait and do it in a hospital. In case—' she didn't finish. 'Seth, you do realize that we think—'

'What if someone else snatches it on the way to the hospital?' scoffed Nightshade. 'If it was me trapped in that thing, I'd just want it opened as quickly as possible.'

Pewter looked at Seth and all he could do was nod.

Pewter moved towards the cage, something already in his hand. He reached towards one side of the intricate metalwork, there was a small click, and Seth saw he had used a tiny key – a small piece of bone carved with symbols – to unlock the firefly cage.

Seth suddenly panicked. What was the hurry? Angelique was right – they should do this some-where safer, better equipped. He moved to stop

Pewter, to snatch his hand away. But before he could, a blinding flash of light filled the room and they all had to turn away.

Seth blinked away the white blobs that floated in his vision. He could see the door to the firefly cage was standing open. And he was looking at a woman, small and delicate, looking wan and drawn, with tiny hands and feet and untidy light-brown hair, but with kindly eyes. A woman he didn't recognize at all, but whose eyes widened as she lifted her arms and stretched them towards him.

And before she even spoke, something inside of him told him who it was.

'Seth, my boy, you found me.'

'Mum?'

She stretched out her arms further and Seth ran towards her – just as she collapsed on to the kitchen floor.

47. SHE WAS ALREADY GONE

Seth knew he shouted something. He'd been thinking, *Pewter didn't know what he was doing. He'd let her out too soon. He had killed her*, but he was too horrified, to traumatized, too out of his depth to do more than garble gibberish at the inspector, who, anyway, took no notice.

'I told you we should have done this in a hospital,' said Pewter.

Angelique and Pewter knelt alongside the prone body on the kitchen floor.

Seth saw the inspector gather air, as he'd seen him do before when he was sparking a light for them to see ahead, or creating a force to throw at something in their way. But this time, Pewter was reaching further, and Seth saw a telltale shimmer in the air.

'I'm taking her to where she'll get the best care, Seth,' said Pewter, scooping his mother into his arms and stepping towards the teleport. And then he was gone. She was gone.

'Where? Which hospital?' said Seth desperately. He'd seen his mother for a few fleeting seconds after years of believing she was dead and now she was already gone.

He turned desperately to Angelique. 'He's taken her. Where have they gone? Can I go too?' he asked in a small voice.

'She's been under a severe magical enchantment and attack for a long time,' Angelique said gently. 'Inspector Pewter's got a brother who's the very best at this kind of thing, or it may be a cousin. He's got a pretty big magical family. He'll come and take you to her – but when the time is right. Seth, you must trust in that.'

'Must I?'

'Has he let you down before?'

'Frequently.'

But she was right. If ever Seth doubted Pewter it was usually because Seth had got it wrong. Pewter, in fact, had never let him down.

Angelique poured him more tea.

'That magic you did, Seth, that was amazing. You have been studying a lot harder than you let on.'

Seth was suddenly back on that windy clifftop, standing side by side with Angelique and Pewter as they'd fired shots and made the waves huge.

'I was just there, Angelique. You, Dex and Pewter were doing all the magic. You may as well know I've been practising basic spells for weeks ...' He thought of that blackened door, the sour burning milk. 'It was all mixed up out there. None of it could have been mine. I haven't been able to master a single spell.'

He felt better and worse at the same time for having admitted it. He was exhausted. He'd been trying to do magic for weeks with only disasters and humiliation to show for it. It would be a relief to give it all up.

He'd captured Tiffany and recovered Dr Thallomius's firefly cage. There was a chance his mother might recover enough for him to one day be with her again. Did he really need magic? He could manage without it.

There was a long silence. Long enough for Seth to start thinking how much he wanted to go home, back to his hotel, to cooking – he was good at that. He guessed someone had to tell Mr and Mrs Bunn that their precious daughter had been found, but that she was under magical arrest. He also guessed that pleasant little duty would fall to him.

The silence was broken by Pewter, who suddenly stepped through the back door. 'OK, we've got one injured, one dead – no, two.' He slapped his forehead. 'The body in the cellar. One of Red Valerian's followers, at least an ex-follower, wouldn't do to leave a body lying around for someone to stumble on. Oh, and Tiffany under magical arrest. It's going to be a long night with some very uncomfortable paperwork. Decided where you want to be dropped off, Seth?'

'I still don't understand why I can't be with my mum.'

Pewter laid a warm hand on his shoulder. 'All in good time, Seth. She's in the best place and there is nothing you can do for her right at this moment. All I can ask is that you trust me with her care.'

Seth nodded, having no choice but to hope Pewter was right. 'Then home, please, Inspector. I'm going back to the kitchen at the Last Chance Hotel.

But don't leave me there with no news – I want to know how she's doing, good or bad.'

Pewter nodded. 'I've done my best to explain everything to the remaining Mintencress party. Don't know if they understood a word of it. One does one's best with magic. I've also explained about the cleaning. Should be safe enough here for them – eventually. I wish that things would work out more simply for me once in a while. I have a feeling two bodies may well make my bosses think I've been rather careless. All in all, though, we've done rather a good job here.'

Seth nodded. Things really had turned OK for him too. 'I'm pretty tired,' was all he said.

'Expect you need a break from magic!' said Pewter, clapping him hard on the back and making Seth slop his tea. 'I understand if you don't fancy giving me a hand for a while.'

'It's kind of worse, you know,' Seth tried to explain, 'knowing about magic but also knowing you're not any good at it.'

He looked up and saw the confused faces of Dex and Pewter. Angelique was shaking her head. He realized the feeling must be totally alien to them.

'I really can't do magic,' Seth whispered. Then said louder: 'I told you, I'm no good at all. I've tried and tried the basics. I know when it's time to give up.'

'Not magic?' Pewter looked at him with his brilliant blue eyes. 'Seth, even terrifically talented sorcerers had to start somewhere. But you – you've got magic pouring out of you. I can smell it on you. You've got enough magic that if you sprung a magic leak you wouldn't even notice it dribbling away. Your trouble is that magic wants to flash out of you like a firecracker. It's the holding it in you're struggling with. It's the controlling it – making sure it doesn't control you. And that is particularly important for you, with your mother, you know that.'

Seth took a moment to take this in. His first thought was not to believe it. Then he was thinking back to that clifftop and how that summoning spell from his mother's book had flown into his mind. He felt the black book glow warm against his chest, his only connection to his mother. Had he really done magic? And if he had, was it of the wrong kind?

'Practising somewhere quiet where no one's going to get hurt is a smart place to start,' went on Pewter. 'Thought the Last Chance Hotel could not be more perfect – in case there were a few false starts and out-of-control explosions.'

'What you need is some nice, safe, simple spell you can demonstrate without blowing anyone's ears off,' advised Dex, who had been silently munching his way through the biscuits. 'It's not doing the magic – it's doing it well and in a controlled way. My advice is to try to avoid turning up at the Prospect and doing a spell that ends up blowing up the Sorcerer General. Might take longer than you realize.'

'I could help,' offered Angelique in a small voice. 'If you'd like.'

Mina, Lark and Alfie arrived before Seth could reply.

Mina looked so different in her smart clothes, her long hair no longer under a cap – it was like looking at a different person to when she'd sort of helped out Seth as the maid.

Pewter turned to them. 'Dazed, beautiful and bruised! But ready to carry on, I hope.'

'Ready to take a holiday!' snorted Lark.

'That will give us the perfect chance to arrange for the Snakesmouth Lighthouse to get a proper cleaning. But that can be completed with little inconvenience to yourselves. Take a short holiday, why not. Builders will probably come back now we've removed the mad woman from your annexe. And no ghosts! Isn't that fortunate.'

He moved forward, extended his hand. 'Good luck with this place. Sure you'll have fun and it'll be a great success, what with all those waves. You could set up a surf school for people who have had enough of just watching them. And so very pleased, Miss Mintencress, that you are not dead.'

Mina was looking at him grimly. 'You don't think we're staying? You are so wrong.'

'But it looks like you'll make a terrific go of this place, now the sinister magic's gone. And not being dead is surely the best news of all.'

'What do you think we've been doing all this time you've been dealing with dangerous witches and dead bodies? We've been packing. We're going back to the mainland.' She took Alfie by the hand. 'I should have listened to everyone a long time ago.'

Lark looked at her friend with concern. 'Are you quite sure, Mina?'

'Everyone's been telling me this place is cursed, but I wouldn't listen. Now I think it's me that's cursed. I managed to buy a building that was being used as a hideout by a criminal on the run from magical police that had once been home to a dark sorcerer who was skilled at getting magical shadows to strangle people for him.'

Pewter shook his head. 'Doesn't sound so bad. Could be worse.'

'I don't need another building project, I need a

holiday,' said Mina. 'Rendleton is welcome to it.'

'Rendleton?' said Angelique and Seth together.

'Yes, I'm giving the lighthouse to Rendleton. Mr Stormforce was right to tell us Zachary has something of a claim on it.'

Dex looked at Angelique and Seth's bemused faces with a knowing grin. 'Come on, I didn't spend a whole day with a guy trying to interest me in ductwork without discovering some of his secrets. Why does everyone think I am totally useless? Weren't all of you curious as to why he was so keen to come out here and stuck it out despite all the setbacks?'

'We had a few other things to think about,' said Angelique.

'He's Snakesmouth's son,' explained Dex. 'His mother fled once she realized how dangerous her lovely husband was. And when she realized she was going to have a baby. She moved as far away from her husband as she could. But Rendleton got curious when he grew up, came to check out his old dad.'

'Luckily, I don't think he has yet grasped the idea that magic can be passed on in families,' said Pewter. 'I predict a bit more damage to this place if he tries to discover if he's inherited any of his father's talents.' He looked at Seth. 'Another one who will have a tricky path to navigate towards magic.'

Mina approached Seth uncertainly, then flung both her arms around him. 'Thanks, Seth,' she said, squeezing him hard, 'for everything. I would never have— Without you I would have— Anyway, if you ever need anything, just call me, OK? I mean, when I get back from this very long holiday. Don't call me for at least a year, OK? Now, Mr Pewter, I believe we were promised a quick, dry route off this island.'

Moments later, Pewter had vanished them away in a teleport, and was just as quickly back, rubbing his hands. 'Holiday? I don't think so. My guess is she'll have another exciting project lined up in no time. This is going better than I thought. We are all wrapped up.' He turned to Seth. 'Next – back to the Last Chance Hotel, you said? No, wait – keep forgetting that body in the cellar!'

Pewter vanished for a few more moments.

'Er . . .' Seth glanced at Angelique. 'What you said a moment ago . . . sure you've got time to help me?' he asked her.

'From what I've seen and heard of your magic, Seth,' grinned Dex, 'you're going to need all the help you can get.'

Angelique simply nodded.

'OK,' said Seth, breathing hard, once Pewter was again standing before him expectantly. He knew the decision to go with Angelique was going to lead to a lot more hard work and would be a difficult path, but he felt strangely prepared for many more disasters along the way. 'I'll go wherever she's going.'

'Great. I love a last-minute change of plan,' said Pewter, rubbing his hands together again. 'Is that everything?'

'I do have one final question, sir,' said Seth. 'Why were you so interested in the seagulls? It's the one thing I've completely failed to work out.'

'Ah. Now there, once again, it's me who failed – failed to prove what I needed to in time. You have no idea the number of barns, deserted outhouses and villages I scoured in this area, all the time looking for a trail of destructive magical activity that would give her away. The stories of ghosts drew me here. And what was the first thing I discovered? Multiple unexplained deaths. I knew I had to be closing in on Tiffany.'

'The gulls?' said Nightshade, suddenly looking up with interest. 'What on earth have they got to do with Tiffany?'

'I wanted to see how they'd died. My guess is that if we could have examined one, we'd have found it was strangled. Probably by shadow. Unfortunately, despite my very best efforts, I failed to find one. All washed away by the stormtides, I assume.'

Seth took this in slowly. 'You mean those gulls are the only evidence that she actually knew exactly what she was doing?'

Pewter nodded.

'Then she's going to get away with it? She's not going to be safely locked up? She'll be back on the streets wreaking havoc in no time.' Seth now had yet another reason to keep practising hard at his magic. 'I fear she will have little difficulty convincing the authorities that it was all an accident,' said Pewter. 'All caused by the firefly cage. Is that your last question, Seth? Then are you ready?'

Seth knew Pewter meant was he ready to leave, but far more important, he felt that he was ready to continue with his struggles. He was ready for the prospect of magic. He nodded.

Nightshade leapt into Seth's arms. 'I'm ready too.'

Pewter raised his silvery eyebrows. 'Ah yes, I almost forgot about the dratted cat.'

ACKNOWLEDGEMENTS

Being given the chance to write a second book is mostly down to the many wonderful people who gave such support to your first book. It's rather humbling to realize just how many people you have to thank for their involvement in you having that chance.

The lovely booksellers from both Waterstones and indies (particularly all at Mostly Books who are attempting to break all sales records with their sterling support). The sales and marketing folk at Bounce, the reviewers, the book bloggers, the heroic librarians, the educationalists tirelessly promoting reading for pleasure, the teachers who tweet, the other authors who generously offer advice and support. From me to all of you, thank you for making the world of books such a pleasurable and supportive place to be part of. Together we will recruit more children to the love of reading.

I would particularly like to mention Joseph Cash Primary School in Coventry, who made the decision to try to teach English in a different way and chose to base all reading and writing lessons for a half term on *The Last Chance Hotel*. It was such a pleasure to meet such enthusiastic children, who knew the story and characters even better than I did.

Particular thanks, of course, goes to my publishing team, including my wonderfully wise agent, Jo Hayes, at The Blair Partnership. And everyone at Chicken House for giving me the chance and then navigating me through the difficulties of a second book. Barry Cunningham, Rachel Leyshon and Laura Myers all have their very important roles to play and great copy-editing from Fraser Crichton. Rachel Hickman and illustrator Matt Saunders I have to thank for another phenomenal job in producing such a stunning design and cover. Thanks, Elinor Bagenal, for regularly sending me joyful news that readers in other countries will get a chance to read about Seth and his magical mystery adventures. Not forgetting Jazz Bartlett for helping me to get started in organizing my school events. It has been a busy year.

Thanks also to my early readers and writing 'fam': Oliver Nicholls, Jo Collins, Sally Poyton, Sandra Simpson and Noreen Miller all kept me on the right track. And again, enormous thanks to the incredible talents of Oliver Nicholls for the unexpected delight of having elements of Seth's world put brilliantly to music.

And as always, I could do nothing without my

wonderful team at home, Mark, Alex and Tim. Always there with a much-needed cup of tea and support at the right moment.

And finally, thanks to you, you lovely readers, particularly those who have been in touch and shared how much you enjoyed reading *The Last Chance Hotel*. I really hope we meet again in the next adventure.

MIDNIGHT HOUR by BENJAMIN READ & LAURA TRINDER

Emily's parents have vanished into the secret world of the Midnight Hour – a Victorian London frozen in time – home to magic and monsters. Emily must find them in the city of the Night Folk, armed only with a packed lunch, a stowaway hedgehog and her infamously big mouth. With bloodthirsty creatures on her tail, Emily has to discover the truth to rescue her parents. What family secret connects her to the Midnight Hour? And can she save both worlds before she runs out of sandwiches?

Anarchic humour, rich imagination and poetic writing, interspersed with elegant line drawings, add up to pure delight — with a stowaway hedgehog as a bonus.

GUARDIAN

Paperback, ISBN 978-1-911490-90-6, £6.99 • ebook, ISBN 978-1-911490-91-3, £6.99

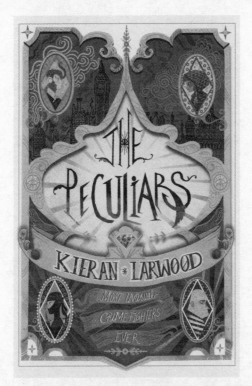

THE PECULIARS by KIERAN LARWOOD

The Peculiars are a band of misfits, trapped in a nightly Victorian sideshow. There's Wolfgirl, Sheba; Sister Moon, who can move at the speed of light; and Monkey Boy, ace climber and human stink bomb. But during the day, in a world of child-snatchers, grave robbers and dastardly doctors, they solve the mysteries no one else cares about – including why London's poorest children are being snatched from the banks of the Thames . . .

. . . reminiscent of Philip Pullman's immortal Sally Lockhart books.
THE TIMES

Paperback, ISBN 978-1-911490-21-0, £6.99 • ebook, 978-1-911490-22-7, £6.99

POG by PÁDRAIG KENNY

After their mother dies, David and Penny move to her family's old house in the forest. Dad says it's a fresh start but it feels sad and empty without Mum.

And there are noises in the attic . . .

A small furry creature is living in the roof. There are other creatures too – less friendly ones – that seem to be multiplying. Only with Pog's help can David and Penny save themselves – and goodness in the world.

If they can resist promises from the darkness.

A fantastical tale of monsters and grief, family and love . . . with real depth and heart.
THE BOOKSELLER

Paperback, ISBN 978-1-911490-39-5, £6.99 • ebook, ISBN 978-1-912626-01-4, £6.99